A Leap Of Faith

by

Nell Castle

This is a work of fiction. Names, characters, places, and incidents are either the product of the author's imagination or are used fictitiously, and any resemblance to actual persons living or dead, business establishments, events, or locales, is entirely coincidental.

A Leap Of Faith

Cover Art by *Kim Mendoza*

The Wild Rose Press, Inc.
PO Box 708
Adams Basin, NY 14410-0708
Visit us at www.thewildrosepress.com

Publishing History
First Mainstream General Edition, 2016
Print ISBN 978-1-5092-0787-9
Digital ISBN 978-1-5092-0788-6

Published in the United States of America

Kate appraised her with a sweeping glance. "You are here to eat, right? Because someone set up a nice bird feeder in the meditation garden if that's more your style."

"Ha ha. I'm here to support the church and eat the food I prepared." Sophia ladled a portion of green beans and a larger serving of salad onto her plate. She turned away her nose as Kate helped herself to a fist-sized roll, hot and fragrant. Progress was slow. Sophia looked behind her to see the line meandering out into the hall. "Good turn-out, huh?"

"Yeah, and I really appreciate your help, Soph. Even the minister said we couldn't have pulled it off without you stepping in at the last minute."

"I haven't seen Reverend Nelson in ages. He's got to be eighty by now, right?" Sophia reached the dessert table and continued shuffling forward, eyeing the bakery slices with regret.

"Reverend Nelson?" Kate snorted. "He was put out to pasture years ago. I told you we hired a new minister. He saw you this morning picking up supplies."

"I never saw him. Was he looking out the window of the rectory?" Remembering the ironic smile of the man who'd helped load her car, Sophia snapped her fingers. "I meant to ask you about the guy who helped me load my car. Mid-thirties, light brown hair? Tall and good-looking?"

Kate sighed. "That *was* the minister, Sophia. This is the twenty-first century. Ministers don't have to walk around in clerical collars every day."

Eyes wide, Sophia turned slowly to stare at Kate. "Are you telling me the minister caught me breaking into church with a bobby pin?

Dedication

For Pattie, who inspired me to begin,
and
for Christine, who inspired me to finish.

Chapter One

Sophia ripped open bag after bag of frozen Italian sausages, sending them skittering across the surface of a ten-foot frying pan. With the white puff of a chef's hat tottering on top of her curly hair, she grumbled, "I feel like the cookie elf." The giant-sized pan had been her idea—a gimmick to promote the housewares department at the Cleveland store where she'd worked the past two years as merchandising director. O'Grady's—a store familiar to viewers around the world after its Santa Slide was featured in a hit holiday movie—never shied away from excess.

But sausages hadn't been part of the plan. Not until Kate had called that morning and thrown her completely off course, as Kate so often did. Sophia had lain in bed an extra few minutes, reviewing all the tasks of the day ahead. *I haven't missed a single detail.* She stretched luxuriously then swung her feet out of bed and shrugged into her bathrobe, grabbing the cell phone from her nightstand and sliding it into her pocket.

She passed the bay window of her living room and paused to squint at the buds of the oak tree near the street. Winter had been exceptionally harsh in East Benton, and spring was a long time coming. The dogwood trees were extravagant with pink and white blooms, but the towering oaks of her quiet suburban neighborhood still looked skeletal against the bright blue sky. Sophia longed for the unfurling of the leaves every spring, her favorite season in her quiet Ohio hometown.

After strolling into the kitchen, she opened the refrigerator door and sighed. A jar of gherkin pickles, a bag of coffee beans, three different kinds of mustard, a bowl of chicken stock, and one hard-boiled egg. Oh, and a container full of pre-cut carrots and celery. Lots and *lots* of celery and carrots. They'd been the mainstay of her diet for the past two months, and the sight of them did little to quiet the violent hunger pangs ricocheting beneath her ribs.

She opened the container and popped a carrot stick in her mouth. If her Italian mother could see her now. She wistfully remembered the comforts of a dining room table crammed with platters of pasta, antipasti, and dessert.

The first few bars of "Born to Be Wild" from her cell phone blasted her back into the present. She fumbled it out of her pocket and hit the Speaker button, placing the phone on the counter and switching on the pot of coffee she'd set up last night. "Hey, Kate, how are you?" Sophia leaned against the counter with her arms crossed as the coffee brewed.

Kate's profile pic was Sophia's favorite. She wore a baseball cap over pigtails, her cheeks pink with laughter. Two giggling boys were encircled by her arms, each wielding an inflatable bat as they mugged for the camera.

"Me? Oh, another day in paradise." Kate breathed hard. "Chasing Randy around the kitchen to get him to pull his jeans back up after his wicked twin pantsed him on the way out to the car. I'm already five minutes late for dropping them at school and getting myself to work on ti—"

"Do you need me to bring you a tranquilizer gun? Or just take them to preschool?" Sophia interrupted when Kate paused for a breath. A single mother since before the boys were born, Kate had a long list of responsibilities to juggle and frequently called Sophia to help with babysitting, driving, and shopping.

"No, I'll get them there—got you!" Kate shouted. "Now pull up your jeans, you little nudist, before Mommy gets fired for coming in late again!"

Sophia heard squeals and high-pitched, uncontrollable giggles moving farther from the phone.

"I got a call from Donna down at the church this morning." Kate returned to a conversational tone. "Tonight's the Italian festival, and the vendor they hired to make all the Italian sausage sandwiches canceled at the last minute. Donna's in a total panic. But I told her I had the perfect solution." A long pause followed.

Sophia recognized the set-up a split second later. "Oh no, you don't. I haven't even been to church in more than two years."

"And don't think I don't know it, missy. You've got the housewares fair going on at the store today, right?"

"Yes. In fact, I have to get moving myself if I want to get in there early." Sophia eyed the microwave clock as she heard Kate clattering pots and shutting drawers on her end of the phone.

"And the huge frying pan was delivered and set up in the kitchen area yesterday, right? The one you said can actually be used to cook with?"

3

"Yeah, the frying pan I'm making *pancakes* in to hand out to customers. I need to leave now, so I can stop at the grocery store to pick up syrup and whipped cream." Sophia loved luring in customers with unusual displays and exhibits, and the ten-foot frying pan sizzling with butter and pancake batter was sure to draw a crowd.

"Well, now you don't need to go to the grocery store, because you're not making pancakes after all. Randy, go into the garage and get in your booster seat *right now,* or there will be *no* cartoons when you get home. You hear me?" Kate thundered into the phone.

Sophia clapped her hands over her ears. "No way will I change my plans at the last minute." She hoped her own no-nonsense tone was forceful enough to end the matter once and for all.

"You can make all the sausages and green peppers and onions at the same time in your giant pan. Just run down to the church kitchen, and you'll find the supplies you need on the counter. I told Donna you'd be coming by ten o'clock, and she'll have it all set out for you."

Kate's tone was placating and confident at the same time. Sophia heard the chiming of a bell as Kate opened up her car door, then the metallic click of a latch, and a moment later, a door slammed shut. "Kate!" She swallowed a mouthful of coffee, burning her mouth in her haste. "I can't change my plans at the eleventh hour! I have to pass out samples, exactly why I chose pancakes. The mix is cheap and easy to make. I've got a teenager lined up to flip the pancakes. Do you think I'd trust him to cook pork and risk giving food poisoning to a store full of O'Grady's customers?"

"Just tell him to leave the sausages on until they

start smoking. How hard can it be?"

"Spoken like a woman who can't boil water," Sophia retorted. "You don't mess around with internal food temperatures when cooking *pork*. And besides, I can't just use the store's special event to make a meal for a church! 'Hey, doesn't this smell great? Too bad, you can't have any!'" She paced across the kitchen floor, her long legs carrying her from the refrigerator to the window in just a few strides.

"Relax. I've taken care of everything. I told Donna to pick up some mini sausages and buns to hand out so you don't get into any trouble with O'Grady's. The church can afford it now they aren't paying for a vendor."

Sophia slapped a palm against her forehead. "But—"

"This is the church you were baptized in, Soph. Will you really let down your church when it needs you most?"

"Oh, brother." Sophia sighed. "Don't you think you're laying it on a little thick?"

"I've gotta go, Soph. I'm late as it is. Just head down to the church by ten and pick up what you need. You're the best! Love you!"

"Wait a minute!" But Sophia was talking into a dead phone. Once more, Kate had dragged her into a messy situation and left her to hold the bag. For the past seventeen years, ever since they were kids, Sophia had gotten Kate out of one muddle after another. *Why can't I ever say no?*

She dashed into the bedroom to get dressed, cramming the rest of the carrot into her mouth and crunching so fast, her jaw ached. She pulled a pale pink camisole over her head and tucked it into a straight black work skirt, frowning at her reflection as she adjusted the tiny gold buttons on her black shrug. "I don't even like Italian sausages."

Pausing for a moment in front of her full-length mirror, she slipped stockinged feet into black pumps and noticed how the heels lifted her muscular calves. This starvation diet might kill her in the end, but she would look good in the coffin. And besides, the only possible way to win Christopher was to become thin and beautiful, like the dancers in his troupe. He would see that April was totally wrong for him, and...

"No time for daydreaming." She grabbed her purse and her car keys. "Sophia to the rescue...again."

****

Twenty minutes later, Sophia knocked at the back door of St. Jerome's fellowship hall. After years of helping her parents cook for church fundraisers, she knew exactly where the supplies should be. If only she could get this door open. She tried the knob again.

Now what? If she had to run to the rectory and find someone to let her in, she'd be late to O'Grady's. Reverend Nelson or Donna, his office assistant, would surely ask about her long absence from church. She couldn't bear to imagine the awkwardness of that conversation.

Sophia pounded the door twice. A small, square window was set high in the door, almost too dusty to see through. She squinted and saw boxes piled on the counter of the deserted kitchen. Again, she rattled the doorknob and sighed. She had no time for this today.

"Darn it, Kate." She leaned against the door and examined her options. Years ago, Kate had used a bobby pin to unlock the basement door and sneak in, unnoticed, long after her foster parents had gone to bed. From her bun, Sophia pulled a bobby pin. She felt a long, curly strand of hair tumble down the back of her neck. Fumbling, she pushed the pin into the keyhole and turned the doorknob.

Nothing. By now, more strands of hair toppled from her bun. She blew upward from the side of her mouth, pushing the thick hair out of her eyes. She slapped her palm hard against the door.

"A key usually does the trick."

Startled by the deep voice behind her, Sophia whirled. The man was a stranger, an unknown face at this church where she used to know everybody. Dressed in snug, faded jeans and worn work boots, he was probably the new maintenance man. Quite an improvement on old Tony, the squat, unibrowed grump who'd chased Sophia and her friends out of empty classrooms when their parents had stayed late after service.

He squinted at the bobby pin she held in her fingertips.

She dropped it onto the sidewalk. This was worse than getting caught by the janitor while using the men's room at the ballet.

Raising his eyebrows, he returned his gaze to her face.

Sophia stood there, frozen in embarrassment.

"Couldn't figure out which way to stick it in, huh?" His brown eyes glinted with amusement.

"That's what she said." She slapped her hand over her mouth in dismay. Why did she *always* have to give a comeback? Because she'd expected Donna or

Reverend Nelson might meet her at the back door. Not a lean, handsome stranger scrutinizing her like some kind of puzzle.

He crossed his arms over his yellow polo shirt.

She slid her gaze to the blond hairs glistening on the tanned skin of his wrists.

Sucking in a quick breath, she started over. "I know it looks like I'm breaking into the church—and I guess I am—but I was told to go into the kitchen and pick up supplies for the festival. I was hoping it'd be open."

Without a word, he reached his arm around her and slid a key into the lock behind her back. The solid flesh of his upper arm brushed against her sleeve.

She tilted her head away in confusion, the clean smell of his aftershave tickling her nostrils.

Unlocking and opening the door in one swift motion, he stepped back and gestured for Sophia to enter.

Hesitating before stepping inside, she cleared her throat. "I don't think we've met. I'm Sophia Anton, and Kate Couvert called me this morning to ask me to help out—"

"With the Italian sausages." He slapped the top of the largest box and slid it off the counter, straining the box's weight against his upper arms as he balanced it against his chest. "Donna sent me over to unlock the door. I'll help you get these boxes out to your car."

The muscles at the base of his neck tightened and drew her attention to the gold cross he wore on a gold chain. Sophia grabbed a large box stuffed with sausage rolls and followed him out the door. "Thank you," she called up the stairs, averting her gaze from the backseat of his blue jeans and the muscles churning beneath the fabric as he climbed. Get your mind out of the gutter, Sophia. You're at church! She braced herself with a firm shake of her head, joining him at the edge of the parking lot where he waited at her car.

Pressing a button to open the trunk, she searched for something pleasant to say.

He lowered the box into the trunk. A cord of tension ran from each forearm and disappeared into the short sleeves bunched around his biceps. Without a glance at Sophia, he turned and trotted back down the steps to the kitchen.

Sophia trailed after him, more heavy strands of hair slipping from the top of her head. The next box she lifted was heavier than the last. She lugged it to her car.

By that time, he'd already delivered another box and disappeared into the kitchen.

Lowering her box with a groan, she flexed her spine, hands on her hips. Time to address her hair catastrophe. Pulling the one remaining pin and tucking it between her lips, she stripped the elastic band from around her ponytail and gave her head a quick shake. With the expertise of a motion practiced over a lifetime, she gathered her thick mane between two hands and swiftly twisted the ponytail into a coil on top of her head.

She fastened the elastic band around the bun and jumped at a quiet throat clearing from behind. Her pulse quickening, she pivoted toward him. With her hands still poised above her head, she was uncomfortably aware of her pink camisole straining upward. But the man's gaze was fixed on her face.

"Sorry you had to carry such a heavy box. This is

the last of them." He balanced a tower of three smaller boxes toward Sophia's car.

Sophia scuttled out of the way, shoving her bobby pin underneath her bun. One pin would have to do for now.

"Thank you so much for your help." She addressed his back as he leaned over the trunk. "I don't know how I got roped into doing this. I wasn't even planning to attend the festival, let alone spend my whole day at work flipping sausages." She touched her fingertips to the damp base of her throat. "I'll probably smell like a slaughterhouse by the end of the day. Anyway, I appreciate you letting me in the building and not calling the police on me. As it is, I'll barely make it to work on time." She glanced at her watch and winced.

He shut the trunk, leaning his weight against it before he turned back to Sophia, a smile playing along his lips. "I won't hold you up then. Good luck today, and thanks for helping the church." Without waiting for her reply, he walked away, crossing the parking lot to the rectory.

Sophia sat behind the wheel, her gaze following his long-legged, purposeful stride. He'd left so quickly, she hadn't found out his name.

He held the rectory door for an exiting deliveryman, brushing his sandy brown hair off his forehead as he smiled a greeting. Before he went inside, he looked across the parking lot at Sophia and raised his arm.

Waving, she started her car and squealed the tires in her haste to leave. A guilty smile dimpled her cheeks. This morning was too busy for enjoying the pleasant buzz of meeting an attractive man. For now, she'd better concentrate on getting herself and her car full of sausages to O'Grady's on time.

She drove out of the parking lot and pulled onto Monroe Street. On both sides were stylish old homes and plush lawns, newly green now that April's showers were coming to an end. The sun had climbed higher in the sky, and tiny green leaves unfolded on branches canopied over the street.

At a four-way stop, she braked. A robin pecking in the lawn beside her lifted its head, exultant, and flew to a nest cradled between two branches of a red maple. Perched on a branch, the bird dipped its beak inside the nest. Sophia's car idled at the intersection as she craned her neck to glimpse the baby birds. Only when a car tapped its horn behind her did she pull away from the curb. She looked at the robin one last time in her rear view mirror, her face softening into a smile.

"Here's to new beginnings."

****

Seated at his desk later that afternoon, Jackson set down the phone and sighed. Sam Newes, a longtime parishioner, was in his final days. A congregational leader who'd devoted himself to the causes of hunger and poverty in their community, he had continued volunteering after retirement. Even after a diagnosis of lung cancer, Sam refused to slow down, spending his days helping non-violent felons find work after release from prison.

Now, according to his wife Franny, he was settling into the final stages of his illness. His doctors told Franny to prepare for the worst, and she called to put Jackson on notice. In the two years Jackson had served as parish minister at St. Jerome's, he'd had his way smoothed by the older couple. They had rallied volunteers for every church event, proving to be not just supporters but trusted friends. What's more, Jackson never failed to be moved by the devotion Sam and Franny showed toward each other in their fifty-year marriage.

Jackson gazed out the window toward the fellowship hall. Volunteers clambered down the steps to serve the meal for the Italian festival, one of their largest and most successful annual fundraisers. The sausage vendor's last-minute cancellation had thrown everyone into a panic, but a back-up plan by one of the committee's members had saved the event.

He'd dressed to get dirty this morning, wanting to be ready to jump in wherever he was needed as they set up the hall for tonight's festival. When he received Donna's text to open the door for the woman who'd volunteered to cook the sausages, he emerged from the basement and rounded the corner of the fellowship hall to unlock the kitchen door.

But she'd beaten him there. The back of a tall, shapely woman surprised him as she vigorously rattled the doorknob. He hadn't intended to sneak up on her, but as he prepared to say hello, he saw her black hair tumbling from the top of her head. He didn't move, his gaze fixed on the heavy locks of hair whispering to the nape of her neck.

His professional composure fled when she turned: her face heart-shaped, with high cheekbones the color of pink roses—naturally pink, painted by exertion. Her dark gray eyes were large and liquid, the fringe of thick black lashes rivaled only by the lushness of the hair spilling down to frame her face.

For a moment, Jackson closed his eyes. For years, he hadn't allowed himself to think of a woman in a physical way. His visceral response to Sophia Anton had surprised him so much he hadn't trusted himself to speak more than a few words.

He swallowed hard and opened his eyes. *All the time I've been spending with Franny at Sam's bedside must be making me sentimental.* The old woman's love for her husband was evident each time she stroked his hand or rested her forehead against his before leaving him at night.

Years ago, as a young man, he'd hoped for the same kind of a marriage. But time had proven him very wrong. Now, at thirty-six, he'd put aside romantic illusions. He would minister to Sam and give comfort to his family during his last days. These were the responsibilities that bound him during and after the years of his own marriage's collapse—responsibilities that had, and always would, come first.

No matter what his own heart yearned for.

****

Sophia had to admit, she'd had fun today. Kate notified the church grapevine that Sophia would be preparing all of the Italian sausages in a gigantic frying pan, and several older members—retirees mostly—stopped by O'Grady's to offer their help. With so many hands at her disposal, chopping and dicing green peppers, onions and garlic, she soon smelled the delicious aroma of sautéed vegetables wafting throughout the entire second floor of the department building.

Henry, a quiet but brawny teen employee, lifted the bags of sausages to Sophia at the platform.

She donned a chef's hat to supervise the actual cooking. Shoppers who drifted into the housewares section, drawn by the smell of Italian seasonings, stayed to watch the rosy-cheeked cook in her chef's hat. Wielding a spatula the size of a shovel, she tossed strips of green peppers and rings of sautéed onions with expert rhythm, her strong arms lifting half a dozen sausages at a time as she traded jokes with the onlookers.

By the time the last batch of sausages finished cooking, she still had a line of customers clamoring for a taste.

Kate had stopped by briefly during her lunch break. "Housewares has never drawn this kind of a crowd before." She climbed onto the platform with Sophia and popped a mini sausage into her own mouth.

Despite herself, Sophia smiled. "I have to admit, Kate, onions and garlic are probably drawing a bigger crowd than pancakes."

"Yeah, you can smell it from the street." Kate's words were garbled, her mouth stuffed with meat. "Have you had a chance to eat yet? I'll hoist the spatula for a few minutes if you want to go in the back and eat lunch."

With a longing glance, she plopped a sausage into a roll and handed it to a young customer. "I sneaked some green pepper strips while we were prepping this morning. I'm good."

Tossing back her chestnut hair, Kate gave her friend a hard look. "You can't live off of raw vegetables, Soph. In case you haven't noticed, you're five feet ten and your body needs real food."

Sophia shook her head, greeting the line of

customers as she handed them sandwiches. "I'm fine. I can live off the fat of the land for a while, believe me."

A short snort from Kate's nostrils warmed Sophia's cheek. "I know what this is about. You're starving yourself before you see Christopher in New York. You're losing weight to compete with the little bag-of-bones dancer he dates. Aren't you?"

Sophia thrust a paper platter of rolls at Kate. "If you must stand here lecturing me, could you at least make yourself useful and feed the hordes? I've loaded sausages for the church into chafers—and by the way, you can help me wash this pan when I'm done."

"I'm not kidding, Soph." Kate's voice was somber as she passed mini sausage rolls to the steady line of customers. "I'm worried about you. A diet's one thing, but starving yourself is another. You are gorgeous, and if Christopher doesn't appreciate you exactly as you are, then he's no good for you."

For ten more minutes, Sophia's best friend peppered her with criticism of not just her diet, but her choice of men. She finally glanced at her watch, squealed with alarm, and dashed back to the school where she worked.

Sophia was relieved to see her go. As much as she loved her friend, she knew Kate would never understand her connection to Christopher. Kate liked the dangerous types—men with facial scars and piercings. She only learned her lesson when Carl Henly, her precious boys' father, left town five years ago without a forwarding address before the twins were even born. After that, Kate grew up fast. As a single parent, she'd had no choice. She swore off the bad boys and took an unexpected pivot back to the church she'd often visited as a teen, with Sophia.

Ironically, Sophia had turned her back on church some time ago. Not intentionally. She had just…drifted away. When she drove by St. Jerome's, she could almost see her parents in the parking lot—her hulking, elegant father leaning an arm on the roof of his luxury sedan as he helped his wife from the car. Her petite mother resting her hand in the crook of her husband's arm as he escorted her to the service. The church was the focus of her family life when she was a child. When her father died and her mother's death followed a few months later, Sophia couldn't face the empty pew they'd always shared up front in the sanctuary.

She met Christopher during that difficult time, the one bright spot in a landscape deadened by her grieving. She'd attended a collaboration meeting with the Ohio Ballet on a snowy winter night. Unwinding a muffler from the tangles of her hair, she walked into the lobby.

When she saw the man leaning against the wall, she caught her breath.

He cradled his cell phone between a dove-gray cashmere scarf and his chiseled chin. Long, blond hair swept off his face showcased eyes of crystalline blue. His gaze locked on Sophia as he continued talking on the phone. A slow, sure smile lighting his face, he mouthed the word "hello."

Sophia stopped at the door and returned a stiff smile. Why had he singled her out? As she heard him make arrangements for a ride home after the meeting, she hurried inside.

Settling her notes at the podium, she reviewed her presentation. Just before she began, she noticed him stroll inside and sit in a folding chair in the front row. She glanced away, her cheeks warm, as he stretched out his legs, relaxing his long frame into the metal chair. With the confidence of a person totally at ease with his body. *Something I've never felt.*

He folded his arms and slouched, chin tilted down toward his chest, his gaze fixed on her. Laughter rumbled deep in his chest at each of Sophia's ad-libbed wisecracks. As the meeting concluded, he led the applause for her presentation.

Disarmed by his approval, Sophia took a deep breath and offered him a ride home. That night, they became fast friends.

Sophia would gladly have opened her arms and her heart to Christopher, but they never quite began dating. Christopher's relationship with April, a dancer with a perfect body and a flawless face, was on and off. April's alcoholism was the subject of many long discussions, and Christopher took her back each time she pledged to give up drinking.

But Sophia bided her time. The flame between Christopher and April would surely die eventually. Appearances aside, Sophia had so much more in common with him than April did.

No man had ever touched her soul like Christopher did. They spent hours wrapped in conversation, deliberating the "deep" questions. He introduced her to de Chardin, Jung, the *Tao te ching*. Thoughts and feelings she'd always understood but couldn't express were reaffirmed by their dialogues.

Kate had no interest in these conversations. Better for Sophia to eat in private, and keep her plans for Christopher sealed off from the rest of her life.

****

Sophia pulled into the packed parking lot at St. Jerome's and saw the sun sinking behind the church steeple. The festival was still going strong. Friendly volunteers who'd helped her prepare the sausages had relieved her awkwardness about her long absence from church. Some of them were friends of her parents, people she'd known since she was a little girl. When they'd left O'Grady's with a dozen chafing dishes of hot sausages, they insisted she drop by the festival and celebrate with them.

Inside the fellowship hall, she opened her purse to buy a meal ticket when Randy and his brother Josh ran behind her and locked their arms around her legs.

"Hang on, you little monkeys!" Sophia knelt and wrapped the boys in her arms, planting noisy kisses on each upturned face as they giggled and squirmed. "Randy, nice to see you chose to wear pants tonight. Josh, b'gosh, have you gotten taller since I saw you last week? You'll be taller than me soon!"

"All right, boys, let Aunt Sophy breathe." Kate undercut her words with an affectionate smile at the twins twisting and hopping inside the circle of Sophia's arms. "You can tell her all about school today while we're eating. Now go and finish your mac and cheese."

Sophia stood and brushed herself as the boys raced back to their table.

Kate appraised her with a sweeping glance. "You are here to eat, right? Because someone set up a nice bird feeder in the meditation garden if that's more your style."

"Ha ha. I'm here to support the church and eat the food I prepared." Sophia ladled a portion of green beans and a larger serving of salad onto her plate. She turned away her nose as Kate helped herself to a fist-sized roll, hot and fragrant. Progress was slow. Sophia looked behind her to see the line meandering out into the hall. "Good turn-out, huh?"

"Yeah, and I really appreciate your help, Soph. Even the minister said we couldn't have pulled it off without you stepping in at the last minute."

"I haven't seen Reverend Nelson in ages. He's got to be eighty by now, right?" Sophia reached the dessert table and continued shuffling forward, eyeing the bakery slices with regret.

"Reverend Nelson?" Kate snorted. "He was put out to pasture years ago. I told you we hired a new minister. He saw you this morning picking up supplies."

"I never saw him. Was he looking out the window of the rectory?" Remembering the ironic smile of the man who'd helped load her car, Sophia snapped her fingers. "I meant to ask you about the guy who helped me load my car. Mid-thirties, light brown hair? Tall and good-looking?"

Kate sighed. "That *was* the minister, Sophia. This is the twenty-first century. Ministers don't have to walk around in clerical collars every day."

Eyes wide, Sophia turned slowly to stare at Kate. "Are you telling me the minister caught me breaking into church with a bobby pin? The guy I made a 'That's what she said' joke to?" She sucked in her breath at the disrespect she'd shown the minister. Her parents must be rolling over in their graves.

"You know…" Kate shook her head. "Your Mom always told you there's a time and a place to be funny. But it's never when the minister's standing behind you." She waggled her eyebrows at her friend, a mischievous grin stretching across her round cheeks.

Sophia froze, her gaze searching Kate's face. Could she be bluffing? Sophia swiveled her head, her gaze lifting from the neat points of a black-collared shirt to the amused brown eyes of the man who'd packed her car this morning. The same man whose jeans she'd tried not to gawk at as she followed him up and down the stairs.

"So, now you wear a collar." Sophia extended her hand, ignoring the hot blush creeping up her cheeks.

Chapter Two

"Don't mind my best friend, Pastor Thomas. She doesn't get out much." Kate cast a wicked glance at Sophia. "You've met Sophia, but she didn't know who you were."

He pressed both hands around hers. His palms were rough against her knuckles, but his grasp was gentle, warming her cool fingers. In the white collar and black shirt, stark against the ruddy skin of his neck, he was no less handsome than he'd been wearing blue jeans and a rugby shirt earlier in the day. But the clerical collar added a dignity not common to most men his age.

"I wanted to thank you earlier when we loaded your car." A smile teased the corners of his lips, and he held her hand a moment longer before letting it go. "But I didn't want to make you even later for work."

Flustered, Sophia waved her hand. "The sausages were a huge hit at O'Grady's. I should be thanking you."

He shook his head. "You jumped in at the last second and cooked enough sausages to feed a crowd of five hundred—and they're the best sandwiches we've ever served. I've been hearing it from everyone."

Her glance swept the crowded hall. Diners at every table munched on sandwiches, oily juices trailing down their chins.

"Sophia is the best cook I've ever known—with

the possible exception of her mother, who taught her everything she knew." Kate nudged Sophia's shoulder, her expression playful.

Shrugging away, Sophia rolled her eyes. "Just your typical Italian family. Food equaled love. And my Mom was old-fashioned, even for her times. She'd tell me as long as I could cook, I could always catch a man." She laughed. "*That* part hasn't worked out so great…"

She trailed off as Kate began wagging her finger. Oh no. Had she opened the door for Kate's big, nosy opinions about Christopher? In front of the minister, no less?

But Pastor Thomas's gaze was fixed on Sophia. "You were incredibly generous to take time from your work day to make the food for this fundraiser. I've heard your family's name mentioned over and over at this church. I'm glad to finally meet one of the Antons."

Shifting to avoid the minister's gaze, she crossed her arms over her chest. "I know, I haven't exactly been active with the church lately—obviously, since I didn't even know who you were—but I'd like to come around more. I've missed the people here."

"Keep talking. The boys are shooting peas." Kate dashed off through the tables

The minister grinned, leaning against a table as he watched Kate's retreating figure. "There's a place for everyone at this church." He rubbed his palm over his chin and gave a sideways smile to Sophia as Kate held her sons' plates high over their heads. "Pea shooters, overworked mothers, even young Italian cooks with ten-foot frying pans."

A smile relaxed Sophia's face as she glanced at the minister. A white collar peeked from between the black tabs of his clergy shirt. His neck, tanned and taut, was peppered with five-o'clock shadow beneath his chin.

"I was just thinking—maybe you could help me with something else?"

Pastor Thomas's voice shook Sophia out of her reverie. For the second time today, she'd indulged in impure thoughts about a man of the collar. What was wrong with her?

"I think you know Sam Newes and his wife Franny."

She nodded. Sam had been a friend of her parents, a music box collector who'd once given her a ceramic jewelry box that played a song from her favorite musical. She still treasured it.

Pastor Thomas hesitated. "I'm not sure if you've heard Sam has lung cancer."

Sophia's breath hitched, and she shook her head.

"He's known it for awhile, but he's kept quiet and worked on projects as hard as ever. You know Sam."

Sam and her father had prepared and served hot meals for the homeless at a downtown park. Beside her tall father, Sam looked almost diminutive: a short man with premature baldness, bushy eyebrows, and a lumpy nose. His homely face transformed when he smiled, his eyes squeezed so tight with merriment, they disappeared behind his round, red cheeks.

"I want to do something special for Sam and Franny." He stepped closer, lowering his voice and dipping his chin closer to her ear. "Something to honor their long life together. I've sat at his bedside the last few weeks while he and Franny have been reliving moments from their past. Years ago, when they'd just had their kids, they lived in Maine. Yesterday, they were laughing about all the hours they spent in the harbor trying to trap lobster."

Pastor Thomas paused, turning to look directly at Sophia. His gaze, dark and warm, made an appeal. She wondered why he hesitated to tell her what he needed.

"If I knew how to cook, I'd like to make them a lobster picnic." He spread his hands in a helpless shrug.

Sophia clapped, bouncing on her heels. "I would love to give them a lobster picnic! We'd just need a wicker basket with a red gingham table cloth to line it. We'll serve lobster tails, and maybe clam chowder, and corn on the cob." She bit her lower lip, concentrating. "We'll need home-baked bread, of course, and Key lime pie for dessert. It'll be *so* beautiful for Sam and Franny!"

Pastor Thomas placed his hand on her back to move her a few steps and allow a parishioner in a wheelchair to maneuver through the aisle. "You don't waste any time. Looks like I've asked the right person for the job."

His touch, as gentle as a feather, whispered against her silk blouse. She shivered, and a warm blush flooded her cheeks. *Get a grip, Sophia!* She forced herself to look at his clerical collar before she answered.

"I've been doing special events for years. O'Grady's pays me to come up with an idea and run with it. But *you're* the one with the great idea. I'll just be the worker bee." She smiled to think of Sam and Franny's surprise at the feast prepared especially for them. "Sam and Franny have always put everyone else first. Making a special meal for them is such a beautiful gesture. I'd be honored to help you." Her palms met in front of her chest like a prayer.

He laughed. "I wish everyone felt so honored when I ask them to help out. Okay then." He clapped his hands once, like a coach going into a huddle. "I'll call you in the next few days so we can make our plans. In the meantime, shop for whatever you need. Donna will reimburse you as long as you submit your receipts." His gaze met hers, warm with appreciation. "I'm glad you've come back to us, Sophia."

Her heartbeat rollicked in her ribcage. The man may be a minister, but he sure knows how to make you feel wanted. Or significant, she corrected herself. Before she could reply, she heard a family seated nearby call out to Pastor Thomas. With a little wave, Sophia made her way down the narrow aisle to join Kate and the boys for what was left of their dinners. Hers was now cold, and she didn't mind at all.

****

The next few days passed quickly. The housewares fair required Sophia to spend long hours at O'Grady's. By the time she got home, she was ready to drop. But during her breaks, she'd enjoyed selecting a set of lobster napkins, bibs, and the perfect picnic basket for the lobster dinner that weekend.

On Friday evening, Sophia arrived at Kate's house with a bottle of red wine, a cheesecake, and a quinoa salad.

Kate met her at the door. "I'll take that and that." She plucked the bottle from Sophia's hand and slid the cheesecake into the crook of her elbow. She narrowed her eyes at the casserole. "What's inside the dish?

"Quinoa with black beans and cilantro." Sophia's smile was so wide, she could feel her dimples straining. Maybe positive reinforcement would help sell her friend on health food.

"Ugh. You can hold on to that one yourself." Kate wrinkled her nose and gave Sophia a one-armed hug as they entered the kitchen.

Like Kate herself, the house was warm, bright, and untidy. A roll-top desk in the corner staggered under its load of textbooks and lesson plans. Kate had won awards for innovative, student-centered math classes at the juvenile detention center. She taught teens who came from troubled families and broken homes, like her own. Although Kate wasn't sentimental enough to admit it, she'd chosen a career to help repair the damages she'd experienced herself in foster care.

She'd first met Kate back in sixth grade. Sophia shrank in her seat when the new girl with the cool jean-jacket and combat boots chose the desk right in front of her. During lunch, when all the girls vied for Kate's attention, she looked right through them, eating her battered bologna sandwich without a word.

The next day during science class, she'd turned in her seat to face Sophia. "Did you do the science homework?"

"Yes." Sophia stuttered her answer, wondering if Kate wanted her to break the rules and let her copy her work.

"Give it to me."

Sophia handed her paper to Kate, who erased Sophia's name and added her own to the top. The assignment provided Kate's only A that year, and Sophia's only zero.

But though their friendship began with an act of bullying, within a week they were inseparable. Sophia was the cherished only child of older parents, elected student council president and prom queen. Kate was a rule-breaking, freak-dating, pot-smoking free spirit. They'd been the odd couple of their high school.

The TV blared from the living room. "Not too worried about the kids' hearing, I guess." Sophia took the wine opener from the drawer and unscrewed the cork.

"No." Kate's reply was emphatic as they settled onto stools around the high kitchen table. "Anything to get them to just sit still for a while. They've been wound up ever since they got home from school. I let them take the cushions off the couch and dive into the pile. They piled the cushions into a tower, and Randy toppled right off the minute my back was turned. Cut his head on the edge of the coffee table." She took a slow sip of wine.

Sophia's eyes widened. "Is he all right? Does he need stitches?" She was poised to grab her car keys and race to the emergency room.

"He'll be all right. He's had worse. I bandaged it and told him if he was lucky, one day he'd have a scar like a pirate. So he ran out to the kitchen, climbed on the counter, and jumped down with a steak knife. He clenched it between his teeth like a pirate's dagger." Kate demonstrated with her finger, her eyes opened and wild like a buccaneer's. "I had to catch him before he fell and cut his own throat."

Sophia gasped as Kate took another sip of wine. "How can you be so calm about it?"

But Kate only shrugged. "I know. I'm amazed that boys ever survive childhood. At least, boys like mine." She left the table and flipped two grilled cheese sandwiches from a skillet onto child-sized plates. As she worked, she continued talking, her back to Sophia. "I finally turned on the basketball game to distract them. They've been sitting and watching it for half an hour, safe and sound."

Sophia shook her head and blew out a relieved sigh. "Thank God you're the mother of those boys, instead of me. I'd chain them to the couch and make them sing show tunes. Don't tell me that's all you're feeding them for dinner!" Her own mother had never served fewer than three courses for dinner.

"No." Kate pulled a bunch of grapes from the refrigerator. She ripped the stem in two and dropped a cluster on each plate. "*That's* all I'm feeding them. And a glass of milk. The question is, what do *I* eat now that I know the main course is rabbit food?"

With an indulgent smile, Sophia looked inside the refrigerator. "Well, let's see what you have to work with. Lettuce, tomatoes, cheese….do you have tortilla chips?"

Nodding, Kate left the kitchen with a plate in each hand to deliver dinner to the boys in the living room.

"How about taco salad?" Sophia called, lining up ingredients on the kitchen island.

"Sounds good." Kate came back into the kitchen for the boys' milk. "I don't have any ground beef though."

"No problem." Sophia scanned the pantry and reached for a can. "You've got kidney beans for protein. They're better for you anyway."

At ease in Kate's kitchen, she set to work.

Kate moved her stool to the island and grated cheese. "So"—she began then waited while the faucet ran—"how goes the planning for the lobster picnic?"

Pumping the top of the salad spinner, Sophia grinned. "Oh, Kate, the day will be so wonderful for Sam and Franny. I can't believe a minister, of all people, came up with this plan. Have you ever known a *guy* to be so thoughtful and…romantic?"

Kate rolled her eyes. "Have you met the guys I've dated?" She winced as her knuckle grazed the cheese grater. "I've known romantic gay men. Straight? No." She rotated the block of cheese to protect her fingers from the sharp metal grooves.

Sophia's eyes widened. Was *that* what was so different about this minister? She set down the spinner and looked at Kate. "Are you telling me—"

"No!" Kate laughed. "Pastor Thomas has been married before."

"Really?" Sophia emptied the lettuce into the salad bowl. "What happened?"

"Don't know. I just heard he was married before, and now he isn't." Kate dumped her pile of cheese over the greens.

"*Sprinkle* the cheese, Kate. Don't drop it like a grenade!"

Kate shrugged and reached for the can of kidney beans.

Sophia moved on to dicing the tomato. "Does he have kids?"

"Nope." The tip of Kate's tongue peeked out from the corner of her mouth as she concentrated on operating the manual can opener.

"Eligible bachelor in the pulpit, then?" Sophia's eyebrows rose.

"Not according to Donna." Kate grunted as the opener loosened its grip. She repositioned it on the rim.

"I once made a crack about the women's ministry throwing him a private banquet, and she shut me right down. Said he'd made it 'perfectly clear' marriage had been a mistake, and he'd be celibate for the rest of his ministry."

"Huh." Sophia frowned as she mixed green chilies and tomatoes into a bowl. She squirted in juice from a plastic screw-top lime. "Do you have any fresh cilantro?"

Kate's only answer was a cocked eyebrow.

"Of course not. Well, this is the best I can do with what I've got." Sophia added salt, pepper, and cumin. The citrus tang of lime rose up from the bowl. She tasted the dressing. Not bad, even without the zip of cilantro. She poured it over the lettuce and looked back at Kate. "So the minister took a vow of abstinence. Too bad."

Kate whirled, her mouth agape. "Sophia, you naughty girl. Do you have the hots for Pastor Thomas?"

"No!" She laughed, mixing the final ingredients into the salad bowl. "I was thinking too bad for *you.*" At the memory of his hand grazing her back in the fellowship hall, she sighed. Some lucky woman should experience the gentleness of those hands.

"Ha!" Kate spread a layer of tortilla chips over two paper plates. "I may have sworn off bikers and deadbeats, but dating a minister is still a bridge too far. Can you imagine me as a minister's wife? Or the boys, God forbid, as minister's sons?"

"God forbid," Sophia agreed, then waved a hand over her plate. "No chips. I'm eating quinoa salad."

"Oh come on, Soph, live a little. It's Friday night. And I can see your ribs. Eat human food!" Kate dipped a chip into a glob of cheese and dressing, waving it under Sophia's nose.

"Well...maybe just one bite." Sophia popped the chip into her mouth. The tang of spicy cheese smothering the crunchy chip almost made her swoon. She reached for another chip just as her phone rang. The peal of Tibetan singing bowls told her the caller was Christopher. With a smile, she dropped the chip and picked up her phone. "Hello!" She beamed at Christopher's profile picture, ignoring Kate's glare.

"Do you have a minute, Sophia? I need you."

Sophia had once written in her journal that Christopher's deep, silky voice was like a warm shot of bourbon. "Absolutely. What do you need?"

"I'm finishing my application for the American Ballet Company and can't remember the name of the summer program I did in Chautauqua. Was it *Les Sylphides/Les Patineurs* or the other way around?"

"The other way around." Leaning her elbows on the island, Sophia twisted a strand of hair around her finger.

"Okay. How do you spell it?"

She could hear hesitant tapping on a computer keyboard. Patiently, she spelled out both French names. Though he could use spell check and other online references, Christopher preferred to verify his spelling with her when he was forced to write. He completed his slow typing and read it back.

"When is the application due?" She was surprised he hadn't asked for her help earlier.

"Tomorrow morning," Christopher answered. "I've been working so hard on my audition program, I almost forgot the paperwork. I wish you could look at it and make sure I haven't missed anything."

"You could scan the application so I could read it," Sophia offered, calculating how much less sleep she'd get after editing Christopher's résumé.

Kate, shoveling another forkful of salad in her mouth, rolled her eyes.

"Nah. I never remember how to scan, and I don't have time for you to walk me through it. I'm running through my routine one more time tonight, and then we're going to dinner."

"You and the other dancers?" Sophia hoped April wasn't one of them.

"Yeah, with friends." His voice was muffled as he said, "Just give me a minute, April."

Sophia stiffened. "I thought you and April were taking a break and thinking things over." Sophia's voice was pleasant, but dismay rooted in her chest.

"We did." He lowered his voice. "She's helping with my audition. She knows what they're looking for. Hey, Sophia." His voice became louder and more brisk. "I've got to get off the phone now. I appreciate your help with the application."

"Just one more thing." Sophia spoke fast before he hung up. "What should I wear for the show you're taking me to at BAM?"

From Christopher's end of the line came silence.

"Brooklyn Academy of Music? The Premiere you're taking me to in two weeks?" She wished she didn't have to prompt him, especially with Kate's cynical presence judging her from across the table.

"Oh!" Christopher exhaled. "With everything going on, I almost forgot. You'll need formal wear, of course. Wear something elegant to showcase your height. Listen, I really need to go now. Talk to you soon, *mi amor*. Good night!"

The line was dead before Sophia could respond. She cradled the phone in her hand for a moment.

"So how's your man in tights?" Kate narrowed her gaze as she took a long sip of wine.

"Don't call him that!" Sophia's couldn't keep irritation from edging her voice.

"He's a ballet dancer, right? Does he *not* wear tights?" Kate clapped her hands over her eyes. "Ugh." She exaggerated a shudder, peeking out at Sophia between her fingers.

Sophia's smile was reluctant as she sipped at her wine. "He's pretty stressed out about this audition. Mikhail Baryshnikov danced in the company. This is the big time."

"I guess." Kate sniffed, toying her fork through her salad while watching Sophia closely. "But where do you fit in the picture?"

Before answering, Sophia swallowed hard on her wine. "I'm going to the premiere with him when I visit in two weeks."

"Yeah, I heard," Kate responded. "But who will Sophia Anton be when Christopher's dancing with the American Ballet? His personal secretary?"

"Our relationship isn't like that, Kate." But her best friend was voicing the very fears she herself wanted to stifle. She gave her shoulders a brisk shake. The connection she shared with Christopher was like no other. *And I'm not the only one who feels it*. "He's told me I'm the only woman he'd ever settle down with."

Resenting the skepticism painted on Kate's face, Sophia struggled to compose her explanation so her friend would understand. "You don't know his emotional side. He shares things he tells no one else. He's vulnerable with me. He trusts me."

"*Everyone* trusts you, Sophia. You're like Mother Theresa."

Sophia blew out an impatient puff of air, but Kate's tone was sincere.

"I don't doubt he lets his guard down in front of you." Kate pressed her hand against her chest. "I just want to trust *his* intentions. I want to know when he'll kick April to the curb for good."

"You and me both." She clinked her wine glass on the edge of Kate's. "He's surrounded by dancers. I don't think he's ever dated anyone he couldn't lift over his head. And here I am, almost six feet tall. Not exactly the definition of willowy." She grimaced. "I've lost thirty-five pounds since I last saw Christopher, but I haven't even told him. I want him to be surprised."

Kate was silent for a moment, her hazel eyes assessing her friend. "Thirty-five pounds in, what…six weeks? Do you think that's healthy?"

"I think any weight loss is fantastic." Sophia forced a laugh.

"I don't." Kate's voice was hard. "Don't you see you're hurting yourself?" She reached over and gripped Sophia's hands. "You have so much to offer any man. You're beautiful exactly as you are. Why can't you see it?" Her eyes were sober, her lips pulled into a tight line.

Sophia pulled away her hand, smoothing a gentle finger over her friend's straight chestnut hair and tucking it behind her ear. "You have to say that," she whispered. "I'm the only thing standing between you and dessert."

Kate slapped Sophia's hand, her expression relaxing. "True. And if you don't hurry and slice it, you'll find yourself chained to the couch watching basketball with the boys."

With a mock shriek, Sophia crossed to the refrigerator and pulled out the cheesecake.

Chapter Three

The phone rang early the next morning. Sophia lurched her head from under her pillow and slapped for the cell phone on her nightstand. The tinny strains of "Nine to Five" gave her an impulse to curse. O'Grady's. On a Saturday?

A minute later, she scrubbed her face furiously as the shower pounded over her shoulders. O'Grady's held ladies fashion shows several times a year. If a model from the Big and Tall department canceled at the last minute, then Sophia received a desperate phone call.

The first time she'd filled in, Sophia had imagined slinking glamorously down the runway in a sexy cocktail dress. Instead, her outfits were as matronly as the clothes her own mother had worn. But Sophia couldn't say no to another manager in a bind. Lord knew she'd dealt with an unreliable work staff too many times herself.

Wet hair springing in ringlets around her face, Sophia slid into a pair of black tights and white canvas flats. She pulled a pale yellow tank top over her damp skin. No sense taking too much time with her clothes. Soon enough she'd sport a pant suit. Pulling her wet hair into a ponytail, she grabbed her purse and keys and flew onto the porch.

Gray clouds swarmed low, flattening the air and intensifying the moldering odor of compost as she locked the front door. In the clammy humidity, hairs stood erect on her bare arms. She'd just have to borrow a wrap at work. She hurried to the car, slamming the door against the chill. Her phone rang again as she backed out of her driveway. Church, the screen read. Shoot! She and the minister had planned to meet this morning and finalize their plans for tomorrow night's lobster dinner.

"Good morning, Pastor Thomas, how are you?" Glancing at the clock, Sophia accelerated faster than usual.

"Hi, Sophia. Please, call me Jackson. Just confirming our meeting at 10:30."

His voice, low and pleasant, flooded her with pleasure. She'd love to listen to it, rather than racing off to work.

"I'm so sorry, but I've been called to work and can't meet you this morning after all. I was just about to call you. Could we try for later in the day?" The phone was silent, and she bit her lip.

"I'm afraid not. I have a meeting in Greensburg later. I was hoping to wrap up the final details before I leave."

Beneath his polite response, she sensed his frustration. "I'm really sorry about this. I got called in at the last minute." A car in the crossroads braked and honked as Sophia's car passed it in the intersection. Glancing in the rearview mirror, she saw the stop sign obscured by an overgrown forsythia at the corner. She winced and gave a guilty wave.

"Listen, why don't I try you later tonight or tomorrow morning? I don't like talking on the phone while I'm driving. Sorry again, Pastor. I mean, Jackson.

Talk to you soon." Gunning the accelerator to beat the traffic light at the end of the township road, she punched off the phone without hearing his response.

Tiffany, the ladies' fashion floor manager, met her at the door to O'Grady's convention hall. Short and fit, with curly, closely-cropped hair and horn-rimmed glasses, Tiffany looked chic in anything she wore. Thanking Sophia for filling in at the last moment, she escorted her to a rack of clothes.

But this time, instead of the usual assorted business jackets and polyester stretch pants, what Sophia saw made her catch her breath.

Lingerie. A lacy peppermint-green chemise with an empire waist. An ankle-length gown with an underwire bra, white and diaphanous. A vintage-looking black bustier with hook-and-eye closures. A wine-red baby doll with matching panties. A royal-blue teddy with full bikini back. And lacier, frilly items hanging behind them.

Astonishment choked at the base of Sophia's throat. "I think you've got the wrong rack, Tiffany. Or the wrong model. I'm Sophia, remember? Of the Easy Spirit shoes and support hose?"

Tiffany snorted. "Only in your mind, Sophia. Have you seen yourself lately? With your height and the weight you've dropped, you're the perfect size to model this lingerie. You'll be able to show off for once." She scanned the busy hall. "I've numbered the hangers. You know the routine: take them to the dressing room and come back for hair and make-up. No 'buts' about it!" she barked. "I wouldn't have put you in lingerie if I didn't think you could do it. Just hurry!"

Hollering for a light technician, Tiffany was gone

before Sophia could argue. She gazed at the lingerie. Beneath the wild fluttering of her heart, her stomach clenched. She swallowed hard and licked her dry lips. She could never…!

Despite herself, she pressed her damp palms into the inviting fabric of a velvet bustier. She loved the look and feel of lingerie. But lingerie wasn't made for a body like hers.

She cast a furtive glance around the immediate area, but no one was watching. Pulling a hanger from the rack, she held a negligee under her chin. With an appraising eye, she scanned the length of her body reflected in the narrow mirror on the wall and angled her knee to peek from behind the skirt. *Admit it, Sophia. The nightgown looks…sexy.*

Her boldness growing, she pouted her lips at the mirror and tossed her hair like a coquette. Not bad. She tilted her right hip against the sheer fabric. Not bad at all.

Browsing the rack of lacy garments with growing courage, Sophia giggled. *I wish Kate could see me now.*

Taking a deep breath, Sophia removed the hangers one by one. For the first time since she was a young girl, she wasn't ashamed of her body. And Tiffany *had* told her to show off.

Time to step up your game, Sophia. You'll never win a man like Christopher until you act like an attractive, confident woman.

Emboldened, Sophia opened the dressing room curtain and arranged the outfits on a rack. Her heart beat fast and her palms sweated as she peeled off her tank top. *Calm down.* The audience for these shows is mostly older women. How critical can they be? She kicked off her flats and stepped into the outfit marked Number One. When she opened the curtain, she saw the hair stylist beckoning. As soon as Sophia was seated, her hair was pulled free of the elastic band.

"Girl, it's a sin to hide these gorgeous curls!" She spritzed Sophia's hair, creating a halo of black ringlets to drape down her back.

The makeup stylist applied smoky eyeliner and a thick application of mascara, smoothing rouge like dusky rose over Sophia's high cheekbones. She dusted a translucent powder over the long, straight bridge of her nose and surveyed her handiwork in the mirror. She squeezed Sophia's shoulder. "You look like a Roman goddess."

"Like Julius Caesar, you mean." Out of long habit, Sophia deflected the compliment.

The stylist frowned, tweezing a few stray hairs from Sophia's tender brow line. "No, like Venus." She gathered Sophia's hair into one thick coil and let it cascade over her right breast. "See? Venus de Milo."

Sophia peeked at her reflection from under lowered lashes. Her fresh-faced, just-tumbled-out-of-bed look was a dim memory. She'd never felt so exotic, so…desirable.

"Five minutes!" Tiffany hollered into the room.

Heart pounding, Sophia thanked the stylist and ran backstage to prepare for her first turn. Within ten minutes, Sophia was having the time of her life. Sure, fear seized her when Tiffany called her name. But as expected, her audience was mostly well-dressed, middle-aged-and-older women. They seemed far more interested in chatting with their friends than watching the catwalk.

On her second trip down the runway, Sophia grabbed a plastic champagne flute from a prop table onstage. Tilting her head far back, she drained the glass, flung it over her shoulder, and strutted down the catwalk, enjoying the satiny swish of the ankle-length gown as it draped and unveiled her long legs with each step.

She modeled more than ten different outfits. Her last was her favorite: a three-piece satin baby doll, cotton-candy pink with a rhinestone pin, a mesh long-sleeved jacket and, underneath it all, a G-string Sophia prayed no one could see. As she made final adjustments on the sleeves, she was sorry the fashion show was over already.

Tiffany walked by Sophia and slapped her on the bottom. "Shows off all your best assets, kiddo." She pushed her back to the catwalk to join the entire crew in a bow. Mindful of the G-string, Sophia curtseyed to the crowd. Most were already exiting the dark conference room.

Her eyebrows arched, her smile ironic. She'd revealed her body to a roomful of strangers, and they couldn't leave fast enough. No doubt, they were late for lunch.

She high-fived another model as she left the stage. So what if no one would remember her performance? She'd never done anything so brave in her life. As she passed Tiffany, she raised her fingers in a V for victory sign, and then returned to the dressing room to don her regular clothes.

****

By force of habit, Jackson steered his car onto the highway, blind to the presence of other cars. He had to fight to see anything but Sophia.

He'd been disappointed, he couldn't deny it, when Sophia canceled their meeting this morning. So he improvised. Stop by O'Grady's and talk with her for a few minutes while she's at work. *After all, O'Grady's is on my way.*

He took a slow walk around the housewares department, but there was no sign of Sophia.

A bored sales associate made a call, and then escorted him to the first floor. "The show just started a few minutes ago." She opened the door and motioned him inside a convention hall. Lines of chairs extended to a stage in the front, where a runway protruded down the center of the room.

An announcer behind a microphone described the fabric and cut of a jacket while another woman walked the runway. He'd stepped into a fashion show. He scanned the room for Sophia.

A well-dressed young man approached. "Take a seat over here." He led Jackson by the elbow to an empty seat behind a cluster of women.

"I'm looking for Sophia Anton," Jackson whispered.

The young man nodded. "She should be out in a minute." He hurried back to stand by the entrance.

Jackson sank into a chair, glancing about him with lowered lids. Women whispered to each other, nodding toward the stage and taking pictures with their smart phones.

The model circled the end of the runway, paused, and sauntered back to the main stage, exiting behind the curtains. The applause was sporadic, almost an afterthought. Most of the audience was absorbed in conversation, so Jackson joined in the polite clapping.

"And for an evening of high romance"—the announcer paused while the stage lights lowered—"we have Sophia wearing an elegant purple floor-length gown."

Jackson froze, his hands stopped mid-clap. Into a cone of light stepped Sophia, her hands on her hips.

"This long, silky, plum gown has a black lace bodice sprinkled with sequins and a sexy ultra-low back with crisscross straps. Turn for us, Sophia."

Twirling so the skirt fluttered up, exposing her ankles and calves for a delicious moment, Sophia paused with her back toward the audience, offering a profile view of her face in a pouty smile. Her hands rose to lift her long mane of dark curls, exposing thin straps crossing the smooth skin of her long, bare back.

"At the end of a perfect evening, what could be more enchanting than heading into the boudoir with your lover's hand on the small of your back? Comes with a thong," the woman added.

Sophia shook her bottom, heart-shaped and stamped with a triangle of plum fabric beneath the silky skirt fabric.

Not until Sophia glided down the runway did Jackson realize his hands were still raised, motionless in mid-clap, in front of his chest. Jamming them into his pants pockets, he slid low in his chair.

He doubted Sophia could see faces in the dark from under the spotlight, but he wasn't taking any chances. Dropping his chin to his chest, he resisted the urge to look. With his head down, his gaze could only strain as high as Sophia's left knee. A long slit in the gown exposed her muscular calf. The pulse in his throat banged against his lowered jaw.

"Thank you, Sophia."

Jackson raised his head. Sophia's bottom was swinging into the darkness of the stage wings. The audience applauded with more energy now. He hunched in his chair for the rest of the show, through each variation of costume change, through each embodiment of Sophia in nightwear.

Now, he shifted in the driver's seat, directing mechanical glances at the rear-view mirror. Sophia didn't want him to know she was part of the fashion show, or she would have mentioned it. What business did he have watching her model lingerie?

He should have left immediately. But, as Sophia's image drifted back into his mind, his throat thickened. Her face tilting toward the spotlight, a smile playing over her full lips, her hair floating over her shoulders...

The sudden blare of a car horn snapped Jackson to attention. A few fat drops of rain spattered the windshield. He flipped on the wipers, tightening his grip on the steering wheel. He gave his head a rough shake, knowing he would be discussing an important policy decision at the district office. If his thoughts kept drifting back to Sophia, he'd cause an accident before he ever arrived.

Why was he so rattled by a fashion show? He frowned a warning at his reflection in the rear-view mirror. Plenty of ministers balanced their personal lives with their ministries, but he required a solitary focus.

When he was first ordained, he'd thrown himself into the cause of social justice. He attended rallies for racial equality, fund-raised to end mass incarceration, and addressed income inequality from the pulpit. The world swelled with misery. His job was to ease the suffering. He didn't have a spare minute to think of his own needs.

But meeting the demands of his large urban parish was exhausting. Especially when he returned each night to an empty apartment.

He didn't realize how lonely he was until he met Laura.

Fresh out of college with a degree in sociology, she worked at the minority services center. Blonde and energetic, she stood out from her burnt-out co-workers.

He hadn't had a girlfriend since he was a teenager. Like a character from an old movie, he asked Laura's parents for permission to date her. He fell into the comfortable routine of seeing her on weekends and phoning her each night. He liked having someone to talk to. Someone who understood the challenges he faced in his job. But his relationship with Laura came under the scrutiny of his entire congregation. When were they getting married? Laura's parents were laying hints at Sunday family dinners.

He *was* fond of her. He'd be relieved to stop all the gossiping at the church. Who could have been hurt by making things official?

Jackson exhaled at the memory of his own stupidity. Flipping the windshield wipers to their highest speed, he applied the brakes as he approached the exit ramp. Rain thundered onto the pavement around him. Who could their marriage hurt? Everyone. He'd carry the burden of his guilt forever.

Stopping at the end of the exit ramp, he hovered his hand over the turn signal. He'd made this drive a dozen times, but now he couldn't remember if the district office was to the left or right.

Taking a deep breath and letting it out slowly, he relaxed his clenched jaw. With his next breath, he raised his shoulders and dropped them. With one more slow breath in and out, he emptied all personal thoughts from his mind. Focusing on the road before him, he flipped on the left turn signal.

As he drove into the district parking lot, he noticed the rain had slowed to a sprinkling. He had important work to do today. Straightening his shoulders, he stepped from the car and slammed the door on any further distractions.

Chapter Four

Sophia slept in on Sunday and spent the rest of the day preparing the food for Sam and Franny's picnic.

Every task had been a joy. Listening to Tony Bennett crooning on her stereo, she baked homemade bread early in the day. Its buttery aroma wafted through her sunny townhouse. She kept a plate of celery sticks handy and crunched on them each time the urge to taste-test struck her.

By the afternoon, the air was suffused with the scent of rosemary and garlic as red-skinned potatoes glistened under a light coating of olive oil on the top rack of her oven. She carefully sliced each lobster tail and marinated them in a mixture of melted butter, paprika, and garlic. A generous squirt of lemon juice followed by a pinch of white pepper completed the seasonings. On a whim, Sophia tucked a roasted chicken in the picnic basket, hoping to keep Sam and Franny well-fed for the next day or two.

She missed cooking with love and intention. But why bother preparing elaborate meals for just herself? She couldn't afford the calories anyway. She patted her flat stomach.

In the spirit of the lobster picnic theme, she wore a pair of denim Capri pants—"clam diggers" her mother had called them—and a red gingham plaid shirt with rolled sleeves. After sweating from the heat of the oven, she opted to pull her hair into a low ponytail, allowing a few loose curls to frame her face instead of wearing earrings.

When the doorbell rang, Sophia was ready. Pastor Thomas—*Jackson*, she reminded herself—stood on her small front porch, so close his cologne tickled her nose.

What was the fragrance? She recognized it from the perfume counters at O'Grady's.

Clean and fresh, it was unmistakably masculine. She snapped her fingers. "White Mountain!"

Jackson's smile faltered, and he cocked his head.

She laughed. "Sorry. You're wearing White Mountain cologne. The sales girls in the cosmetic departments spray samples on the men when their wives come in to shop."

He nodded, his smile uncertain.

In a crisp denim shirt with a pale yellow tee beneath it, damp hairs curling up at his temples, he didn't look like a minister.

Sophia hesitated, her hand resting forgotten on the doorknob. His eyes were so gentle.

"I smelled your cooking as soon as I got out of my car."

Jackson's words broke Sophia's spell. She blushed, waving him inside. "I've had a blast. I can't remember the last time I spent all day cooking a meal from scratch." On the kitchen table sat a wicker basket with six ears of corn arranged around the rim. A bag of silvery clams was propped next to bright yellow lemons peeking through an orange mesh sack. The loaf of bread, wrapped in a snowy-white linen kitchen towel to keep it warm, stood on its end next to a bottle of white wine. Supported by careful placement of the lobster, potatoes, and chicken, a Key lime pie nestled in the center of the basket. "And I can even shut the lid." She pulled it down, careful not to graze the whipped peaks of the meringue.

Jackson gave a long whistle. "When I asked you to help me, I never expected a feast like this. I don't even think a caterer could have done such a great job."

When he turned to face Sophia, his face was frank with admiration. A thrill of satisfaction surged through Sophia, but she waved off his praise. "I had a great time doing it. Could you hang on just a second? I have one more thing to bring. You carry the picnic basket out to the car, and I'll be right out."

"No problem." With a sweep of his hand, Jackson slid the basket off the table onto his forearms. Resting the basket against his chest, he waited as Sophia opened the door, and then eased onto the porch with measured steps. "Precious cargo," he called over his shoulder as he walked to the car.

Sophia trotted back to her bedroom, unable to squelch her grin. She'd hadn't agreed to cook a feast just to have her ego stroked. But she couldn't deny Jackson's appreciation made the night ahead even sweeter.

The neighborhood where Jackson drove was only minutes away. Sam and Franny lived in a community of old brick homes with freshly painted shutters and manicured lawns. The first flowers of spring—tulips, daffodils, and crocuses—bloomed from mulched beds.

As they walked up the flagstones to Sam's house, Sophia plucked a pale cluster of purple lilacs from the bush beside the garage.

Jackson raised an eyebrow.

"What? Flowers are the finishing touch. And lilacs are my favorite." She draped the delicate purple blooms over the basket.

Franny met them at the door. A trim woman with closely cropped white hair wearing a youthful French sailor top, she looked younger than her seventy-five years.

She wrapped Sophia in a tight hug. "Look at how beautiful this little girl has become! A little bonier than I remember, though." Holding Sophia at arms' length, she surveyed her from head to toe. "I was so tickled when Jackson told me you were preparing the meal. If anything will bring Sam's appetite back, it's a home-cooked meal cooked by one of the famous Antons! Your mother made a great cook out of you—and a beautiful young lady, too." Franny beamed at Sophia, then grabbed her and hugged her again.

Same old Franny—generous, warm, and outspoken. Even her husband's terminal illness hadn't changed her positive outlook.

Nestled into the kitchen nook was a table set with fresh flowers soaking in the waning afternoon sun. Jackson unpacked the picnic basket while Sophia and Franny caught up with each other. With the ease of a practiced cook, Sophia boiled the corn in one pan and steamed open the clams in another while she helped Franny set the table.

After lighting two short pillar candles in the center of the table, Franny left the kitchen to fetch Sam.

"Do you think he'll be able to sit here and eat dinner?" Sophia asked Jackson. "We could have the picnic in his bedroom."

"Sam insisted on having the picnic out here."

Jackson set his glass of water on the counter and smiled. "He wanted to sit on a blanket in the yard, actually, but Franny put her foot down. He may be weak, but when his mind's made up, there's no arguing with Sam Newes."

Sam came into the kitchen, leaning on his walker and breathing hard with each step. Sophia had tried to prepare herself, but his appearance shocked her. Her father used to joke his friend was as wide as he was tall, but now Sam's chest was shrunken, ribs straining visibly against his immaculate white t-shirt as he breathed in and out. Sam had been mostly bald for years, but chemotherapy had left his gaunt face without eyebrows.

"Hey, Sam!" Sophia greeted him as heartily as she could manage.

Sam paused to catch his breath. As ever, a smile lit his face. His eyes crinkled, and deep dimples appeared on both sides of his mouth.

"There's the little doll." His voice a wheezy breath of air, he held out his arm.

Sophia dashed to his side, squeezing him as hard as she dared. She turned away her face to hide the tears threatening to spill. Sam patted her back for a moment, but he soon needed to rest a hand on his walker to steady himself. "So what'd you cook for us tonight, Sophy?"

Moving back to gesture at the picnic table with a flourish, Sophia swallowed hard and forced a smile. Jackson set the walker in the hallway and offered his arm to lean on. Franny came to Sam's other side, propping her shoulder under his armpit. They lowered Sam into the seat of honor, cushioned with a donut hole and a pillow for his back to rest against.

"I could eat a horse." Sam was finally settled comfortably at the table. "But I guess lobster will do." He winked at Sophia as Franny scolded him for his bad manners.

Sophia was grateful to laugh. Sam's physical presence was badly diminished, but his sense of humor was clearly intact. She took her seat at the table, Sam to her left, Franny to her right, and Jackson sitting across from her, his back to the window. The setting sun cast a golden glow over his hair and down the sides of his face.

His gaze held hers for a moment, warm and gentle. Still holding her gaze, he put each of his hands over Sam's and Franny's.

Sophia's heart stirred. He closed his eyes to bless the food, and she closed hers in confusion. She knew he was ministering to the table, but the message in his gaze seemed to convey another meaning. Something meant just for her.

After he blessed the food, he clasped his hands together for a moment and looked at Sophia with a wide smile. "Sam and Franny, when I heard about your lobster trapping days, I knew exactly what kind of meal I wanted to make you. In some small way, I wanted to try to thank you for everything you've done in this community. I wanted you to realize what you've meant to the life of our church. The smartest decision I made was to ask Sophia to take over the planning. So I propose a toast to the chef, Sophia Anton, who cooked this meal not only with great skill, but with a loving and generous heart." He lifted his wine glass, and Sam and Franny followed suit.

"No, no!" Sophia raised her hands to stop them. "This toast is for Sam Newes, advocate of the homeless, my father's old friend, devoted husband and father, and the person who introduced me to musical theater."

From the box she'd placed on the floor under her chair, Sophia carefully removed a small ceramic jewelry box, delicately etched with trails of ivy cascading down its sides. After setting it in the middle of the table, she opened the lid. A song from a Broadway musical, its haunting lyrics on the memory of times past well known to all of them, twinkled brightly throughout the quiet kitchen.

Sophia raised her glass toward Sam, her eyes bright with unshed tears. "To memories."

"To memories," they all repeated.

Franny squeezed Sophia's hand tightly and sipped from her glass. Her smile was pained, but it didn't dim the bright gaze fixed on her husband's face.

Sophia hadn't had a dinner like this in ages. Not since her parents died, she suddenly realized. And Franny was just as interested in piling food on Sophia's plate as her own mother had once been. To distract her, Sophia asked Franny to tell her about the old days of trapping lobster.

"Of not trapping lobster, you mean."

At his wife's reply, Sam snorted in agreement, his mouth full of roasted potatoes.

"We didn't have much money for entertainment back then, so we tried to find free things to do the kids would like. They were really little then—Garrett was three, four?" She looked at Sam for confirmation, and he nodded. "Danielle had just started walking. Someone had left a little leaky rowboat in the backyard of the house when we bought it, so we patched it up and took it out on the weekends. Other people would be out there in boats, too. The kids loved to see the cages come up with a lobster trapped inside, clicking its claws and thrashing around." Franny snapped her fingers and thumbs together to mimic claws.

"They never got to see it in our boat, though," Sam joined in. "We couldn't trap a lobster to save our lives."

Franny nodded, picking up her corn on the cob and waving Sam on.

"We were new to Maine, so we asked the other people in the boats what to put in our cages. We tried everything they told us, but no matter what we used, the lobster didn't touch our bait."

"Finally we figured they were giving us bad advice because we weren't townies," Franny added. "But we never did get the hang of pulling the lobster trap straight up. If we ever caught anything, chances are we were tipping it straight back into the water."

"I used to feel so bad whenever I pulled up the cage." Sam continued the story, his breath becoming more labored. "Garrett was sure we'd caught a big one. He'd be so excited every time, leaning over the side of the boat to see what we caught. But when the cage came out of the water, sure enough: nothing in it but a hot dog. Or less." Sam shook his head, breathing hard for a moment, and then tucked into a forkful of lobster meat with gusto.

"But he never lost hope," Franny reminded Sam, who nodded, smiling as he chewed. She paused, her lips pressed into a tight line. "Tell them about the time he fell in."

"I didn't even see him go in. I just heard him plop into the water." He coughed hard.

Franny pushed his glass of water into his hand and waited for him to drink before she took up the story again.

"Garrett leaned out over the edge of the boat to watch the chain rise. Sam tried to keep the cage level as he pulled it out. I must have been busy with Danielle, because I heard a big splash. I wasn't even sure what happened until Sam jumped right into the water, clothes and all."

Franny took a drink of her wine, shaking her head. "You set lobster traps into the rocks. The water had to be a good ten or fifteen feet deep. Deep and cold and dark. We couldn't see a thing." Franny's gaze was faraway.

Sophia's heart beat faster. Even though she knew the story ended well, she didn't like where it was going.

"And of course, Garrett didn't swim yet. Oh, my heart skipped a beat when I realized my baby was down there. I didn't think Sam could even see him. And you still had on your shoes, didn't you?" She looked across the table at Sam.

He swallowed, and then shrugged. "Had to do it in the Navy. Twenty minutes of treading water, fully clothed, boots, too."

Franny cast him a fond look. "So Sam goes under once, comes up for air. Nothing. Takes a deep breath, goes under again, this time for longer. Nothing. At this point, I'm screaming. The men in the boats around us are taking off their clothes and shoes, getting ready to jump in."

Wide-eyed, Sophia stared at Franny. All she could

think of were Randy and Josh, Kate's incorrigible twins, who were always getting themselves into trouble. She never stopped fearing they would seriously hurt themselves one day.

"And then I felt him grab my leg." Sam spoke to Franny as if they were the only two in the room. "The little bugger had gone deeper than I did, even in my shoes. So I went down again, grabbed him under the armpits, and yanked him up to the surface."

"All the people in their boats cheered. And tell them what Garrett said, Sam," Franny prodded.

"He said, 'What took you so long, Daddy?' He wasn't crying or anything. Brave little guy." Sam chuckled as he sopped up butter with a heel of bread.

"He knew his Daddy would save him. Never doubted it for a second." Franny's voice was quiet, her face lit with tenderness.

Sam looked at his wife for a long moment. As if on cue, they leaned forward and touched their wine glasses together.

The kitchen was bathed in a peaceful stillness. Sophia could feel the love radiating between Sam and Franny as tangibly as the light from the setting sun warming her through the window. The moment was such an intimate expression of emotion, she almost felt like an intruder. Slowly coming out of the spell of the story, she glanced across the table to see if Jackson was as moved as she had been. But his expression was one of naked grief. She diverted her eyes instantly, floundering for a way to ease back into normal conversation.

Sam rapped his knuckles against the table and looked at the minister. "So, Jackson, what do you think of our Sophia here? Obviously, she can cook." The minister smiled so swiftly, Sophia wondered if she'd imagined the sadness she'd seen.

"This one's a keeper, Jackson." Franny patted Sophia's shoulder, beaming. "Beautiful, smart, and a hard worker."

Sophia pressed her fingers against her closed eyelids. *Just like my parents,* she thought. *Singing my praises to any unmarried man in the room.*

"And she's got a heart of gold," Franny continued. "She organized a group of volunteers to make enough meals to feed thirty people every month over at the family shelter on Twelfth Street. How many years did you do that?" Franny asked Sophia.

"Three," Sophia said, "but—"

"And she was the youth group leader for a while, until she got canned." Sam burped quietly into his hand.

"Sam!" Franny glared across the table.

Sam only shrugged.

She turned back to Jackson. "He's giving you the wrong idea. Sophia was a wonderful youth group leader. She had those kids doing all kinds of service projects. Toiletry collections for the domestic violence shelter, sewing wraps for premature babies over at Mercy Hospital, walking animals at the Humane Society. And she helped them lead youth services, too. Sophia was the best youth group leader we ever had."

"The teens didn't think so." Sam spooned up the last of the garlic butter with another piece of bread. "They petitioned Reverend Nelson to have her replaced. Said they were tired of always doing for everybody else and never getting to do anything fun for themselves." Sam smiled mischievously at Sophia.

"Those teens were spoiled brats!" Franny glared at her husband.

Sophia's shoulders rolled with silent laughter as she fought to keep her face serious. "I don't know how they could prefer laser tag and pizza parties to crocheting scarves for the homeless every Saturday night. You just can't please some kids!" Her shoulders rose in an exaggerated shrug.

"You were too good for them." Franny patted Sophia's hand. "So Jackson, what do you think?"

Jackson's arms were crossed as he sat back in his chair, an amused smile playing on his lips. He tilted his chin and smiled at Franny. "I agree. Sophia *was* too good for them."

"That's not what I mean!" Franny said with an exasperated laugh.

Oh no, please don't. But there was no stopping this speeding train from going off the tracks.

"I mean, maybe the two of you can go out some time."

Sophia choked on a mouthful of water.

Franny handed her a napkin.

"Of course we're not dating." Sophia couldn't bring herself to look at the minister. "Pastor Thomas and I just both happened to agree you and Sam are wonderful people, so we worked together on a meal for you."

"*Pastor Thomas?*" Sam teased. "This young guy? He looks more like a plumber than a pastor."

While listening to Franny rebuke Sam, Sophia stole a glance at the minister. He seemed much less uncomfortable than Sophia felt. If anything, he was amused by Sophia's embarrassment.

"It's true. When I wear the collar, I earn the title of 'Pastor.'" He winked at Franny. "But I don't wear the collar very often. I go by my first name. Just like everybody else."

His smile was easy and open, but Sophia was still flooded with embarrassment at Franny's matchmaking. To hide her agitation, she arose and cleared the table for coffee and dessert.

Jackson had invited Garrett and Danielle to come over and share the Key lime pie with their parents.

The old couple urged Sophia and Jackson to stay.

But both blamed an early start to the work day. They knew Franny and Sam's children would appreciate time alone with their parents, especially now when Sam's time was so precious.

Sam gave her a long hug goodbye from his chair. "What Franny and I have—your parents had it, too. It's time you find the right fella and get married."

His rasping voice showed the evening had taken its toll.

"I will, Sam. Don't you worry." Sophia kissed the top of his head tenderly, meeting Franny's gaze with a sad smile.

Franny rose to thank them, extracting a promise from Sophia to come back to church.

Jackson leaned in to hold his face close to Franny's for a moment while she grasped his shoulders in silent gratitude; then, with a tremulous smile, she prodded him toward the door.

Once outside, Jackson opened the car door for Sophia.

She looked back at the house after he shut her door. Through the candlelit bow window, she saw Franny had moved to the seat she'd vacated. The couple's hands were joined on top of the table.

When Jackson slid into his seat, he sat still for a moment, looking straight ahead. Suddenly, he turned to Sophia. "Would you like to stop for coffee before I take you home?"

****

The Silver Spoon, a local institution in East Benton, was dimly lit when they walked in. A younger crowd came out after dark, and a teenager with a guitar perched on a stool in the corner, softly strumming.

Jackson stepped up to the coffee bar to order the pot of mint tea they'd agreed to share.

Sophia found a spot at a small round table near a bookcase stacked with eclectic titles. On the bottom shelf was a chessboard and a variety of card games.

They weren't likely to see anyone from church at this place. Sophia stared down at the table, her brow furrowed at the implication of her thought. Why should they care if anyone from the church saw them? *Don't let Franny plant ideas in your head.*

Jackson returned, carrying a tray with a pot of tea and two cups. He spooned sugar and cream into his cup.

The cuffs around his wrists slid back to reveal the golden brown hairs she'd noticed when she'd first met him.

His fingers, long and graceful, stirred the spoon with care.

He seemed as absorbed in preparing his tea as she was in watching him. With his head bent in the half light, eyes lowered, he resembled a man at prayer—gentle, strong, accustomed to hardship. She suddenly recalled his anguished face earlier in the evening. What memories rattled his tranquility?

He raised his head and smiled to see her gaze on him.

Disconcerted, she raised her cup hastily to her lips.

"No cream or sugar for you?" He took a sip of his own tea.

"No, I take my tea straight. Like my men." She'd added the lame quip before she could stop herself. *What is wrong with me?* Why did she always have to put on the clown shoes and red nose when she was talking to men?

"The sad thing is, it isn't even true." She could feel her cheeks coloring. "I actually have a history of dating men who are gay. Whoever I'm dating can take bets his next girlfriend will be a guy."

Jackson pushed himself back from the table, a quiet laugh rumbling from deep in his throat. His eyes flashed with humor. She thought again how little he resembled any minister she'd ever known.

"Don't apologize. I needed the laugh." He rubbed the corners of his eyes. "Being with Sam and Franny tonight, knowing how soon they'll be saying goodbye to each other, after a lifetime of total devotion—even in the ministry, I don't see it very often. Let alone in my own life." He raised his teacup, his gaze far away as he sipped.

Sophia put her hands around her teacup, nodding. "I know. All I could do while I watched them finish each other's stories was wonder if I'll ever find a love like theirs. One I can count on for the rest of my life."

Jackson cocked his head. "There's no one in your life right now?"

"No." She hesitated. "Well, yes. At least, I think

there is. Or I hope there will be. It's complicated." Her words trailed off.

Jackson's eyebrows rose, but he didn't speak.

Uneasy in the silence, Sophia tried to explain. "I have a friend in New York. Christopher. He's a ballet dancer. And no, this one's *not* gay."

Smiling, Jackson dipped his head to encourage her to continue. He leaned back in his chair to listen, arms crossed.

"We've been friends for a couple of years now. I met him here in town, but he moved to New York a while ago to dance with a bigger ballet company. I'll be visiting there in another week, and I'm hoping we'll be moving our relationship to a new level."

Sophia nodded at her own words. She wanted Jackson to agree with her.

But he continued observing her in silence.

"He tends to date toxic personalities." She hadn't meant to keep talking. Obviously, this minister's trick of the trade was to stay quiet long enough for people to reveal themselves. And it was working. The idea of remaining silent beneath his long stare was even worse than the babbling she was doing.

"He was dating a dancer who's an alcoholic. She's terrible for him, and he knows it. He tells me everything about their relationship and how she neglects him and verbally abuses him. He says he only has clarity when he's talking to me."

"Do the two of you talk a lot?"

"Almost every day." Sophia paused. "He calls me when he needs help."

Jackson's expressive eyebrows rose again.

"I know how it sounds," Sophia hastened to say.

"Like he's just using me. But our relationship is much more. There are things we talk about we've never shared with anyone else. Either of us."

As he took a long, slow sip of tea, his gaze remained fixed on hers. "I'm glad to hear it. Relationships without common interests don't tend to last."

"We like the same kind of books," Sophia blurted. "We introduce each other to new ways of thinking and it's such a...delight. I know it sounds corny, but we love sharing our philosophical perspectives."

Carried away on her own memories, Sophia let down her guard. "One of the first times I invited him to my house, I was chopping vegetables for dinner. He put his hand over mine to stop the knife for a minute, and he talked about the life force in vegetables. He told me Eastern cultures honor the vegetable for giving up its life to the people who eat it. And then he said a little prayer of thanks to the vegetables for giving us their nourishment." Her hand drifted to her collarbone. Christopher had touched her heart that day. "When he did that, I was hooked. It may sound silly, but now I always thank my fruits or vegetables before I eat them." She refocused her gaze on Jackson, smiling at the soulful picture of her boyfriend she'd created.

Jackson's arms were crossed over his chest. A crease wrinkled his brow again.

"Very noble," he remarked finally.

Sophia nodded, hoping she'd done justice to Christopher's spiritual side.

"So"—he cleared his throat—"what do you do before you eat meat? The dance of the seven veils?" Jackson's eyes glinted.

Sophia gasped, crumpling her napkin and throwing it at him. "No. The Macarena," she shot back. The ball of paper bounced into his teacup and sank.

"How about a prayer for my desecrated cup of tea, Sophia?" Fishing out the sodden napkin with his spoon, he dropped it onto the saucer and met Sophia's gaze.

"Maybe *you'd* better start praying, Reverend." She waved her own spoon threateningly at him, but she couldn't help smiling. She always had trouble explaining how sensitive Christopher was.

"Now I'm sorry I missed the preliminaries with the lobster," he teased. His face grew serious a moment later. "I don't mean to make fun of your beliefs. I agree. In our society, we take food for granted. Christopher sounds like someone who thinks deeply about"—he gave a tiny shake of his head—"all sorts of things."

Sophia nodded. She wished she hadn't brought up Christopher. Somehow, she only succeeded in making him sound pretentious.

"You said when you visit him you're hoping to take your relationship to the next level. But he's involved with another woman. What's going to be different this time?"

She stared into her empty teacup to avoid his gaze. "Physical health and beauty are important to Christopher. I've lost a lot of weight recently. I think he might see me differently now. As a potential, I don't know…girlfriend, I guess, instead of just a best friend." She trailed off into a whisper, staring at the floor. The last thing she wanted was to look at Jackson's face and see pity.

His hand closed over hers, rough and warm and so large, it all but concealed hers. He didn't say a word, speaking only through the pressure of his palm. Like a protective shield, his touch pushed away her awkwardness.

He's gifted at putting people at ease, she thought, remembering how serenity descended on Sam's and Franny's table during Jackson's blessing. She raised her chin and found Jackson's gaze fixed on her.

"I haven't known you long enough to have any right to tell you what to do, Sophia. But I'm sure you know, love goes deeper than appearances. I hope your friend, or boyfriend, understands that, too." He paused. "If you ever need to talk, you can stop by the rectory anytime." He pressed his fingers over hers once more before leaning back in his chair.

Her skin felt naked when he pulled away. She dropped her hands in her lap, twisting the ring on her finger. *What am I doing here?* As they'd talked tonight, she'd almost forgotten his calling. She hadn't expected to be so comfortable spending the evening with a minister. She'd planned to be on her best behavior. But tonight, he'd made them all relax. He'd even gotten past her usual defenses—the jokes she used to distance herself. She never confided her plans about Christopher to anyone.

Sure, Jackson Thomas was the head of her church—her spiritual counselor, if she needed one. But had she confused the man with the minister? Remembering the warmth of his hand on hers, she shivered. When her gaze drifted back to his face, she found him studying her.

"What do you want from life, Sophia?"

She weighed the question. *Remember, he's asking as a man of the cloth.* "The usual things, I guess. I like my job. It's fun. It allows me to be creative and meet interesting people."

She paused, stirring her cold tea. "But I don't see myself in merchandising forever. I want to do more than build a company's profit for stockholders. I want a more fulfilling career."

The hint of a frown wrinkled Jackson's forehead as he leaned in closer.

Sophia sighed, looking at her hands in her lap. She may as well seek spiritual advice. How often was she out for coffee with a minister? "To tell the truth, what we did for Sam and Franny tonight was more gratifying than any project I've done at work. I want to make a difference in peoples' lives. In a way, I'd like to do the kind of work you do: help the people in my community. Make the world a better place."

"And you can have that life with Christopher?" Jackson raised his eyebrows, but his tone was gentle.

"Maybe. I don't know. Because the other part of the equation is, I want a husband to love. I want to be a mother more than anything in the world. I'm almost thirty years old, and I can't wait forever for the right man." Her gaze held a challenge. "Sometimes you have to take what life gives you, even if you've dreamed of bigger things."

Jackson tapped his index finger against the table. He cocked his head to the side to regard her, and then nodded. "I wasn't planning on asking you for another favor. If you really are interested in doing meaningful work in the community, I have a situation, and I could use your help. Before you go off to New York. If you have the time."

"My schedule's light this week, since I put in a lot

of extra hours for the housewares fair. What do you need?" Her heart beat a little faster at the idea of collaborating with Jackson again. *Stop that right now.* She clenched her fingers in her lap.

"Do you know Hazel Bracca?" he asked.

Sophia nodded, puzzled. She hadn't thought of Hazel in years. She and her sister, Marie, had been constant fixtures at all church events when Sophia was a child. She'd considered them a little unusual because they'd never married, even though they were her own mother's age.

"Hazel's been living at the Downtowner. Last week she was evicted. They threw her and all her belongings out into the street."

Sophia winced. The Downtowner was famous in East Benson for housing the mentally ill. "How did she end up there?"

Jackson shook his head. "Hazel didn't attend church when I first came to St. Jerome's. One day in the rectory, Donna mentioned passing her in the street. Donna seemed alarmed at how Hazel had changed. So I started asking questions downtown. When I found out where she lived, I visited her every week or two. She's experiencing memory loss, so it's hard to hold a conversation with her. I couldn't get anywhere asking about her past."

"Is Marie dead then?" Sophia couldn't imagine Marie would allow Hazel to live at the Downtowner.

"I haven't found any record of her death, but I haven't tracked her down either. Hazel seems sure her sister is alive, but she can't, or won't, tell me where to find her." He rubbed at his forehead, then dropped his face onto one hand. "Anyway, Hazel was barely hanging on. I arranged for Meals on Wheels to bring her food, but she ate like a bird. I think she threw most of it away. I tried to get information from the management about how she was paying her bills," he continued, "but Hazel wouldn't sign permission for me to talk to the landlord or to the utility companies."

He ran his palm from his forehead to his neck, sighing. "The situation came to a head today. The landlord called this morning to say he'd evicted Hazel last night. Said he'd already given her a thirty-day warning, and she'd shut the door in his face. He didn't seem too broken up about throwing an old woman into the street."

Sophia's eyes widened. "That's terrible! How could anyone do that?"

Jackson shook his head, bouncing his knuckles on the edge of the table. "I spent half the day trying to find Hazel at the shelter, at the downtown motels, the library…and then I just drove along the streets looking for her. I finally found her under the overpass by the hospital. I tried to get her into my car to take her to the shelter, but she started yelling so loudly, a policeman stopped to question me." Jackson tapped his throat with his index finger, and grimaced. "I didn't have my collar on. The policeman wanted to take her to the station, but I asked him to give me a day or two to figure something out."

"You left her under the overpass?" Imagining tiny Hazel Bracca wandering through the most dangerous part of town, Sophia shuddered.

He narrowed his eyes. "No, I walked her down into the park since she wouldn't get in my car. Then I called Mona over at the shelter and asked *her* to pick up

Hazel. Hazel agreed to go with her, but just for one night. I have until tomorrow to come up with a plan. Unless—*you* can help?"

Allowing herself just the hint of a smile, Sophia looked at him over the bridge of her nose. "After all that bunk I gave you about wanting to make a difference, how can I say no?"

Jackson folded his hands in his lap and leaned back, grinning. "Right. No excuses now." Then he straightened, his face serious again. "I'd like you to go down to the shelter and talk to Hazel. Persuade her to go somewhere safe while I arrange for a space for her at a nursing home. Stop by the church tomorrow morning. I'll have money waiting in case you need to put her in a motel for a night or two. She's not just mentally unstable, Sophia. She's physically withering away and needs to be under medical observation."

Elbows braced on the table, he propped his chin on his clasped hands. "She's not crazy about men, so I'm hoping she'll listen to a woman. She might even remember you from when you were younger. Her mind wanders through the past more than the present."

Sophia nodded. She couldn't bear the thought of a helpless old woman adrift on the streets of East Benson. She'd find a way to reach Hazel. "I don't work until four o'clock tomorrow. I'll have plenty of time. Hazel worked on all kinds of church events with my parents. I'll remind her of happier times. Maybe then she'll trust me. Don't worry, Jackson." She nodded, confident in her plan. "I'll find a way to get through to her."

"My own Girl Friday." Jackson's mouth curved into a smile, his gaze lingering on her face.

In the dimmed light of the coffeehouse, his eyes

were as dusky as coal. She could get lost in those eyes. *There I go again.* Heat rose from the base of her neck, flooding toward her face. She stood before her cheeks could betray her emotions, keeping her head ducked while she cleared the cups and saucers from the table and brought them to the bar. By the time she returned to the table, she was back in control.

She reached for her purse. "Sounds like my day starts early tomorrow. I'd better head home and get some sleep." She kept her tone businesslike. Her minister had requested her assistance. She was only volunteering her time to the church.

By the time they emerged out into the cold April night, she'd almost persuaded herself to believe it.

Chapter Five

The next morning, Sophia pulled up to the front entrance of the women's shelter. A gray cement block building, its foundation crumbling along the ramp leading to the entrance, the women's shelter squatted like an afterthought among the drugstores and pizza shops on Sixth Street.

Hazel perched on a bench by the door, clutching her handbag to her chest.

Gathering her courage, Sophia braced her shoulders. She'd already dealt with one challenging woman this morning. Open hostility from Donna had greeted Sophia when she arrived at the rectory to pick up the money Jackson left for Hazel's recovery mission.

"I don't know why Pastor Thomas is going to so much trouble for Hazel Bracca. The woman doesn't appreciate a thing he does. He's too nice for his own good." Donna retrieved an envelope from the back of a drawer, shaking her graying helmet of hair. Magnified behind bifocals, Donna's pale eyes were as hard as nickels. She handed Sophia the envelope, staring with open unfriendliness at the younger woman. "Interesting. We haven't seen you in church for ages. Then when you meet our new minister, you seem to be running for Volunteer of the Year."

Her face flushing with a mixture of embarrassment

and irritation, Sophia managed a tight smile. "Well, I pulled my friend Kate into the church years ago when she needed it. I guess now she's pulling me back in. I'm glad to be able to help."

"Hmmph," Donna sniffed.

Sophia forced out a stiff goodbye and fled the room, Donna's stare weighing on her like cement.

Sophia's confidence continued plummeting as she drove to the shelter. *Had* she agreed to help from a sense of duty to one of her parents' old friends from church? Or was she just looking for an excuse to spend more time with the minister?

Thunderstorms through the night had transformed the potholes of late spring into craters filled with water. Gutters running with rain earlier in the morning pooled with standing water now as the sun burned in the clear blue sky. The temperature was cool, almost cold this morning; but the sun was starting to warm the air.

Climbing out of the car with a wide stride to avoid the water, Sophia planted a smile on her face. She stepped toward the old woman, willing herself to appear calm and friendly. "Hi, Hazel. Do you remember me? I'm Phil and Estelle Anton's daughter."

Hazel tilted her head toward Sophia, exposing a face shrunken and etched with lines. Her eyes blinked rapidly, and the cords in her throat stood out as she strained to speak. "Sophia?"

Relief washed over Sophia. She sat beside Hazel and hugged her gently. The woman felt as fragile as a baby bird.

Hazel clasped one hand around Sophia's wrist and peered at her face. The old woman's eyes were almost hidden by a frayed black beret sliding down her forehead. "What are you doing here, Sophia? Are you on the streets, too?"

Sophia patted Hazel's hand. "No. I was looking for you, Hazel. I'd like to help you find a place to stay."

But Hazel gazed at her through a cloud of confusion. "I don't need help. I have my bag." She gave her handbag a little shake. "Plenty of money in here. I'm just waiting for the bus." She peered down the street. Her mouth turned down, she stared at her purse again and fell silent.

Had she forgotten Sophia was there? She raised an uncertain finger to the shoulder of Hazel's frayed orange poncho. "Hazel, I remember the wonderful *pizzelles* you made. You used to give them to me when I was a kid. I always asked my mother to use your recipe."

Hazel raised her face to Sophia's, her aged forehead wrinkled with concentration. Suddenly she smiled, exposing two rows of yellowed and broken teeth. "Nobody makes *pizzelles* like I do."

Sophia bobbed her head up and down. Hazel seemed very pleased with herself.

"The bakery on Cherry Street makes *pizzelles,* too. Have you ever tried them? They're almost as good as yours." She squeezed Hazel's hand, needing to get the old woman off this bench and into her car. Maybe the lure of *pizzelles* would do the trick.

"Ha!" Hazel scoffed. "They're no good. I wouldn't give a penny for them."

Sophia leaned closer to the old woman, placing her hand over Hazel's bony fingers. "But I've heard they're *really* good! Why don't we get in the car and run down to the bakery and find out? We'll have some coffee, too. Just us girls!" The confidence she was trying to radiate was wearing thin. *Please, get off this bench!*

Hazel swiveled her head toward the car. "Is that our ride?" She stood, swaying in a wide arc to the left.

Sophia grabbed her elbow to support her.

With overstated dignity, her head and shoulders thrown back, Hazel stepped to the car. At each footfall, the support hose visible beneath her wool skirt slid toward her ankles. When they reached the curb, she waited for Sophia to open the passenger side door, nodding her thanks as if Sophia were a paid driver.

Shoulders shaking in silent laughter, Sophia offered her arm while Hazel lowered herself with difficulty onto the seat. During the short drive to the bakery, Sophia chattered about the stores they passed. She peppered Hazel with questions, but Hazel only smiled and stared out the windshield. Sophia had hoped to see a sign of recognition on the old woman's face when they pulled into the bakery parking lot. This Italian establishment was a favorite of her parents and their friends. But Hazel's gaze remained cloudy and unfocused as she walked unsteadily to the bakery door.

The odors of freshly baked pastries and rich coffee brewing in old-fashioned percolators were an assault on Sophia. She'd eaten only a half cup of cottage cheese that morning. Placing a stern hand over her growling stomach, she helped Hazel lower herself into a booth by the window. She hurried to the counter to order a bag of *pizzelles* and two cups of coffee. Returning to the booth, she opened the bag of Italian cookies and placed one on a napkin in front of the old woman. With a sigh, she closed the bag and placed it at the end of the table, out of reach of both of them.

Frowning, Hazel stared down at her napkin and broke off a tiny piece of the flat cookie. Placing it in her mouth, she chewed with effort, the bolus of food bulging against her paper-skin cheeks.

Sophia was transfixed. Had Hazel forgotten how to swallow? What had the vet told her about making her cat swallow a pill? Stroke its throat? She eyed the ropey tendons extending from Hazel's jaw and grimaced. Uh-uh.

Hazel opened her mouth and let the soggy remains drop straight down on the table. "No good." Her wide eyes accused Sophia.

Like I'm poisoning her. Sophia swallowed a giggle and swept the sodden cookie into a napkin, folding it into a tidy lump. "You don't have to eat any more. Why don't you have some coffee?"

Staring out the window into the parking lot, Hazel sipped from her cup. Keeping the woman's mind from wandering was so difficult. As a face from Hazel's past, she'd hoped the old woman would show more interest. But Sophia was having no more luck communicating with Hazel than Jackson had. "Hazel, I remember your sister Marie. How is she doing?"

Hazel sighed, a trickle of coffee sliding down her chin.

Would she be disrespectful if she wiped the woman's mouth?

"Marie's my sister," Hazel said finally. She took another sip of coffee, the cup clattering against the side of the saucer when she placed it back down.

Sophia slid a napkin on top of the brown puddle sloshed over the side. "Does Marie live around here?" she asked. "Could we go see her?"

Hazel's eyes were unblinking. "Who'd you say you are again?" She swiped the corner of her mouth with a wrinkled fingertip.

"Sophia Anton." She dropped her chin to her chest. She was getting nowhere. Lifting her head, she pulled her cell phone from her handbag to text Jackson.

—Hazel doesn't remember me. Need help—

"I knew your father."

The woman's abrupt words startled Sophia. She nodded to Hazel with an encouraging smile. Finally, the old woman was remembering the Anton family.

Hazel smiled into her coffee cup. "He wore a black tie decorated with chili peppers."

"Right!" Sophia said. "I bought him the tie for Father's Day. You knew both of my parents, remember, Hazel? You and my Mom were in charge of the mother-daughter banquet every year."

"I *knew* your father. In the biblical sense," she added, her lips prim.

Sophia, in the act of raising her cup to her mouth, set it down hard enough to splash the coffee right over the side. She clenched her hand around the cup and forced her voice low and even. "Hazel, that's not true."

The woman's wizened face wore a coy smile. She twisted a lank strand of hair around her finger. "We were lovers!" She covered her mouth with her bony hand and giggled.

Sophia stared at the old woman, disbelief dropping her jaw. The pulse of the cell phone in her lap distracted her. She was happy to look away from Hazel's preening face and read Jackson's reply.

At a funeral. Please keep her till I can get to you. Thx

Sophia raced her thumbs over the keyboard.

—*She says my dad was her lover!!*—

After hitting Send, Sophia forced herself to again look at Hazel. The old woman wore the secret smile of a woman remembering a stolen moment of passion. Sophia's stomach clenched with a rising feeling of nausea. Her phone pulsed again.

LOL!

Did he think she was joking? Sophia glared at the screen. A moment later, another message appeared.

I know you can handle this

Sophia swallowed hard. With all the firmness she could muster, she told Hazel, "We need to find you a nice place of your own to stay."

Hazel's dreamy expression morphed into a mask of fearfulness, her penciled-on eyebrows lifted high, her mouth opened into a quivering oval. "What will you do to me?"

Her tone dissolved into a high pitch of distress. Customers seated at the counter turned their heads to look.

Rising, she knocked her bony hip against the corner of the table and made a piteous cry.

Sophia hastened to help her to her feet. She could feel disapproving stares drilling into her back. "We're just going for a drive, Hazel. It's a beautiful morning. Wouldn't you like to take a drive in the country?"

Her lip trembling, Hazel gazed at Sophia. "Where are we going?" Small as she was, the old woman held firm against the coaxing pressure of Sophia's hand under her elbow.

Sophia put on her most winning smile, too embarrassed to meet the gazes of the other patrons.

"Just for a nice ride into the country. And then I'll take you wherever you want to go. Okay?"

Hazel's eyes suddenly went vacant, the intensity of her gaze disappearing like water down a drain. Yielding to the pressure of Sophia's hand under her arm, she let herself be led out the door and back into the car. Once settled, she twisted her head to face Sophia with a sweet smile. "I'd like to go visit your father." She folded her hands in her lap and looked out the window.

Lord, give me strength. Gritting her teeth, Sophia backed out of the parking lot onto the deserted one-way road leading out of town.

The movement of the accelerating car lulled Hazel. She stared straight ahead as if in a trance.

Sophia pressed the automatic door locks and headed to the highway.

****

Two hours later, Sophia had crossed the county twice. If she slowed to a stop, she risked rousing Hazel from her reverie. She didn't want Hazel to try to escape again. If she only knew where the funeral was, she'd drop Hazel with Jackson and let *him* deal with the woman.

What a sucker she was. The second anyone made her feel needed, she dropped everything to take care of another person's problems. First Kate, then Christopher, and now even the minister of her church.

She forced herself to check her speed. Her racing pulse was making her press too heavy on the accelerator. She glanced at the fuel gauge—down to about an eighth of a tank.

Pulling into a service station, she slowed to approach the gas tanks. As she feared, she noticed the old woman awakening from her trance.

Hazel's crooked hand scrabbled for the door handle.

"Hi, Hazel!" Sophia called, her voice hearty. "You stay here while I pump the gas, okay?" She grabbed her purse and tripped out of the car, closing and locking the door behind her. Keeping one thumb on the lock button of her key pod, she used her other hand to swipe her banking card and unscrew the gas cap.

The door handle rattled as Hazel tried to get out. Her struggle intensified, rocking the car.

Where did this tiny woman find the strength? Sophia filled the tank as fast as she could. She jumped back into the driver's seat, avoiding antagonizing Hazel with any further eye contact. In Hazel's current state, she might turn and strike Sophia.

Hazel wrestled harder with the door handle, her veined hands shaking.

What am I supposed to do? Feeling at a loss, Sophia reached for Hazel's shoulder.

The old woman's head spun toward Sophia, her eyes wild. "Let me out of here!"

Sophia closed her eyes. She'd never felt so exhausted by another person's need. Maybe she should just give up and let Hazel go. But how could she abandon an old woman who wasn't in her right mind? Sure, Hazel had concocted an unforgivable lie about Sophia's father. *But how had Hazel remembered her father, and his tie, with such clarity?*

With a shake of her head, Sophia pushed the thought away. She was no closer to moving Hazel to a safe place than she'd been when she first found her at the shelter. No matter what Sophia was feeling, she had to protect Hazel.

Remembering how Jackson had calmed her by laying his hand over hers, Sophia took a deep breath and wrapped gentle fingers over the woman's wrinkled knuckles. "It's all right." Sophia kept her voice soft while she nodded her head, imitating her mother's technique for calming her upset daughter many years ago.

Frozen with fear, Hazel allowed Sophia to stroke her hand. A few moments later, Hazel's cramped shoulders relaxed against the seat.

Sophia had to find a way to leave the gas station. She took another deep breath. "Come visit my house, Hazel," she said, giving the old woman's hand a gentle squeeze and watching for a change in the woman's attitude.

Hazel's face slackened again, wiped clean of the anxiety and distrust of just moments before. She stared into the younger woman's eyes. "Who are you, honey?" Her finger swiped back and forth under her nose.

Sophia restrained Hazel's hands, lowering them to her lap. "I'm Sophia Anton. Will you come for a visit?"

A smile wobbled from Hazel's wrinkled face. "Why, I sure will! Will your father be there?"

Releasing Hazel's hands, Sophia gripped the steering wheel until her knuckles turned white. She stared out the windshield at the woods facing the gas station. The scent of honeysuckle perfumed the car even though she'd dared to lower the windows only a crack in the heat of the day. Exhaling a slow breath, she slid the gear into Drive and returned to the road. She could feel Hazel's gaze as she waited for an answer. Grudgingly, Sophia responded. "Maybe."

Hazel folded her hands in a smooth, unhurried motion and beamed out the windshield.

****

After an hour of waiting for Sophia's father to arrive—*Good luck with that*, Sophia thought—Hazel fell asleep at the breakfast table over her cup of coffee. She slumped against the kitchen wall, a faint snore rumbling from her throat.

Hardly daring to breathe, Sophia tiptoed into the living room. She plucked a pillow off the couch and, with care, propped it between the old woman and the wall. Sophia caught her breath again when Hazel's eyes flew open, releasing it only when the old woman settled back to sleep with a chest-rattling exhalation.

Sliding her cell phone off the counter, she sneaked into the bathroom to call her department and explain she wouldn't be in to work today. Exhausted, Sophia crossed the living room and sank on the couch. From where she sat, she could keep an eye on Hazel's still form.

Her chin lifted with each steady inhale. Propped against the wall, her upper body dwarfed by the pillow, she seemed even more frail and vulnerable.

In utter bewilderment, Sophia gazed at the old woman, searching her memory for an explanation of Hazel's outrageous claims about Sophia's father. She'd known Hazel only from church dinners. Hazel was the smaller of two sisters: lively, talkative, darting back and forth between the church kitchen and the fellowship hall to wipe tables or refill empty water pitchers. Marie, bulkier of frame and much quieter than her older sister, stayed behind the scenes, washing pots and pans and mopping the kitchen floor.

She remembered her parents chatting and laughing with Hazel—*both* of her parents. Surely, Hazel's outrageous claims were nothing more than the fantasies of a mind unglued from reality.

Her gaze drifted to her parents' wedding photograph hanging on the wall. Her father, tall and handsome, wore a smile softening his stern features. His hands were big enough to encircle her mother's waist. She leaned back into his arms, her short, dark hair curling like ivy around her gentle face.

Sophia had often wished she'd inherited her mother's slight stature. Other than having similar hair, she favored her father. Would she ever find a man who could fold her into his arms the way her father embraced her mother? Someone tall, protective, strong, but gentle. Her Dad had forever been her model for the perfect husband—up until this moment. He'd been a charmer; she couldn't deny it. Sophia's mother used to tease him about "fending off the church ladies" when he helped in the kitchen. Women flocked to work at his side. Debonair even in an apron, a kitchen towel tucked into his back pocket, he ambled from station to station, lending a hand and encouraging the volunteers. He lifted spirits. Sophia had been proud of her father's irresistible personality.

But she'd been a child then, and thought like a child. Was more going on behind the scenes than she knew?

This is ridiculous. Instead of going to the gym, or taking a nice, long walk, or doing anything I'd like to do, I've spent the day trying to reason with a woman who's probably senile. And somehow she's managed to plant her crazy ideas into my head. I'm missing work and I'm trapped here while she snores all over my breakfast table. If I move her, I'll wake her and get her started all over again. I can't even leave my own living room in case she starts to slide off her seat.

Sophia jumped up and paced the carpet. *Whose job was this, anyway?* The minister had asked for a favor, and she'd jumped at the chance to help. Her parents would have expected nothing less. They'd taught her to answer the call of the church.

Be honest. It wasn't the church *she was trying to please.* Jackson's intense brown eyes, his mischievous smile, the warmth of his hand enclosing hers. She squeezed her eyes shut, her stomach clenching as she recognized her true motive. She'd offered her help because of the man who'd asked for it. She'd wanted to please him, to do the job no one else could get done. She wanted to show him he needed her.

Sophia stood stock still in the middle of the living room. *Just like I do with Christopher. Because the only way I think he'll ever want me is if he needs me.* She shook her head hard. "No!" She clapped her hand over her mouth and held her breath.

Hazel stirred for a moment, and then dropped her chin lower onto her chest.

A car engine's hum sounded through the window screens. Sophia hastened to the door to look through the diamond window.

Jackson's faded black sedan sat in the parking lot next to her coupe.

Her stomach flipped as he emerged in his clerical black suit. She watched him tug off the white collar and push it in his pocket. Scrabbling for the door handle, she opened it before he could knock. She motioned him inside with a finger on her lips, her gaze on the white strip of cloth dangling from the pocket of his trousers.

He started to speak.

Instead, Sophia shushed him and gestured toward the couch. "Do you want coffee?" She could trust herself to speak only in a monotone.

He shook his head.

She could feel the intensity of his gaze as she locked her attention on the refrigerator. Her heart thudded in her throat. "Water? I don't think I have anything else." As she swiveled toward the kitchen, she felt his hand trap her wrist.

"Sophia. Sit," he commanded, his voice gentle.

Perched on the edge of the couch, her hands in her lap, she lowered her eyelashes so her face wouldn't betray her.

"You're upset. What happened?"

Sophia lifted her chin to stare at Hazel. "I got her here safe and sound, just as you asked." Crossing her arms and pressing her lips together, she fell silent.

Jackson propped his elbow on the back of the soft leather couch, his body half-turned toward her. With his fingertips supporting the weight of his head, his face was angled in her direction, but he too looked away.

In the distance, a lawn mower sputtered to life. Sophia shifted away from Jackson. Her ears hummed with the silence between them.

Jackson cleared his throat. "So she wasn't any easier for you to manage than she was for me."

If he'd hoped to break the awkward silence, he was mistaken. She bit her lower lip between her teeth. *This time,* he *can do the talking.*

"Did she remember you?" Jackson continued.

Sophia turned to Jackson with an acid stare. "Obviously. Otherwise, she wouldn't have spent all afternoon telling me about her affair with my father." Her tone was low—her "lethal voice," as Kate called it. Sophia's heart raced. She'd never dreamed she'd speak this way to a minister.

His gaze solemn, Jackson dipped his head.

But Sophia had seen his fleeting smile before he smothered it with his hand. She slapped her hands to her side and sat up straight. "Is this *funny*? My father was the only man I've trusted my entire life. The kind of man I hoped to find for myself someday. And today I learned he was unfaithful to my mother!"

"Sophia, you can't trust Hazel. She's lost her grip on reality." He placed his hand on Sophia's, but she snatched it away.

"*Today's* reality, maybe. Her eye for details from the past are accurate, though. She remembered my father's favorite tie—the one *I* bought him for Father's Day. She remembered making *pizzelles* and keeping the recipe a secret." Not that it was uncommon for a woman of Hazel's generation to keep her recipe a secret. But still. "Do you think I had fun spending all day learning about my father's infidelity?" The sarcasm felt good, like popping a festered blister. "Spending hours driving an old woman around the county because if I stopped, I knew she'd jump out of my car."

Sophia was breathing hard now, but the words kept tumbling out. "Hours I could have been doing something I get paid for, like my *job*! Do you realize I had to miss work today because of this little assignment? I'll bet you didn't, because you barely took the time to respond when I texted you I was in over my head. You were busy with your *other* parishioners, taking care of everybody else at the church while I took care of *your* responsibilities. Well, what about me? Aren't you supposed to be *my* minister, too?"

Jackson dropped his elbows to his knees and clasped his hands together, squinting at the carpet between his feet. "Of course I am." A muscle in his jaw twitched. "You're right. Hazel was my responsibility, not yours. I'm sorry I couldn't come as soon as you needed me."

"Don't be." The threat of tears clogged the back of her throat. "This is just…what I do. The need to ride to the rescue is like a sickness. You didn't twist my arm to take care of Hazel. I *wanted* to be the savior. But today my martyrdom"—she spat out the word—"backfired. Hazel didn't *want* my help. Whether she meant to or not, she poisoned my view of my father. Today, *I* needed help. I needed someone to swoop in and save *me.* And no one was there." With the knuckle of her hand, she brushed an angry tear off her cheekbone, hating the self-pitying sound of her own voice.

His forehead creased with lines, he straightened to face her. Grasping gentle fingers around her shoulders, he drew her close, bending his neck to place his cheek against hers.

She closed her eyes and shivered as a faint hint of whiskers grazed her skin. Cradled against his chest, her body yielded to the familiar warmth and reassurance of his hands.

He leaned back.

Her eyelids flew open. Jackson's face was mere inches from hers.

His lips drawn into a tight line, he traced a finger

across her jaw and cupped her chin in his hand.

Sophia's breath caught as she gazed into Jackson's eyes, as dusky and deep as a pool of chocolate. She melted toward him as his fingers slid into her hair, combing through the long locks all the way from the nape of her neck. His lips sought hers, only a gentle brushing. He cupped Sophia's head in his hands and gently drew her face away from his. His heart beat against her flat palms as she pressed them into the rough fabric of his black shirt.

His gaze on her parted lips, he coaxed her mouth forward again, this time allowing his lips to linger and trail down her jaw to her throat.

She moved closer, curling her fingers into the thick hair over the back of his collar, her desire for him cresting like a wave. His heart pounded against hers as she yielded her throat to the demands of his kiss.

But he pulled away.

The absence of his warm skin and throbbing heart dashed her ardor like a bucket of ice water. Opening her dazed eyes, she pulled her hands away from his shoulders. She hugged her elbows close to her body, peeking at Jackson from under lowered lids.

He slid to another cushion on the couch, pressing his elbows to his knees and clasping his hands. A muscle in his jaw twitched as he stared at the carpet, just as it had the moment before they kissed.

Twisting her damp hands together, she waited for him to speak. Her cheeks grew hot as she endured the silence. She opened her palms against her thighs and stared into them, blinking. Had the kiss even happened?

The blare of a car horn from the street roused them. Sophia lifted her gaze to Jackson.

He unclasped his fingers and spread his palms wide. Without a glance at her, he rose from the couch. Pausing as he reached the door, he kept his back to the room and rested his hand on the knob. The clerical collar he'd half-tucked in his pants pocket swayed to a halt. Head bent, he whispered, "I'm sorry." He walked out the door, shutting it behind him with a quiet click.

Her pulse still racing, she raised a palm to her throat. What had they done?

Hazel's voice, high-pitched and sharp as she called across the kitchen, whipped Sophia's conscience. The old woman's eyes were open and staring at Sophia. "You can't have him."

Sophia froze, unable to reconcile the old woman's presence with what had just happened on the couch. She'd never felt such passion before. Never. And the look in Jackson's eyes before he leaned in to kiss her— surely, he'd wanted it as much as she had.

Or had *she* leaned in? The suddenness of his departure stunned her, and now she wasn't sure what had happened between them. She'd been so angry, hurling furious words. His arms had come around her. His rough cheek against her skin. And then, they kissed. But who initiated the kiss?

A dawning horror prickled her skin. Had she thrown herself at the minister? No. He'd put his arms around her, pressed his face against hers. She shivered again just at the thought.

But hadn't she seen him press his cheek against Franny's last night? And Franny hadn't lost control. Sophia's cheeks flamed. She struggled to answer Hazel. "Did you have a good nap?" The words scraped Sophia's throat.

"You can't have him any more than I could have your father." Hazel's lips turned down at the corners, and the thin skin around her eyes crinkled.

The woman looked sorry for Sophia. Never in her life had Sophia been so uncertain of her next step. She'd made advances toward her minister, and he'd raced out of her house. The old lady who claimed to be Sophia's father's lover had witnessed Sophia's own crime of passion. Closing her eyes, she clasped her fingers into praying hands. If only the earth would open and swallow her.

She half-opened one eye to see Hazel frowning from across the kitchen. No sense waiting for divine intervention. Sophia rose, forcing her feet to walk to the freezer. When she wanted to distract Kate's boys, she fed them ice cream. Maybe Hazel could be soothed into forgetfulness with a bowl of butter-brickle. Sliding a dessert bowl in front of Hazel, Sophia handed her a spoon.

Squinting, Hazel grasped the spoon and dipped it in the bowl. Confusion drained from her expression as she licked her spoon.

Encouraged, Sophia chattered about Sam and Franny Newes and other older members of the church. With any luck, the memory of what Hazel had witnessed from the kitchen would fade into the ether.

Spooning up the last of her ice cream, Hazel wiped a napkin over her mouth. "I need to use the ladies' room," she announced with a regal sniff.

Sophia was grateful for the diversion. She could almost see shame nodding to her from the shadows whenever silence fell. She sprang up to help the old woman to the bathroom, turning her back as Hazel used the toilet. Sophia wrinkled her nose. Hazel needed a good washing. "How about a nice, warm bath?" Sophia filled the tub with warm water. She could lift Hazel's tiny frame if necessary.

Hazel shook her head as the water filled the tub, taking a firm hold of the towel rack with one hand and the toilet paper dispenser with the other. But her eyes widened as she watched Sophia pour bubble bath into the water. She reached out her hand to touch the frothy white heaps, almost losing her balance until Sophia caught her arm. Eager now to get out of her clothes, Hazel cooperated as Sophia helped her step out of her slacks and shrug off her blouse.

Holding Sophia's hands, Hazel stepped one cautious foot, then another, into the bathtub. She lowered herself into the fragrant mountain of bubbles with a contented sigh.

Hazel needed a good long soak, Sophia decided. She settled the old woman against a bath pillow, tucking two rolled up bath towels under her armpits to prevent sliding. Gathering Hazel's clothes, Sophia dashed down the hall and threw them into the washer on a short cycle. As she poured detergent into the dispenser, she heard her cell phone ring from the bathroom. When she ran for her phone, she recognized the number of the church. Her heartbeat drummed in her ears. Taking a deep breath, she pressed the green button. "Hello." She hoped her voice sounded less quavering than she felt.

"This is Donna, from church."

Sophia laid her palm against her chest to quiet her heartbeat. She was relieved not to speak to Jackson. But didn't he owe her the courtesy of checking in on Hazel himself? As she listened to Donna list the nursing homes who had been contacted, Sophia's heart sank. So this was how it would be. Jackson—Pastor Thomas—would keep his distance.

"Are you still there?" Donna's voice cut through the line.

"Yes, Donna," Sophia answered with an effort. "Whatever Pastor Thomas works out is fine. Hazel's okay here now. She can stay until he finds a more permanent home."

"But you can't leave Hazel alone." Donna's tone was sharp. "We're drawing up a list of volunteers to stay with her while you're at work or whenever you have to leave."

Sophia's heart lurched. She couldn't allow members of the church to hear from Hazel what had happened between Sophia and the minister. "No need. At least, not yet. I'm off for the next two days, and I'm happy to take care of Hazel," she lied. Plenty of co-workers owed her favors. One of them would trade days off.

Sophia punched off her phone to rescue Hazel. She was sliding down in the tub, her mouth getting close to the water. Sophia yanked her up from under the armpits.

Hazel stared up at her, wide-eyed. "What are you going to do now?"

"That's what I'd like to know." Sophia sighed, sitting on the toilet and burying her head in her hands.

Chapter Six

Jackson turned off his car and sat at the end of the driveway. The engine ticked with heat before it settled into silence.

The house he'd grown up in was over two hundred years old, tucked at the end of a graveled lane that cut through dairy farms and fields of corn. The home stayed cool in the shade of towering oak trees. His mother wouldn't step outside for a rest in one of the Amish-made rockers until the afternoon sun warmed the front porch.

The honeysuckle-scented air promised another sunny, hot spring day. A good morning for a ride. He climbed out of the car, leaving his keys dangling in the ignition as the front door opened and his mother stepped outside.

She wiped her hands on her jeans. "It's about time!" she called. At seventy years, Lou Anne Thomas was as strong and energetic as a woman half her age. She watched her son cross the lawn and bound up the three porch steps in one stride. Leaning in for Jackson's kiss, she clasped him by the shoulders with large, capable hands and rested her cheek against his. "So what brings you out here on a weekday? I didn't think I'd see you until next weekend, what with all the funerals."

Crossing his arms, he looked down at his boots.

"I've had a lot going on the past few days. When I woke up today, I decided to take a few hours for myself." He shifted his glance to his mother's face.

Lou Anne's slate gray eyes were as piercing and perceptive as ever. "You're going for a ride."

Jackson nodded, scuffing the toe of his boot against the uneven porch boards.

"Want some breakfast first?" Her straight brown hair swung against the side of her round face as she tipped her head toward the house.

"I ate already." Jackson had already turned toward the barn. He was itching to be gone.

Lou Anne opened the screen door to the house. "I'll be in the garden." The wooden door slammed shut behind her.

His old brown motorcycle sat beside the tractor in the barn. He'd bought it as a teenager when he couldn't afford a car. The bike wasn't much to look at: brown, dented, vinyl peeling from the seat. A leather jacket hung from a nail on the wall beside the bike. He shrugged into it, zipping it all the way up, and then strapped on the weathered black helmet balanced on the back of the seat. Leading the motorcycle through the double barn doors, he pivoted the bike to face the driveway. Priming the engine, he kick started the motorcycle. After a few sputters, the engine revved to life.

He rode down the lane in second gear, opening it up as he hit blacktop. Cool wind whipped against the back of his jacket, but the sun warmed his face and chest. He followed the swells of the road, passing farms and fields of corn. Cats lay peacefully in front of red wooden barns, baking themselves against planks of wood in the morning sunshine. Blooming lilacs perfumed the air.

In the hard years after his father had died, when Jackson worked in a diner four nights a week to help his family pay the bills, he managed to save enough money to buy this battered old bike. Riding his motorcycle let him escape from responsibilities and be alone with his thoughts.

Cresting a rise in the road, he lifted into the air and dropped back onto the seat as he raced down the hill. He needed time to think things through this morning, but he dreaded facing his actions. His indiscretion with Sophia Anton over the weekend was an ethical breach that made him question whether he should remain in the ministry.

His first mistake was asking her to volunteer for the church when she'd only recently returned to the congregation. After all, he didn't know why she'd left, or why she'd returned. Compounding the error, he'd asked her—twice—to assist him in matters he should have handled himself.

Involving Sophia in Sam's and Franny's dinner had seemed practical. They were old family friends, and Sophia was an experienced cook. All Jackson had wanted was to celebrate Sam's life. But sitting at the table, listening to an elderly couple relive their devotion to family, he'd ached with the loss of his own.

Then Sophia had confided in him about her man in New York. The vulnerability in her eyes unbalanced him. He wanted to protect her from making a mistake. And he wanted more time with her. Seeing her in the pews during Sunday service wouldn't be enough.

So he enlisted her help once again. He'd hoped the

same magic Sophia had cast over the evening with Sam and Franny could be used to make Hazel Bracca cooperative. Only when he walked into Sophia's home and saw the look of naked bewilderment and exhaustion in her eyes had he realized his plan backfired. Whether or not Hazel's accusations about Sophia's father contained a shred of truth, her faith had been shaken. Jackson had caused this shock. And he'd wanted to comfort her.

He was flying now, doing eighty miles an hour on empty country roads stretching across the horizon as far as he could see. This morning, he'd been lucky, passing just three cars, with no tractors slowing him down. Riding for the first time since last summer, he knew now what he'd been missing. He leaned into a curve. Like another part of his body, the machine followed.

As he accelerated out of the bend and up a slight swell in the road, he found his mind trailing to the moment on the couch when he'd reached for Sophia. As he'd done with so many parishioners who needed support, he'd placed his cheek against hers. As his own mother had done all his life. But touching Sophia was like firing a pilot light inside. He blazed with the desire to kiss her.

She'd raised her gaze to his. Unable to deny himself, he slid his thumb to her chin and pulled her mouth toward his. Her lips, parted slightly, were full and soft. He kissed her, drawing back and catching his breath while he still could.

Sophia had moved closer, reaching her hands over his shoulders and resting them on the back of his jacket. He'd stroked her thick hair back from her face, drinking her in with his gaze. Those dark lashes against the pale smoothness of her brow. Her lips wet; her eyes huge and vulnerable.

This time he crushed his mouth against hers. The sweet softness of her lips intoxicated him. He was struck by the urge to pick her up and carry her into the bedroom, undressing her slowly so he could delight in every secret curve, every dark hollow of her long and lovely body.

He wanted to know every inch of Sophia.

His lips ventured down her throat, feeling her pulse beat against his lips. Surely, his own heart hammered louder. Sophia's fingers clenched the hair at the back of his neck, making him strain against the constrictions of his clerical shirt to get closer to her—

The blare of a horn rocked Jackson on his bike as a truck roared past him in the other direction. His back was soaked with sweat under the leather jacket. Easing back his speed to fifty-five, he unzipped his coat to the brisk air and glanced at the gas gauge. The tank was almost empty. He'd spent enough time reliving the thrill and the shame of that day. At the next intersection, he'd make a turn and head back to his mother's place.

****

He found his mother on the back porch, overlooking a downward sweep of yard fighting a losing battle with the encroaching woods. She'd set the picnic table simply: a thermos of coffee, two mugs, and a box of donuts.

"Thought you were going to the garden." He slid onto the bench and plucked a glazed donut from the box.

Lou Anne smiled as she twisted the top from the

old silver thermos.

Her hands, gnarled and roughened from years of cleaning houses, were as familiar as his own.

She poured coffee, black and steaming, into Jackson's mug. "You come out on a Monday for a bike ride, I figure you might need someone to talk to." She stared at her son over the rim of her cup.

He sipped his coffee. "I'm surprised you don't already know what the problem is, psychic as you seem to be this morning."

Her eyebrows rose. "Oh, I know the problem: a woman."

Jackson set down his mug hard. "What is this—black magic? Or do you have spies tailing me now?"

Elbows on the table, Lou Anne pushed her bangs to the side of her forehead and rested her homely face between her palms. "A mother can tell what's going on inside of her boy. You're not very complicated."

"I'm not a boy anymore either, Mother." Jackson's response was sharper than he'd intended.

Lou Anne's voice was soft. "I know. Who is she?"

His mother's bird feeder had attracted a female cardinal. He scanned the bushes for its more flamboyant mate. "Someone at my church." Rustling the leaves of the flowering chokeberry, the male flitted to the side of the female.

"Married?"

Jackson's eyebrows shot up for a second. He frowned a warning.

She raised her palms to placate him. "Then what's the problem?" she persisted.

"The problem is I'm a minister," Jackson snapped.

"You're a minister, not a monk. You have every

right to a personal life, just like anybody else."

"No, Mother." He hated when his mother forced personal conversations. "I tried marriage once. You remember what happened. My job doesn't allow me to shut the door, turn off the phone, and call it a day."

"Your job has a lot of demands other people don't have to face, true." Her eyes narrowed.

Whatever she said next would be the knock-out punch. Mentally, he braced himself.

"Then again, you've turned all your energies toward serving others so you can ignore the hole in your life where a woman should be."

He grunted, absorbing the hit in his gut. "Thanks, Ma. And here I thought I had a calling for the ministry."

Grimacing, Lou Anne shook her head. "Laura was the wrong woman for you. She wanted a big house, new cars, and vacations. Your wedding vows never promised those things."

Jackson leaned his elbow on the table, kneading his fingers into his forehead. He'd never had enough vacation time or money for the luxury cruises Laura's sisters invited them on. She'd pressured him to transfer to a wealthier congregation, leading him into arguments that only got uglier over time.

God, he hated reliving those days. But he couldn't shut down his mother when she was on her soapbox. "You can't blame a wife for wanting better out of life than a two-bedroom apartment and one old car. Or for wanting to go on vacations."

"I can blame her for making you miserable." Lou Anne's voice was sharp. "For not respecting your calling. For quitting her job and putting all the pressure on you to support her."

"That's what a husband does, Mother. He supports his wife." The muscles in his chest tightened. Defending Laura was useless. His mother had never cared for her.

Lou Anne put a hand over Jackson's. "You were both young. You followed your dream, but she didn't know what she wanted from life. How could you know she'd burn out on social work?"

"No woman wants the kind of life I have, Mother. I take calls days, nights, and weekends. The ministry comes first. Not a popular viewpoint with today's women." Swallowing the ache in the back of his throat, he tried to keep his tone ironic.

"What about what *you* deserve?" Lou Anne's voice pitched higher and louder. "Who takes care of you while you're busy taking care of everyone else?"

"I don't need anyone to take care of me. I'm a grown man. I cook, I clean, I do my own laundry. I can balance a checkbook. And I can run my life without your advice, Mother." He leaned back from the table, folding his arms across his chest and striving to look nonchalant.

"Then why are you out here mooning over a woman?"

Lou Anne wore the same smug expression she'd use when they played chess and she positioned her queen for the final attack. He bit hard on his lips, refusing to dignify the question with an answer.

Tapping the table twice, Lou Anne sighed. "Truce."

He nodded back, his shoulders stiff. His mother meant well, but talking to him about relationships always led to an argument.

"Tell me about the woman," Lou Anne suggested. "I understand you don't want to marry again. But maybe she's someone you could just date?"

He shook his head. "No such thing as 'just dating' when you're a minister. I live in a fishbowl. Every single thing I do is seen, reported on, and discussed by my congregation. Especially if I got involved with a church member. If I dated this woman, I could be accused of playing favorites or abusing my authority."

Lou Anne sighed. "I really think you're overcomplicating this."

Jackson balled his fists beneath his armpits. He couldn't take much more of this conversation. "There's a reason the Catholic Church doesn't allow its priests to marry."

"But you're not a Catholic priest," Lou Anne shot back. She shook her head. "Well, could you date her secretly?"

His derisive snort made her flinch. "Keep her a secret. How fulfilling for a woman, to be with a guy she can't admit to dating. Pretending not to have feelings for each other, never going to dinner or being anywhere alone for fear someone from the church would find out. And they eventually would—let's not kid ourselves. *Nothing* happens in a church without someone knowing." He leaned his forearms on the table.

"And even if she was willing to keep our relationship a deep, dark secret, she'd never be happy, because she wants to be a mother more than anything." His hands clung to the coffee mug. Most of its warmth was gone.

Lou Anne squared her shoulders, propping her

elbows on either side of her coffee, and stared.

A stare that meant she clearly weighed the decision to speak or stay silent. Jackson prayed the second option would win.

"When Laura lost the baby—" she began.

He shot his hand out to stop her. The tremor in his fingers was almost imperceptible.

"I've respected your right to privacy. We haven't talked about it for all these years." Her voice quavered. "But I'm your mother. For once, would you show *me* enough respect to hear me out?"

He hadn't seen Lou Anne Thomas cry for years, and he wouldn't be the cause for tears now. Easing back onto the bench, he folded his arms tight across his chest, shielding himself from whatever was coming.

"You've never forgiven yourself for Laura losing the baby. But it was not your fault."

Like a poisoned fog, Lou Anne's words seeped into the quiet morning air, threading down his throat to squeeze his heart. He forced himself to draw a ragged breath. He'd had nightmares like this, when he replayed memories of Laura's accident in his dreams until he was sure his heart would break open from the pain of bearing witness.

Overburdened with groceries, she'd fallen at the top of the stairs leading to their apartment. Greasy Chinese food had broken through the sodden bag, causing her to trip.

A neighbor opened his door to see a pregnant woman fall ten steps to the landing. A stream of oranges had spilled from the sack and rolled down the steps after her. They bumped to a stop next to her body, smeared with blood.

The scene was as vivid as if he'd been there. But of course, he wasn't. He worked late that night, so he had the car. Laura had walked ten blocks to pick up Chinese food for dinner. By the time she lugged her bags all the way home, she'd exhausted her body. And she still had two flights of stairs to go.

"Jackson."

He gasped, lifting his head and resurfacing from the horror.

His mother's face was carved with lines of concern. "It was an accident. God only knows why such things happen. We have to pick up the pieces and do our best to get on with our lives. You can't keep blaming yourself. You weren't even there."

His mouth tasted like ashes. He tried to stretch his lips into a smile.

Lou Anne's face blanched.

Did he look as ghastly as he felt? "You're right. I wasn't there." He stood from the bench, his eyes dry and raw.

Lou Anne rose, upsetting her mug in her haste. "I don't know how to help you, Jackson. You've drawn so many boundaries around your heart, I don't know how anyone can get through." Her gray eyes glittered with tears.

He forced his hand to reach for hers through air as heavy as tar. For a long moment, he squeezed her fingers. "I have to get back to work." He scraped the words from his swollen throat.

Holding tighter to his fingers, his mother shook her head.

Straightening his shoulders, he pulled his hand free and exited through the kitchen, letting the door bang behind him.

****

Sophia sat on a kitchen stool in her bathrobe. Her hair was pulled back in a messy ponytail, and her eyes were dry with fatigue. The late-morning cup of coffee would have to make up for the sleep she didn't get the night before.

She'd expected Hazel to drop with exhaustion at the end of the day. Instead, the bath revived her and the older woman refused to settle into bed until close to dawn. Wandering from the front door to the back, she rattled and pulled at the knob, then paced back to the other door to start the cycle again.

Even with the doors dead-bolted, Sophia couldn't chance Hazel figuring out how to open them. Sophia sat in the living room on the couch, head propped dismally on her elbow as she lounged against the cushions, willing herself not to stretch out and fall asleep.

At least Hazel had stopped talking about Sophia's father or the minister. Once Hazel was back in clean clothes, she'd paced in silence.

She was still sleeping now as Sophia scrolled through social media, sipping coffee. Christopher had sent a private message. She was too tired to feel the usual surge of excitement. They hadn't talked on the phone in days, or even texted.

Sophia opened the message. He'd taken a selfie. His blond hair was brushed back and gleaming, displaying a chiseled face stretched in a confident smile. She squinted to read the tickets he held in his hand. "Tickets to the premiere, you idiot," she said aloud. Over the past few days, she'd completely forgotten her trip. Two weeks earlier, she would have jumped up and down to read this message. But she had other things on her mind today. Problems to handle.

She minimized Christopher's photo and sent a message to Kate. Could she stay and watch Hazel while Sophia shopped for food? She couldn't just feed the old woman cottage cheese and celery sticks.

Not wanting to waste precious moments while Hazel was quiet, Sophia dressed quickly, spritzing her hair and brushing her teeth before checking Kate's return message.

"Left boys with the neighbor. Be there in twenty." Kate had written ten minutes ago.

Sophia calculated. She could be back from the store in half an hour. Kate would insist on catching up, but Sophia could plead a headache. She could wrap up this whole business in an hour, if she was lucky. She crossed her fingers. *Please let Hazel sleep 'til Kate is gone*. The last thing Sophia needed was Kate to catch a scent of what Hazel had witnessed in the living room yesterday.

Luck was with her. When she heard Kate arrive, Sophia passed her friend in the driveway and dashed to her car.

"Hey!" Kate protested, holding two specialty coffees.

"I'll be right back!" Sophia assured her through the window. "Don't let the door bang on your way into the house! Even the tiniest noise might wake up Hazel."

At the grocery store, she headed straight to the frozen food aisle and tossed an assortment of prepared meals into her cart. No time to shop for a home-cooked meal. Grabbing an extra toothbrush and a box of tissues, she hastened to a register just as it opened.

Starting her car in the parking lot, she glanced at the digital clock in the dashboard and smiled. She was ahead of schedule. Maybe today things would go her way. But her heart sank when she opened the front door a few minutes later. Hazel sat at the kitchen table with Kate, drinking from one of the cups her friend had bought.

"That's *my* latte!" Sophia banged through the door with her arms full of grocery bags and lowered them onto the island. She was afraid to look at Kate. "So, how are the boys?" She busied herself with putting the groceries into the freezer.

"They're fine. But we have more important subjects to discuss. Hazel's just told me an interesting story."

Kate's voice dripped with extra meaning. "Oh?" Sophia's heart beat against her ribcage as she rearranged the freezer. She avoided looking at her friend.

"Very interesting. Someone's been a naughty girl."

Sophia murmured an unintelligible response, buying time as she refilled the coffee pot, keeping her back to the table and the expectant presence of the two women.

"She claims someone was stealing kisses from a forbidden man. And he couldn't get enough. Do you know anything about this, Soph?"

Sophia measured two scoops of coffee into the filter, closed the lid, and pressed the button before facing the table. "Hazel likes to tell stories, don't you, Hazel?" She smiled at Hazel and glanced at Kate just long enough to widen her eyes and shrug.

"Well, this story would rock the church." Kate

challenged with an arched eyebrow.

Resentment smoldered in Sophia's chest. The humiliation of what she'd done yesterday was too fresh. She never lied to her best friend, but couldn't she nurse her wounds in private? She pressed her lips into a hard line. "Hazel gets confused. You do realize that, don't you?"

"Of course I realize she gets confused!" Kate flicked her hair off her neck with an impatient hand. "But do you?"

Sophia frowned. Kate's tone had changed from playfulness to irritation.

"I can tell when something's upsetting you. You get this plastic smile on your face, and you won't look me in the eyes." Kate came to Sophia's side, dropping her voice. "Come on, Soph. This old lady's been living on the street and starving herself to death. She needs to be medicated. Why in the world would you believe anything she says about your dad?"

In relief, Sophia sagged against the island. So Hazel had only spilled one story. *Better this one than the other.* "All I said is, Hazel gets confused." Her tone was slow and measured. Staying calm was the best way to de-escalate tensions with Kate. "Just like you said."

"But I can tell you believe her. You're so gullible! When will you stop listening to what people *say* and pay attention to what they *do*?"

Sophia tapped her foot on the floor. Of all the things she didn't want, a lecture from her best friend topped the list. "Fine, Kate. So I *was* upset by Hazel. I'm not whining about it or making it your problem. I'm getting on with my life anyway. What's the big deal to you?"

Holding on to the corners of the island, Kate's muscles stood out in her forearms as she faced down Sophia. "Because you're *not* getting on with your life. You allow other people to hold you back. You get fooled by their b.s. and can't see them for what they really are."

Sophia shook her head, hoping to clear the fog and make sense of what Kate was griping about. "What are you talking about? *Who* are you talking about?"

"I'm talking about you being naïve. Trusting whatever people say. I'm talking about you acting like the walking wounded just because an old woman"—she indicated Hazel with a jerk of her thumb, and dropped her voice—"made up a crazy story about your dad."

Sophia put up a warning hand. Her body was exhausted, and her brain was so tired, it buzzed in her skull. If Kate wanted to pick a fight today, then Sophia would be more than her match.

Kate slapped away Sophia's hand. "Or how about you thinking if you can just lose enough weight, you'll get the Happy Ever After with Christopher? When will you wake up to reality?"

Sophia's jaw dropped. So Kate's anger wasn't because of Hazel at all. She was just taking another opportunity to badmouth Sophia's relationship with Christopher. Her heart pounded against her ribcage. "I can't believe you're lecturing *me* about reality. How many losers did *you* date? A dozen? And when everyone else judged you, who stood behind you?" She slapped a hand against her chest. "Me. I always had your back, no matter what I thought of your boyfriends. Because I always respected *you,* no matter what." She took a deep breath.

"And when Carl left, who held your life together? Who rocked the babies when you were so depressed you couldn't get out of bed for days on end? Who cooked your meals and fed your boys? Who changed their diapers?" Sophia's voice spiked with anger, but she couldn't stop herself.

"I've been your friend through thick and thin, Kate Couvert. I always had faith in you, faith you'd figure out your life sooner or later. Because that's what friendship is to me—supporting your friends no matter what. Helping them wherever you can. Trusting they know what's best for themselves. Not telling them they're idiots because they make decisions you don't agree with."

Fighting the urge to grab Kate's coffee and throw it against the wall, Sophia twisted her lips. "Sometimes when you're a friend, the best thing you can do is keep your mouth shut."

Kate shook her head hard. "Sometimes you *can't* keep your mouth shut, Sophia. Sometimes you shouldn't. Not if you see your best friend is about to make a huge mistake. Not if you can see as plain as day she's being suckered by a guy who doesn't love her and is only going to use her—"

"What do you know about how Christopher feels about me?" Sophia slammed her hand on the counter. "You met him once, and you summed him up? Every time you hear me talk about him, you shut me down. You have no idea what our relationship is because you, the all-knowing Kate Couvert, made up your mind a long time ago not to like him. Now nothing will ever change your mind."

Clenching her fists, Sophia fought to control the

trembling of her chin. She would *not* show weakness. "You don't care if Christopher sees things in me nobody else has ever bothered to look for. Or that besides you, he's the only other person in the world I can be totally open with. Yeah, he *does* like thin girls, so yeah, I *am* getting thin for him. I'm not changing who I am inside. I'm only changing the outside. And I don't care what you think about it."

Raising her palm between them, Kate opened her mouth to reply.

But Sophia was done listening. "You have no idea what it's like to be overweight." She jabbed her finger at Kate. "You can be charming, funny, smart, and everything society considers attractive, but you'll never be considered *sexy* if you're heavy, too. I'm twenty-nine years old, Kate!" Her voice cracked on the number. "I can't keep waiting for Mr. Right to show up at my doorstep."

She took a deep, shuddering breath. When she saw Kate open her mouth to respond, Sophia cut her off again. "Christopher loves me. He's told me I'm the only girl he'd ever consider having a family with. I know he isn't attracted to me because I'm not the willowy type he desires. So I'm doing whatever I can to change. Because at my age, I'll *take* a man who shares his feelings. Who appreciates me for who I am. Who has a great career and a bright future. Because he can be the father of my children. And if I have to diet for the rest of my life, I'm willing to pay that price."

Kate banged her knuckles against the table. A vein throbbed against the thin skin of her temple. "Your plan won't work, Soph. You can't *make* a guy love you by pretending to be someone you're not."

Blood pounded in Sophia's ears. "And your vast wisdom on the subject of men comes from where? The twins' father who got you pregnant and left? Or all the drug users and Harley riders who came before him?" Sophia swallowed hard. She'd never said anything so nasty to anyone. But for the first time in her life, she wasn't pulling any punches.

Kate's hazel eyes flinched. "Okay, I'm not an expert on great relationships. Listen, Sophia." She raised her palms in front of her chest and spread her fingers wide. "I'm not trying to kill your happiness. That's the opposite of what I want. You're my family, Sophia. I'd never have the kind of life I have now if I hadn't met you. I didn't even know what a normal life *was* until I met you." She shrugged, dropping her hands to her sides. "Yeah, I still dated a lot of jerks, and I still made a lot of mistakes. But you and your parents gave me the courage to go to college and get a degree. Your mom and dad gave me a place to stay until I could find a teaching job."

Kate rounded the island, grabbing Sophia's hands. "The truth is, the only way I figured out how to be a halfway decent parent to the twins was from watching your parents raise you all those years. And they loved each *other*, too, no matter what Hazel tells you. I owe your parents, Sophia." She squeezed Sophia's hands before continuing. "And the one thing I can do to repay them is tell you when you've gotten messed up with the wrong guy."

Snatching away her hands, Sophia crossed to the other side of the island. She never shared a bad opinion to Kate about the guys she was interested in. *Never.* Why couldn't Kate show the same courtesy?

From the table, Hazel gazed with interest at the younger women as she sipped her coffee.

Kate pressed her palms against the counter. "Maybe I haven't found the right guy myself yet. But even I can tell a relationship is doomed if you have to quit eating, for God's sake, to get him to notice you."

"Knock off the drama, Kate." The explosion of vitriol Sophia had unleashed left her too tired to argue. "I eat. I'm not starving myself. Obviously." She pinched the skin of her waist as proof.

"Yeah?" Kate challenged. "Then when's the last time you had your period?"

Sophia jerked up her head. "What did you say?"

"When I was here a couple of months ago, I borrowed some of your female supplies under the sink." Kate's words rushed out. "Last month you had exactly the same number as the month before. And when I looked this morning, guess what? Same as the last two months."

Sophia's mouth dropped. "Are you telling me you're *stalking* my menstrual supplies?" She knew Kate disliked Christopher's influence, but she'd had no idea how far Kate would go to prove her point.

"I'm telling you I'm scared for you, Sophia! Your relationship is unhealthy." Kate drew a deep breath. The vein at her temple ticked. "I'm saying, I think you need to talk to someone."

Sophia put her hands over her heart in a futile attempt to stem the pain Kate's words had inflicted. Her best friend thought she needed help. Psychiatric help.

Making a strangled sound of distress, Kate flung her arms around Sophia.

Sophia jerked away, marking the distance between

them with each step back.

Kate dropped her arms to her sides. "I don't mean you're crazy, Soph. I think you just need someone to talk to. Someone who'll help you figure out everything."

"I don't have time to argue anymore." Sophia crossed in front of Kate to catch Hazel as she slid sideways on the kitchen bench. "I don't know how long Hazel will be staying with me, and I've got quarterly reports to finish while I'm stuck here at home. Would you like to watch some TV, Hazel?" Hoisting Hazel by the elbow, Sophia steered her to the living room couch. She clicked the remote to a game show and raised the volume, keeping her rigid back toward Kate. "Thanks for coming and hanging out with Hazel while I was gone. Give the boys a hug." She busied herself with papers in her briefcase, laying them out on the table. Her lips were a thin, bloodless line.

She heard nothing but silence behind her. Then Kate sighed and walked to the front door. "I will. Love you, Soph."

"Mm-hmmn," Sophia responded vaguely. "Thanks again. Gotta get back to work." She fixed her gaze on the reports until she heard the door close. Then she buried her face in her hands.

Chapter Seven

Sophia spent the rest of the day at home, grateful to be alone with Hazel.

True to his word, Jackson called on volunteers to assist Sophia. She politely rejected offers of help, claiming she'd planned to stay home anyway.

Hazel dozed on the couch in front of the TV most of the afternoon, allowing Sophia time to phone O'Grady's and complete her paperwork. Twice, she ignored Kate's calls. Kate had been her best friend for most of her life, but no one—no one—had the right to invade her privacy the way Kate had.

In the late afternoon, Sophia prepared their food and served it on a tray in the living room. To Sophia's immense relief, Hazel hadn't mentioned the minister or Sophia's father all day. Sophia was surprised to find herself enjoying their conversation on the couch while they ate sautéed vegetables and grilled chicken breasts.

Hazel came to life when Sophia asked about the older woman's childhood in East Benton. She had grown up during the Depression, but her memories were idyllic—fetching groceries at the corner store for her mother, pushing her baby sister in a pram around the block. She'd watch the boys play stick ball in the field by the tracks, waiting for the train to come by on the hour, blowing its whistle so loudly she had to plug fingers in her ears. Lost in reverie, she paused three times to ask Sophia her name, but she no longer appeared anxious or scared. Food and rest were doing their healing.

Sophia opened her laptop to show Hazel how to play Solitaire. Hazel was entranced. Each time she clicked on a card, she made a small noise of self-congratulation. Watching the cards cascade whenever she cleared a deck, she clapped her hands.

Collecting her phone from her purse, Sophia took the opportunity, while Hazel was occupied on the computer, to check on Sam Newes.

Franny thanked her again for the picnic dinner, recounting how happy Sam had been the entire night. "I haven't seen him so energized since before he got sick." Unfortunately, the night had taken its toll because he hadn't been out of bed since. Franny brushed off Sophia's appalled apologies, insisting the evening was exactly what she and Sam had wanted.

Wishing Franny a good night, Sophia plugged her phone into the charger and curled up on the loveseat. Even after Sam passed, Sophia sensed Franny would endure with grace and good humor. So different from her own mother. Estelle Anton had been lost when her husband died, fading a little more with each passing day. She followed her husband in death just a few months later. Sophia hadn't been surprised, really. Her father's larger-than-life personality had always fueled their household. Her mother had been content to circle him like a satellite.

Again, Sophia thought of what Hazel had said about her father. Had he really been unfaithful to her mother? Was the model for love Sophia had built her hopes on nothing but a fake and a fraud? If only the ghosts of the past would stay there. She eyed the tiny woman on the couch, grateful Hazel remained transfixed by the shuffling card deck on the computer screen.

Her mind drifted back to yesterday's kiss—Jackson's palm cupping her face, the intensity of his lips moving against hers, the pressure of his mouth roving down her throat. Her heart fluttered, and she rubbed her eyes to erase the memory.

Get a grip, Sophia. She had enough discipline to deprive herself of calories when her body was screaming to be fed. She could control her wayward heart the same way. All she needed to do was face the consequences. A perfect kiss didn't end with the man pulling away and leaving without a backward glance.

Her cheeks flamed with embarrassment. Years ago, her father had warned her no one would buy the cow when they could get the milk for free. She and Kate used to mimic his deep voice delivering the old-fashioned cliché, but she couldn't deny she'd been influenced by the idea.

An unwelcome memory pushed at the edges of her awareness. Even after all this time, when she recalled the night of her first dance, shame radiated through her nervous system.

She'd had her first real date at sixteen when a fellow student council member asked her to the spring semi-formal. He was good-looking and popular. She was heavy—forty pounds over her target weight—and two inches taller. She slumped her shoulders so he wouldn't notice the height difference. When she accepted his invitation to the dance, she was sure her life was finally beginning.

Sophia's mother helped her dress that night, fussing over the peach taffeta gown and tightening her straps to cover Sophia's *décolletage*. Later, when Kate drove Sophia to the dance, she unfastened Sophia's straps and tucked them into the cups of her bra.

She tugged at the neckline while she danced, her bodice slipping ever downward with the weight of her breasts. Her date's gaze had constantly lifted from her chest when they talked. She never should have allowed Kate to mess with the dress.

Sophia's date took her to his car before the dance ended, opening the door and helping her slide the bottom of her gown inside. He fiddled with the radio station, and Sophia worked at calming her breathing. She'd never been kissed and was afraid of doing it wrong. Lowering her eyelashes, she glanced down to make sure she wasn't spilling out of the bodice. A lot more cleavage showed than when she'd left home.

Feeling the boy move closer, she lifted her chin and closed her eyes. He pushed past her lips with his tongue and rotated it like a beater in a mixing bowl. One hand gripped her shoulder, and the other slid up and down her bare arm.

This wasn't the kiss she'd expected. Sophia planted one hand over her bodice and the other on the dash, straining to withstand the whip-like motion of the boy's tongue.

He explored with his hands, pushing hers away from her neckline.

Her shoulders stiffened in protest, and she tried to escape from his mashing mouth. When she felt his fingers inch toward the cups of her bodice, she wrenched away, sliding across the seat to the passenger door.

"Come on, you know you want it."

She couldn't see his face in the dark car, but she heard him panting for breath. Pushing a tangle of hair back from her face, she fumbled for the door latch. Her gown twisted beneath her as she climbed out the door. She tugged it back just before she slammed the door and ran inside.

How stupid she'd been to believe he liked her. Boys didn't like girls who looked like her.

A clap from Hazel on the couch brought Sophia back to the present.

"I won!" the old woman told Sophia, beaming from her wrinkled face.

"Yay," Sophia responded with a wan smile. She wouldn't risk anymore humiliation with the minister. Picking up her phone, she deleted Jackson's contact information. She scrolled back to Christopher's message. "Hi," she began. "I've missed you."

****

By the next day, the minister had pulled strings to get Hazel into a nursing home immediately. Donna called with the news. "He'd like to pick her up at two o'clock."

"Bad idea," Sophia blurted. "Hazel's gotten used to me. If I take her to the nursing home and get her settled, I guarantee she'll have an easier time. The minister didn't have much luck with her before. He told me," she added, holding her breath as she waited for Donna's response. Seeing Jackson again after the way he'd left the other day was too fresh a humiliation.

Donna grunted. "If you say so. He said whatever works for you is fine. He's already done the paperwork, so you can just drop her off and go. But he wants you to call if you have any trouble." With a grudging word of thanks, Donna hung up the phone.

Sophia nodded. She'd woken with a firm resolve to move forward with her own plans. Once she delivered Hazel to the nursing home, she'd put the whole sorry episode with Jackson behind her.

Two days of consistent meals and regular sleep were keeping Hazel more lucid. She made comments about TV programs and questioned Sophia about her job. While Hazel napped, Sophia had removed her parents' photos from the walls. Since then, Hazel hadn't spoken once of her "tryst" with Sophia's father. Steering clear of church discussion, past or present, Sophia hoped Hazel's memory of what she'd witnessed between Sophia and the minister would also fade into something like a dream. As long as Hazel didn't see Sophia in the same room with Jackson, both women might put the memory to rest.

Sophia took her time driving Hazel the short distance to Oak Hill Manor. Sunlight through the leaves of two hundred-year-old oaks dappled the red-brick streets of East Benson's oldest neighborhood. Craftsman-style brick homes and neat white clapboard houses stood close to the road in shortened front yards. The nursing home sprawled against the edge of a park bordering the neighborhood to the west. Sophia slowed to a stop at the entrance.

Hazel looked at Sophia, the corners of her mouth downturned. "I don't want to move here. I like living with you."

"I know." Sophia squeezed Hazel's hand. "But you need more friends than just me. I have to work a lot. I want you to have lots of people around to talk to or play cards with. I'll visit you all the time." She would, too. She'd gotten fond of the old woman after all. Knowing Hazel had no family to check on her, Sophia looked forward to stopping after work and bringing Hazel the ice cream she so enjoyed. She bent toward the old woman until their foreheads rested against each other.

With a shaky smile, Hazel planted a wet kiss on the tip of Sophia's nose.

Sophia laughed. Giving Hazel's fingers a final squeeze, Sophia opened her door and stepped out of the car. She glanced inside the sliding doors of the lobby as she walked around the hood to the passenger side. Bending over the desk and signing documents was Jackson, his face turned to the young receptionist collecting his papers.

Sophia's heart lurched. She pressed her palm over it, fighting the urge to get back in the car and keep driving. She'd revealed far too much, even before she'd sat with him on her couch: her vow to lose weight, her plans for Christopher, her eagerness to start a family. She couldn't bear the pity in his eyes she was sure to see if she walked through those doors.

The pink-and-white azalea bushes clustered near the entry were just beginning to open their buds. She'd parked so close to the curb Hazel's door swept leaves off their branches. Sophia groped for Hazel's hands to help lift her out of the car.

Hazel gazed into the younger woman's face. "What's wrong, my dear?"

Hearing the tenderness of Hazel's tone made Sophia's chest hitch. She could use a mother's love right now. She wrung out a smile and pulled the old woman toward her for a quick hug. She'd better gather her courage.

"Hello, Hazel. Miss Anton." Sophia pivoted to find the young receptionist standing behind a wheelchair. The sliding doors were open, and the lobby desk stood empty. Sophia's knees sagged in relief. She helped Hazel into the wheelchair, prattling about the fun Hazel would have riding upstairs in a wheelchair, ordering everyone around like she was a queen.

Reaching for the purse Sophia held out, Hazel smiled. "Let's get going."

Sophia hesitated. "Has all the paperwork been signed?"

The receptionist nodded. "The minister finished it just as you pulled up. He's gone ahead to Hazel's room to put away some things."

Sophia's mouth was dry. Jackson seemed as anxious they avoid each other as she was. She knelt in front of Hazel and put both her hands on the old woman's cheeks. "Hazel, I have to go now. But I'll come back after work to see how you've settled in." As she saw the old woman's brows knit together, she kissed the top of Hazel's head and straightened.

The day was breezy, and she hugged her arms around herself as the receptionist pivoted the wheelchair.

Chatting to Hazel in a bright voice, the receptionist steered through the sliding glass doors and into the building.

With a sigh, Sophia started her car. Passing quickly now through the red-brick streets, she took the first turn off the main thoroughfare to access the byway. She drove the familiar four-lane highway to O'Grady's, passing through countryside free of billboards and other signals of civilization. In the plowed fields, green sprouts of corn stood an inch high in the soil, straight rows stretching for miles to the right and left.

For the first time in days, she was alone. Why wasn't she happy?

Only a week before, she'd cooked sausages for the church festival. She'd passed a magical night with Sam and Franny, retrieved Hazel from the shelter, heard shocking allegations about her father, and tended an old woman around the clock for the past two days. So much had happened so fast.

And the kiss.

But she was putting it all behind her. Clearly, she couldn't return to the church. Best to avoid Jackson Thomas until the end of her days.

Work would keep her busy. She needed to organize a Fourth of July spectacular—something to outdo the twelve-foot frying pan that had been such a hit during the housewares fair. And she still had to find the perfect dress for the theater event in New York. She'd show Christopher a side of herself he never knew existed.

A sigh escaped. She just wished she felt more excited.

Chapter Eight

During the long drive to New York City, Sophia streamed an audiobook with enough twists and turns to shove all stray thoughts from her mind. Eight hours later, she circled Christopher's neighborhood three times before she lucked into a space just a few blocks away.

Inside the narrow foyer, she waited for him to buzz her in, and then walked two flights of stairs to his apartment. His building was quiet, with worn, clean hallway carpeting and walls coated in pale yellow. She rolled her suitcase behind her and stopped at Apartment 313. She leaned on his door to catch her breath. Would coming downstairs to meet her have killed him? She caught herself as the door opened without warning.

Christopher posed in ballet's third position: right arm flung to the side, left arm curved at the elbow with the hand poised over his head. From behind a long-stemmed red rose clenched between his teeth, his wide mouth grinned.

Before Sophia could speak, she saw his eyes widen.

In one fluid motion, he swept his left hand to his waist in time to catch the red rose he spat out. He circled Sophia, appraising her from head to toe, even lifting her arms with a long, slow whistle.

She tilted her head with a wry smile,

accommodating him with a 360-degree turn. "You love your dramatic moments, don't you?" She leaned in to receive her customary kiss on the cheek.

"*Tu es belle*!" Grazing his lips over her left cheek then her right, Christopher pressed an unexpected kiss on her mouth. Underneath the expert application of kohl black eyeliner, his eyes were bluer than ever.

Ha. I told you this would work, Kate. Sophia hadn't spoken to her best friend in a week. Proving Kate wrong was even sweeter than seeing Christopher's surprise. She reached a fingertip to Christopher's jaw line. A layer of ivory foundation made his skin luminescent. "My God, your makeup looks better than mine."

He laughed. "Today was makeup rehearsal. The crew decided on this look. I didn't wash it off, because I knew you'd like to see me made up for the stage."

His tawny blond hair had grown since she'd last seen him, and the ponytail he wore showcased the symmetry of his flawless bone structure. His lips, full and sensual, had often brought Sophia to a state of helpless longing when he curved them into the slight, suggestive smile he wore now.

She rolled her suitcase into his apartment. Her lower back ached, and she rolled her shoulders to relieve the muscles. Plenty of time for swooning after she had a little rest.

Christopher sank onto the loveseat, one of the few pieces of furniture in his minimalist living room. Stretching his arms behind him and cupping the back of his skull with clasped hands, he extended his lanky legs to the side, crossing his ankles so his feet relaxed on the floor.

Sophia had to step over his legs to take her seat, losing her balance at the last second and dropping inelegantly onto the cushion. Christopher looked at her with his usual mixture of affection and amusement. She drew her feet up onto the couch, tucking herself into the space Christopher hadn't claimed. Glad to be out of the car, she closed her eyes. A glass of water would be nice.

Christopher's knee nudged her, and she opened her eyes.

He stared, waiting.

As always, Sophia obliged him. "So how's the show going?"

Listening to Christopher relate the details of his day, she felt her attention drift. She kept her gaze locked on his, but her peripheral vision gathered other information—his languid posture, his long physique filling the space.

Like Jackson's, in a way. Both men were tall, their physical presences imposing, and they carried themselves with a self-assuredness she envied.

Their eyes were different, though. Christopher's darted in every direction, marking time to the animation of his speech. Jackson's eyes locked on hers when they talked, as if he was pulling her thoughts from her before the words emerged from her lips.

Talking to Christopher was more like watching a performance. He did most of the talking. Whereas talking to Jackson—she just needed to close her eyes for a second, just to give them a little rest—was like stepping into a warm bath. The heat of his palm against her cheek as he looked deep into her eyes and drew her mouth toward his—

"Am I boring you?"

Her eyes flew open as Christopher's voice cut into her reverie. Despite his smile, he sounded nettled. She laid her hand on his cheek and shook her head. "Of course not. I've been driving half the day, and work kicked my butt this week." Why was she thinking about Jackson when she was seated on the couch with the love of her life? "I'm sorry. You know I love to hear about your work. Maybe I should have a cup of coffee."

Christopher pulled his legs in front of him so Sophia could stand. "Sounds good. I'd like some, too. I've got some Columbian beans in the fridge. You'll just need to rinse the French press." He stretched his arms behind him, his long fingers reaching back in a perfect arc.

Opening her mouth to retort, she snapped it shut and walked to the kitchen.

"What is it?" He sat straighter, gazing at Sophia with a furrowed brow.

She shook her head, placing the kettle on the stove before opening the refrigerator. The coffee canister was pushed to the back of the second shelf, surrounded by containers of take-out food and jars of gourmet condiments. She ground the beans and poured them into the press before she glanced at Christopher. "It's nothing," she said to reassure him. "Being here in your kitchen while you talk to me from the couch. Just feels like old times."

"Really?" He frowned. "Because you seem different to me."

Shrugging, she opened her hands wide. "Nope. Same old Sophia."

He tapped his fingers against the back of the couch

where his hand rested. "You've never looked better—but the difference isn't just your looks."

Sophia knew Christopher would never make an indelicate comment about her weight, but she appreciated his acknowledgment. She tilted her chin upward and turned her profile to him. "Maybe *my* fabulous new makeup makes the difference."

"You seem more confident." His eyes narrowed as he studied her. "Not as"—he paused—"eager to please."

Sophia rinsed a dishrag to wipe off the counter. "Because I'd have been pleased if *you* offered to make coffee after I've driven eight hours to get here? Don't worry, I'm still willing to clean your kitchen for you, see?" Camouflaging her irritation, she waved the rag in the air. But when she saw his shoulders sag, she dropped the rag and hurried to him. Kneeling, she grasped his hand. "I'm kidding! You know I like fussing around in the kitchen. And we both know the coffee you brew is way too strong." She brought his hand to her lips and kissed his knuckles with a flourish, and then rested her chin on her hands. Next thing she knew, she'd be batting her eyelashes and pouting.

Christopher's face relaxed. He pulled her beside him on the couch and rested her head on his shoulder. He traced his slender index finger over her nose, his face inches away from hers.

She didn't move a muscle in her face, knowing how the tiniest movement in an extreme close-up could distort her features. She hoped her breath mint was still working.

Christopher picked up her hand, resting her fingers against his palms to admire her nails. She was glad she'd made time for a manicure yesterday.

On the tender skin of Sophia's inner wrist, the pressure of his lips was no more than a ghost kiss. For the past two years, she'd dreamed of this moment. His mouth brushed her skin, leaving a tickle over her pulse. He raised his gaze to her face, looking all the world like a prince in a fairy tale. She waited for the romance of the moment to sweep over her. For her heart to beat faster. To feel the flush of desire. To feel something of what she'd experienced with Jackson on her couch. But the mahogany mantel clock over Christopher's fireplace ticked faster than her pulse.

She gently pulled away her wrist from Christopher's mouth, allowing her fingers to linger against his cheek. "Let's have some coffee so I don't fall asleep on you again." She rose from his lap with as much grace as she could muster.

"Okay." Christopher's heartiness didn't quite veil the uncertainty in his voice.

As she drank coffee on the couch and discussed work, Sophia noticed a hesitancy in him she'd never before seen. *I've put him off balance.* She smiled into her coffee cup. Glancing at her watch, she excused herself to prepare for the evening ahead.

Christopher removed her hand from her suitcase and rolled it into the bedroom.

A thrill of accomplishment warmed her. This will be fun, she promised herself as she closed the bedroom door.

****

Two hours later, she surveyed her reflection in the full-length mirror. Earlier in the week, Tiffany, O'Grady's fashion consultant, had helped her choose a gown for the premiere. Sophia still wasn't sure she had the courage to wear it. A floor-length chiffon, its ivory Empire-style bodice emphasized her hourglass figure. The flowing black skirt was snug but smooth around the waist, due to the two spandex waist cinchers she'd poured herself into. A sheer band of chiffon draped her neck, leaving her shoulders and back bare.

She turned, assessing her hair with the aid of a hand mirror. Tiffany had encouraged Sophia to try a different look, teaching her how to craft her hair into a towering chignon. A thin, faux-diamond headband gave Sophia an added sense of hold. The sparkle of silver and pearl scroll ear cuffs matched the single pearl resting on a thin chain over the dimple of her cleavage. Completing her ensemble were powdered-ivory satin peep-toe pumps and a vintage beaded box clutch.

Setting down the hand mirror, she picked her clutch off the bed and pressed a palm to her stomach. With all the spandex strapping her in, she'd be lucky not to faint.

A knock came at the door. "Almost ready?"

Drawing as deep a breath as she could manage, she opened the door. Christopher was the picture of elegance in a black tuxedo, his sleek blond hair just brushing his shoulders. Beneath the immaculate white of his collar, his tan looked airbrushed.

Placing his hand on his heart, he fell to one knee. "Venus!"

Her eyes rolled before she could stop them. She placed a neat toe against his knee and tapped, just enough to send him off balance.

He sprang up and took both her hands, holding her arms out to the side so he could scan her up and down.

"Your dress is perfect, Sophia. And I love how you've done your hair. You've completely transformed yourself!"

She placed her hand on her squashed stomach. *You have no idea.* She was relieved to walk rather than stand still, but stairs would be problematic. At least Christopher's building had an elevator. His hand cupped her elbow during the descent to the lobby.

He stopped Sophia before they walked outside. "Look at us." He tilted her chin toward their reflection in the glass doors. "We make a beautiful couple, don't we?" His face smiled at her in the glass.

But Sophia's smile faltered. Everything Christopher said was all she'd hoped to hear months ago when she'd planned this trip to New York. So where was the fire she'd always felt inside when he touched her hand? Where was the shiver of excitement when he smiled? For the first time in her life, she was on the verge of having all her dreams answered. She needed to fill the emptiness she'd been enduring ever since Jackson turned his back and walked out her door.

Sophia placed her hand on Christopher's arm. In her heels, she was almost at his eye level. "I'm so glad to be here with you tonight, Christopher." Maybe if she said it out loud, they would both believe it.

****

The night should have been magical, Sophia argued to herself as she struggled to unzip her dress in Christopher's bathroom.

He'd known the entire cast and half of the audience at the premiere, but he'd never been more attentive to her. She couldn't remember the names of all the people she'd met tonight, but for the first time in her life, she'd fit in with the beautiful people. All night long, Christopher had murmured in her ear, alerting her to the stares she was attracting. His hand never strayed from her waist as they mingled with the elegant crowd.

He'd treated her to dinner afterward at a little restaurant frequented by dancers and entertainers. A famous actor of stage and screen had smiled and exchanged pleasantries with her while they were waiting in line.

"Stop looking like a tourist," Christopher teased as they took their seats. He was hailed by one person after another. A master of social small talk, Christopher peppered his banter with just enough questions to his audience to suggest real interest. He enjoyed the attention she was receiving, too. Probably more than she was. He hadn't questioned her when she barely touched her food, though he insisted she raise a glass of champagne with him.

Somehow, the evening failed to sparkle. Trussed tight in her under-layers of artificial body shaping, conscious of the unfamiliar weight of a new hair-do, she felt like an imposter.

A mutual appreciation of each other's wit had sparked their friendship. Common philosophical beliefs had cemented it. Crafting her appearance to please Christopher, she'd thought, was the final piece of the puzzle. But tonight, being together had felt like an elaborate act.

Sliding her gown into a puddle around her feet on the bathroom floor, Sophia coaxed the top layer of latex over her hips and slid it down to her ankles. She flexed her fingers and settled into grim battle with the second layer. The fabric clung to her skin, resisting. She felt a little woozy as she clenched and tugged the rubbery fabric centimeter by centimeter down from her navel. What a sight she'd be if Christopher opened the door now.

She straightened tall and sucked in her stomach to relieve as much tension as possible on the spandex. As she finally wrested free of the body shaper, she groaned in relief. She kicked her foot and sent the spandex sailing over the shower curtain. It made a rubbery smack against the porcelain floor of the bathtub.

With what energy she had left, she peeled off her lacy underwire bra and donned a comfortable cotton sports bra. After pulling a soft, faded green t-shirt over her head, she climbed into a pair of flannel pajama bottoms. She'd brought lingerie in case the night took a turn toward romance. But after all those hours squeezed like sausage into a casing, she wanted nothing more than comfort.

She lathered her hands with Christopher's luxury soap and washed every trace of makeup from her face, pressing a hand towel to her cheeks when she was done. Finally, she stripped off the diamond headband and unfastened the bobby pins. Her hair had taken on volume throughout the night. Even without pins, most was still gathered on top of her head, slowly sinking toward her shoulders. She leaned over and shook out her hair, scrubbing her fingertips into her scalp. The pressure from her up-do faded and she let out a sigh. She brushed her hair with strong, quick strokes to remove the tacky residue of hair spray and gel. When she stood and looked in the mirror, she looked much more like herself. She swung open the bathroom door. Stepping into the living room, she drew a quick breath.

Christopher had lit candles on the walls, on the counters, and on every flat surface. He sat on the floor in front of the couch with casual cross-legged elegance. A choice selection of fruits and nuts were spread on an elevated tray in front of him. He uncorked a bottle of wine, passing her a glass as she lowered herself beside him.

Her midsection unrestrained, she took a grateful swallow from her glass.

"You look nice," he told her. He'd changed from formal wear into a thin cotton pair of sweatpants and a soft gray jersey that stretched like a second skin over his muscled torso.

"You make sitting look so easy." Sophia groaned as she braced her elbow against the floor and stretched her legs, lounging on her side. "I'd rather be comfortable than elegant." She lifted her glass in an awkward tilt against her lips and took a sideways swallow.

He swiped at a trickle of wine escaping from the corner of her lips. "As long as the wine gets into you, I won't complain." He caressed her cheek and gave an affectionate smile.

"Why, sir, are you trying to seduce me?" Sophia drawled, turning her face to kiss his palm. Now that she could breathe again, she'd quit overthinking her feelings and enjoy Christopher's lavish attention.

"Yes. How am I doing so far?" He eased his hips onto the floor, positioning his face and shoulders just inches from hers. His legs stretched in the opposite direction. Parting his lips, he took Sophia's lower lip between his, pulling tenderly.

Sophia blinked, and then closed her eyes. They'd

never kissed like this. Christopher had perfect technical skills, synchronizing every movement of his hand through her hair to the unhurried rhythm of his lips. He never lingered too long in one spot. Every so often, he pulled back, gentle and unhurried, to gaze into Sophia's eyes.

The choreography was perfect. The trouble was, she felt like an onlooker to her own make-out session. What was going on tonight? Balancing her weight on one elbow, she slid her hand behind his head. She twisted his hair between her fingers and gave a gentle tug. Hmmph. No corresponding surge of passion. She needed to put her heart into this. Closing her eyes again, she slid back into the memory of Jackson's embrace— his rough jawline rubbing against the soft skin of her cheek, pulling her mouth toward his. She felt again the riptide of longing he unleashed with just one movement.

Her kiss became more urgent. She pressed her elbow against the floor to avoid rolling into Christopher. She could feel Jackson's mouth on her throat now, *his* fingers caressing her skin, as she entered the fantasy more deeply. She sighed as Jackson's hands slid down her bare arms. The thin skin over the palm of her hand tingled as his long fingers traced a delicate pattern. She shivered when he raised her palm to his lips, gazing into his tender, dark eyes.

She met his ardor with her own, folding herself into his strong arms until her heart pounded against his. On this night, their love united them into one spirit, one body—

"Sophia?" Christopher's voice came from far away. When she opened one eye, she plunged back to

Christopher's apartment. He'd fallen back on his elbows, his hands flat against the floor. She was stretched out, pressing one elbow to the floor while her other hand gripped the soft fabric of Christopher's jersey. She scrambled to sit up.

Christopher's hand on her leg restrained her. "I didn't mean to stop you. I just—I just needed a breather." He gave a shaky laugh.

Closing her eyes and swinging her head to the side, she obscured her face with a curtain of hair. She'd let herself pretend she was in Jackson's arms again. The disappointment of finding herself with Christopher instead swept through her like a hurricane wind. She struggled to calm her breathing before speaking. What kind of person kissed one man while she was thinking of another?

Christopher reached for her hand.

She turned a reluctant gaze toward him. He was a gorgeous man. Why wasn't *he* making her pulse race?

"That was some kiss." Christopher had never sounded so shy.

She squeezed his hand then released. Taking a long swallow of wine, she set her glass on the floor and made a face. "Maybe I've had too much to drink tonight. I got a little out of control."

Taking a measured swallow of his wine, he leaned back against the couch and patted the floor beside him.

Sophia scooted over to his side. She'd never let him suspect just how unmoved his kiss had left her.

He grasped her hand, staring toward the ceiling, and then he shook his head. "This has been an incredible day for us. After all these years of being such good friends"—he squeezed her hand for emphasis—

"the universe seems to be telling us it's time to move to the next level." He leaned over and bumped his shoulder against hers. "What are you thinking?"

That I'm going to Hell. She pressed her fingers hard against her temples, attempting to erase her desire for the minister and substitute it with Christopher's presence. After all these years of trying to win this man's heart, how could she hesitate now, when the finish line was finally in sight? She turned to face Christopher. "What about April?"

The wave of his hand dismissed the question. "I told you. We're over."

"But she was at your apartment two weeks ago when we talked on the phone," Sophia reminded him.

"Just to help me with my audition. And anyway, after being with you today and seeing how good we are together, I wouldn't consider going back to April. Not after seeing the kind of chemistry *we* have." He chucked Sophia under the chin with his knuckles.

Only when I pretended you were someone else. "Christopher, my expectations for a relationship are serious, and I'm not sure you're ready."

"Like?" Christopher asked.

"Like I'm not interested in casual dating. I'm too old to play games. I'm looking for a serious commitment. Marriage. Children."

He twined his fingers in Sophia's. "I know your list of demands, Sophia. You always said life won't be complete until you're married and have kids. And I admired your honesty. You're not like everyone else I know—all about looks, appearances, ambition, getting ahead. You just want a family to take care of." He placed her hands on his shoulders, and then slid his arms around her in a loose embrace. "Do you remember when I told you you're the only woman I could ever imagine having children with?"

Sophia nodded. Up until last week, no words had ever made her happier.

"I was being rhetorical."

Really? Sophia raised her eyebrows. Two weeks ago, this confession would have devastated her, instead of just sounding insulting.

"But somehow, everything has changed. Today, the future steps closer, and I can *see* our family." He rested his cheek against hers. "I see us walking on the beach, holding hands. Everyone turns to look as we walk by. In front of us are a boy and a girl. The girl is blonde like me, and the boy has dark curly hair like yours. They're doing cartwheels and somersaults."

"On the beach?" Sophia asked. "Or in the water? Either way, *I* see sand up the nose." She was just buying time. She'd never expected him to be so comfortable talking about having children. No man had ever talked this way about a future together. She'd once told Kate if she wasn't a mother by age thirty, she'd accept the proposal of any man with a pulse. And here was Christopher, one of her best friends, and a man with so many accomplishments. A man with a perfect body and a flawless face. A man who, she realized, *wanted* her.

Christopher leaned back to look at Sophia. "I think I'm ready for a commitment, Sophia. I think you're just what I need."

She traced a finger over Christopher's elegant nose, imagining him leaning over her hospital bed as she cradled their newborn baby. Seized with a tremor of joy, she laid her head on his shoulder. For the next hour, they spun dreams about the house they'd own, the vacations they'd take, and the dog they'd buy for their kids.

Later that night, Sophia hugged her pillow close. She tried to lull herself to sleep imagining children who melded Christopher's traits with hers. But somehow the proportions changed, softening into other faces framed by brown hair, eyes as warm as cocoa. Giving up on sleep, she flung back the sheets and played a mindless game on her phone until exhaustion swept her under in the early hours of the morning.

Chapter Nine

Jackson sat behind the desk of his office, the door open. He'd learned the people who most needed to talk were more inclined to locate him after service than make an appointment during the workweek. The afternoon was more quiet than usual. He took advantage of the time by absorbing himself with his next sermon. When he heard a quiet knock on the door, he looked up.

Peering into his office was Kate Couvert, the young single mother of twins who volunteered at church festivals—and Sophia Anton's friend. Kate's round face wore a polite smile, but her eyes glittered with determination.

He didn't know Kate well. When he'd first arrived at St. Jerome's and learned she was raising her sons with no family support, he'd offered the church's help only to be rejected in no uncertain terms. He stood to welcome her, hoping whatever had brought her to see him today had nothing to do with Sophia. "Hello."

She lowered herself into the chair opposite his desk. "I wanted to talk to you about Sophia."

Great.

"I'm worried about her, and she won't listen to me. I'm hoping she might listen to you."

Kate's forehead was wrinkled like trench work. Jackson leaned back in his chair, crossing his legs to buy time. He tapped his fingers on the desk and concentrated on keeping a neutral expression. This was Sophia's closest friend. Did she know what he'd done to Sophia? The only way to learn would be to hear her out. "What worries you about Sophia?"

"Well, I wouldn't be talking about this if I weren't so concerned." Kate sighed, pushing her straight brown hair back from her face. Her mouth opened and closed twice before she finally spoke. "Since her parents are gone, I don't know who else to turn to. I could tell she really made a connection with you. Plus, Sophia's faith is so important to her. So I thought, maybe if *you* talk to her, she'll actually listen. All she does is tune me out." Her hands were planted palms down on the desk as she met his gaze.

Jackson waited, and then prompted her. "What's your specific concern?"

"Oh!" Kate's eyes widened, and she gave a little laugh. "I thought you might know already. Sophia told me you've talked a lot. She's in New York this weekend visiting the ballet dancer." She made a face. "You might not realize it, but Sophia's lost a lot of weight over the past couple of months. A *lot* of weight," she repeated.

"She seems happy with her weight." He was relieved Kate wasn't confronting him about taking advantage of Sophia, but he wasn't sure what Kate's target was.

"Oh, she's happy, all right. That's the problem. She thinks if she keeps losing weight, she'll magically become the woman this guy wants. Christopher is his name. She's been in a dysfunctional relationship with him for years. He calls her up to ask her to spell words, and remind him how to turn on his washer, and other garbage. Seriously! Anything she's asked, she does for him."

"Did he ask her to lose weight?" Jackson interrupted. His fingers drummed harder on the desk.

"No," Kate admitted. "At least, she didn't say so. He likes to date dancers who are thin to the point of being anorexic. Sophia's decided the one thing standing between them is the way she looks. And you know how beautiful Sophia is."

Kate's comment was rhetorical. He nodded anyway, remembering Sophia walking down the runway in lacy lingerie. He cleared his throat. "In matters of the heart, there's not much we can do for the people we love except be there to support them if the relationship doesn't work out."

"I know!" Kate snapped. "I've butted out of this for the past two years, figuring sooner or later either Sophia would wise up, or this Christopher guy would move on to someone else. The problem is he hasn't moved on. He strings along Sophia, acting like he's the only one who sees the 'real' Sophia. He tells her she's the only one who understands him, too. He makes me want to puke." She jumped up from her chair, making it roll out behind her and hit the bookcase. "Sorry." She pulled the chair back to the desk and stood behind it. "I get worked up."

Jackson gestured for Kate to sit again, shrugging when she remained standing. "You're a good friend to Sophia, and you're worried about the choices she's making. There's not much I can do. Just remember: if she makes a bad choice with her boyfriend, she'll need your friendship more than ever."

"You don't understand. I'm not worried about what will happen in the future. She's already hurting herself right now." Kate slapped the chair twice to emphasize her last two words.

"How is she hurting herself?" His voice was tight, as if his vocal cords were being squeezed.

Kate sighed. "She's lost so much weight she's stopped having her period. Not exactly the kind of thing she'd like me telling the minister, but I have to get you to understand. She's *already* in trouble. I confronted her about it, and she was furious. Now she won't answer my calls. No one else knows how far she's taking this. If I can't get her to talk to somebody, I'm really afraid of what will happen. I know about anorexia from my work at the detention center. Sometimes people with eating disorders reach a point of no return."

Frowning, Jackson nodded. A family in his former parish had been torn apart by their daughter's disease, helpless as her body wasted away despite counseling and treatment. But Sophia seemed so healthy. "Sophia doesn't fit the profile of someone with anorexia," he said finally. "She seems like one of the happiest people I've known. She likes her job, and she has strong relationships in her life. She makes time to do things for other people, like the dinner for Sam and Franny Newes—"

"You're right," Kate broke in. "She always *has* been happy. And she always *does* do a lot for other people. That's why I'm so worried about her losing weight for Christopher. She thinks she loves him. If she goes out of her way for people she just *likes,* how far will she go for the man she thinks she loves*?*"

Kate stared at Jackson like an attorney who'd just

made a watertight closing argument. She was right to be worried. He knew enough about female anatomy to know what Kate described was a serious situation, unless—

He cleared his throat, hesitant to ask such a personal question. "Could Sophia be pregnant?"

"No." Kate barked out a laugh. "She's never had sex with this guy. We tell each other everything. I see you look skeptical, but I'm telling you, there's no way she's pregnant."

Seems like she doesn't tell you everything. Sophia's face loomed before him, her eyes wide and gray as his fingers finally touched the dark curls that had tantalized him from the moment he saw them spilling onto her shoulders at the back door of the church. With effort, he pushed aside the image and forced his attention back to Kate. He clasped his hands on the desk in front of him and bounced them on the surface. "You want me to talk to Sophia."

Kate nodded hard.

"But when you tried, you said Sophia tuned you out. I can't imagine why she'd listen to me."

"She respects you. You're her minister," Kate assured him. "A minister's like a parent to Sophia. She's old-fashioned. Honor your father and mother, honor the minister…"

Where was my *honor?* The thought punished him for the hundredth time. He'd left Sophia's house stunned by his behavior. He was a thirty-six-year-old man who'd mastered his impulses years before. But that day, he'd unleashed his passion like a teenaged boy— and on one of his own parishioners, no less. One who'd turned to him for support. All week, he'd grappled to understand why. He'd just have to put the past behind him, he'd finally decided. Avoid Sophia Anton and resume his daily responsibilities with all the humility and self-control he could muster.

But now he was being asked to counsel the same vulnerable woman he'd taken advantage of. "She should talk with a female minister. I know one in a parish not far from here. I'll ask her to speak to Sophia." Jackson pulled a directory from his desk drawer and flipped through the pages. The defiant thrust of Kate's chin answered him.

"She'll never talk about this to a stranger, Pastor Thomas. Female or not. She trusts *you*."

Her words cut him like a knife. As he picked up the phone, he shook his head. "Sophia will like this minister. She's compassionate and knowledgeable."

"No." Kate crossed her arms, her gaze boring into him. "I could've found a female counselor for her myself if I cared about gender. I asked *you.*"

Jackson rubbed his chin. The thought of lecturing Sophia about her boyfriend nauseated him, but how could he explain that to her best friend? Kate's gaze, locked on his face, never wavered. With a sigh, he replaced the telephone. Imagining he wouldn't have to face Sophia at some point was just wishful thinking. Sooner or later, he had to ask her forgiveness, even though he would never be sorry for holding Sophia in his arms just one time. "When does she get back from New York?"

Kate sank into the chair wearing a smile.

****

Placing her phone on the table, Sophia sagged against the kitchen chair. In the few days she'd been

143

back from New York, she'd ignored Kate's phone calls and texts. But the message she'd just read on Kate's social media page was one she couldn't ignore. Sam Newes had died the night before after one week of hospice care. The church funeral committee was organizing meal donations for the family.

His passing was peaceful, Kate texted back to Sophia. The closed-casket memorial service was in two days, followed by a family-only gravesite funeral.

Sophia was grateful Kate made no mention of their argument. Over the years they'd had spats, but none like this. Sophia was pained by the silence between them, even though she refused to answer Kate's calls. She sighed and pressed her palms to her eyes. Kate wasn't her only problem. She recoiled from the idea of seeing Jackson again when she paid her respects to Sam. If she could just avoid the minister—forever—she could get him off her mind and move forward with her life with Christopher.

Jackson would probably be so busy with official duties he wouldn't notice her. She could sit in the back during the service then stay in the kitchen helping with the luncheon afterward. Once she'd offered her condolences to Franny, she'd leave.

Determined not to worry, Sophia took a pack of cards from her desk drawer and grabbed her keys. Tonight she was teaching Hazel double-handed Solitaire. Her visits to the nursing home were in the evenings ever since Hazel had told her the minister visited after lunch. She'd managed to avoid Jackson since she'd come back from New York. She just needed her luck to hold during Sam's memorial service.

****

Never had Sophia seen the church so crowded. By the time she and Kate arrived, they were lucky to squeeze themselves into a pew in the back.

"Yikes! I hope we have enough food to feed everybody," Kate whispered as they took their seats.

"A lot of these people will have gone by the time the family returns from the cemetery." Sophia was a veteran volunteer of funeral events. Kate looked relieved.

The organ thrummed to life, its deep bass chords vibrating Sophia's eardrums. As one, the congregation rose when Jackson walked to the pulpit. Over his black clerical shirt, he wore a white stole to honor the deceased. From the lectern, his gaze found Franny in the front row. His face reflected the sadness of her loss as he joined the congregation in the opening hymn.

Sophia bowed her head. Today wasn't about her. This service was a celebration of a man's life. She relaxed into the grace of the moment as a chorus of voices reverberated from the high arches of the ceiling. As she listened to Jackson eulogize Sam, peacefulness seeped into her like a steady rain over parched earth. She gazed at the high windows of the church. As a child, she'd studied each stained glass panel over years of weekly Sunday attendance. This was the first service she'd attended since her mother's funeral. Again, she bowed her head, feeling like she'd come home.

When they heard the organ strike the opening notes to the final hymn, Sophia and Kate slid from their pew and exited the sanctuary to prepare lunch in the fellowship hall. The sky was gray and low, and menacing clouds threatened to break overhead. Rain at the cemetery might push up the timing of the luncheon.

They'd better work fast.

They'd just taped the vinyl tablecloths to the banquet tables when the first guests appeared. Kate banged through the swinging half-doors of the kitchen wearing a wild-eyed look of panic. "They're here. Help me get the chafers out."

Sophia and two other helpers sprang into action, hauling heavy rectangular basins of rigatoni, fried chicken, mashed potatoes, green beans, and buttered rolls to the serving table at the head of the room.

Kate dashed off to find matches to light the chafing candles.

Sophia heard a familiar voice behind her. "And this is the young lady who made it happen." She whirled to see a hale forty-year-old woman with eyes as blue as Franny's. Beside her, Franny looked frail in a navy tunic dress. Her face powder was streaked with a trail of tears. As she raised her arms for a hug, she swept away the shadows of sadness with her customary smile.

"Oh, Franny!" The words caught in Sophia's throat as she put her arms around the older woman. "I'm so sorry about Sam!"

"Now, now." Patting Sophia on the back, Franny adopted the role of consoler. "No tears, Sophia. This is a celebration, just as Sam wanted."

Smiling through her tears, Sophia drew back to gaze at the widow. "You're a pillar of strength, Franny. No, you are," she insisted as Franny waved a dismissive hand. "After fifty years, you and Sam acted like a couple of kids in love. And here you stand, comforting an idiot like me." Sophia pulled a tissue from the inside pocket of her skirt and blew her nose.

Franny laughed. "Laughter and tears go hand in

hand at a funeral. In life, too." She extended her arm to the younger woman beside her. "Do you remember my daughter Danielle? I know you haven't seen each other in years. She and Garrett loved your Key lime pie. We told her all about the lovely picnic you and Jackson put together. Dad talked about it for days, didn't he, Danielle?"

More people streamed in, and Franny called over other relatives to meet Sophia. Like Sam and Franny, their family was gracious and good-humored. Sophia enjoyed their quips and funny stories about Sam.

Before long, though, she felt a sharp poke on her shoulder blade. Behind her stood Kate, widening her eyes and jerking her head toward the kitchen. Excusing herself, Sophia followed Kate into the kitchen to help slice a dozen pies.

Covering the plates with plastic wrap, they filled each shelf of the rolling trolley. As Kate brewed another pot of coffee, she directed Sophia to set the dessert table.

As soon as she entered the fellowship hall, Sophia saw Jackson. He was seated at Franny's table, surrounded by children. They played a game, she saw, thumping the table with their fingers and flashing hand gestures. Lips clenched, he thudded the table and watched the signals flash. When his turn came, he held two fingers along either side of his nose like a peace sign before motioning to the child beside him.

Adults at other tables stopped talking, bemused by the activity. Sophia couldn't help laughing as she rolled the dessert cart toward the empty table. She recognized the game from college fraternity parties. A good way to channel the energy of kids at a table—minus the beer.

As she unloaded slices of pie onto the table, she watched Jackson's table from the corner of her eye. Everybody else was watching. Why couldn't she?

The tempo of the thumping increased, and the hand signals flew faster until the circle collapsed in laughter. The children pointed and laughed at the minister as he raised his arms in the air to proclaim his innocence. "What?"

"You missed your signal!" a child's voice shouted.

"I did not!" He crossed his arms over his chest and scowled at the faces circling him.

A little girl in a flowered shirt and tights, hardly older than a toddler, raced around the table and thumped his knee. "You lose!" Her light brown hair spilled from her barrette onto a face shiny with chicken grease.

Jackson caught her around the waist and lifted her to eye level. His large hands spanned the width of her back as she wiggled. He lifted her over his head, turning her upside down until her shirt slid toward her armpits while she screeched with delight. With a fluid rotation of his wrists, he set her feet back on the floor.

She jumped up and down in front of him, and her black patent leather shoes squeaked with each bounce. "Again! Again!" she implored. By now, more little children surrounded the minister, raising their arms.

He picked up one child after another, gently lifting the shyer ones and dangling rambunctious children by their ankles.

Sophia had never seen him so relaxed.

"He's like the Pied Piper," Kate said in her ear.

Transfixed by Jackson and the kids, Sophia hadn't noticed Kate's arrival.

"Too bad he's sworn off having kids. He'd be a great dad." Kate slid plates to the back of the table as she nodded toward the minister.

Emotion clogged Sophia's throat as she collected plates from the lower shelf. She saw a woman, a baby boy in her arms, approach Jackson.

The young mother put a restraining hand on the head of a girl, presumably her daughter, to stop her from jumping up and down and shouting.

Jackson stretched out his arms for the baby, smiling as the child slid into his arms and stared up at a new, unfamiliar face. Jackson's hand curved around the baby's back while he ran another palm over the child's soft, downy hair. When he saw the baby reach a chubby fist to the golden cross hanging over his clerical collar, Jackson drew it away before the baby could pull it into his mouth.

The child's mouth twisted into a cry.

Standing, Jackson walked from the noisy table, lightly jiggling the child and continuing to murmur as he settled down.

"One more load. Wait here," Kate ordered as she spun the dessert cart back toward the kitchen.

Sophia stood alone at the table, feeling her pulse quickening as she watched the minister, still gazing at the baby, make his way toward her.

She couldn't take her gaze off him. His gentle expression when he looked up from the baby made her knees weak. "You're good with babies." *Lame. At least try to be casual.* "And with older kids, too. Although I have a sneaking suspicion the game you taught them was something you learned in a frat house."

Jackson laughed, his eyes mischievous. "Don't tell

anyone. I have a reputation to uphold."

Wriggling in Jackson's arms, the baby turned his open gaze to Sophia.

She leaned her face close to his and shook her curls, smiling. The baby reached for her, and Jackson slid him into Sophia's arms.

Forgetting the awkwardness she'd felt a moment before, she cooed as the baby wrapped tiny fists in her hair. When she saw him steer his hand to his mouth, she whispered a gentle reproof. "No, no." She extricated her hair and planted kisses on the soft top of his head. Closing her eyes, she inhaled the scent of powder and baby lotion as she rubbed her cheek against his downy scalp.

When she opened her eyes, she saw Jackson smiling and chuckled. "Don't tell anyone—I'm a baby addict, and I need help." She rocked back and forth as the boy began to drowse. Jackson's tall figure harbored them from the noise and commotion of the hall. Lowering her eyes as she hummed, she stole a glance at the minister.

His gaze moved from the baby, cheek crumpled against Sophia's blouse, to Sophia.

"Uh-oh, who let you hold their baby? Run! I've got your back." Kate's joke shattered the stillness.

The baby began to cry.

Sophia shot her a reproachful look and patted the baby's bottom, whispering in a sing-song voice until he settled.

"I used to have to fight Sophia to hold my own twins when they were his age," Kate told Jackson, smiling fondly at her friend.

He dragged his gaze from Sophia to Kate. "Good

thing you had two."

From the corner of her eye, Sophia saw Kate shoot the minister a meaningful look.

Jackson shook his head, looking back at the baby.

What was going on? Sophia frowned.

"I'd better get this little guy back to his family." Jackson extricated the sleepy boy from Sophia's unwilling arms.

He stood close enough for her to smell his aftershave and feel the warmth radiating from his cheek. She blushed, her gaze averted until he backed away with the child. Crossing her hands over her chest, she rubbed her arms, feeling more barren with each step he took.

Kate called for the guests to choose their desserts, and then stood against the wall with Sophia as a line formed in front of the table. "You like him, don't you?" Kate asked in a low voice.

Sophia fiddled with the hem of the apron protecting her blouse. Was Kate just fishing, or did she suspect Sophia had feelings for the minister? She swallowed hard. "He's good with kids."

Her gaze followed him as he handed the baby to Franny. He ran a hand through his own wavy brown hair, his expression softening as the older woman laid her cheek against the child's.

"He's good with adults, too," Kate said.

Sophia's face flamed. She studied her fingernails to avoid Kate's stare.

"So how'd the weekend go with Christopher?"

The muscles in Sophia's face tightened at the abrupt subject change. "You don't really want to hear about it, do you?"

Kate shrugged. "Not really, but I don't like fighting either. How was the premiere?"

"Fabulous," Sophia snapped. She stood next to Kate in tense silence as Franny's guests selected plates of pie. She'd promised herself to make this day about Sam, and here she was arguing with Kate again. Drawing the kind of cleansing breath she'd learned in yoga, Sophia pulled her cell phone from the pocket of her slacks and showed her new screensaver. "Tiffany, from ladies fashions at O'Grady's, helped me pick my outfit."

Kate whistled. "Wow. You look like a princess." She touched the screen, enlarging Sophia's image and pushing Christopher into the margins.

"I rocked that dress." Sophia's voice was smug. They both laughed.

"So—did Christopher approve of the way you looked?" Kate handed back the phone.

Sophia looked at her feet, tapping her toe against the linoleum. "Yeah."

After a long pause, Kate said, "'Yeah'? Can you tell me more?"

Looking up, Sophia saw Jackson had found another playmate. He held on to a little boy's hands as he bounced the child on his knee.

The boy giggled uncontrollably, sliding side to side like a rider whose saddle was slipping off the horse.

Sophia dragged her attention back to Kate. "Christopher thought I looked beautiful." Right now, Christopher felt very far away.

"And…?" Kate prompted.

"And, he told me how glad he was I'd come. And—we kissed," Sophia finished.

"You kissed?" Kate's voice was loud as ever.

Her cheeks reddening, Sophia shushed her friend.

"Are we talking about more than his usual European cheek kisses?"

Sophia nodded again.

"With *tongue?*" Kate wrinkled her nose and shuddered.

"We made out, okay?" Sophia whispered in vexation, drawing Kate from the table. "I'm twenty-nine years old, Kate. I'm allowed to kiss." She glared at her friend, knowing Kate would insist on hearing the whole story. Fine, then. She may as well hear it all. "He's broken up with April. He wants us to take our relationship to the next level."

"The next level, huh? And what's the next level?"

She braced herself. Kate's brow was massed like a thundercloud over suspicious eyes. But Sophia refused to be bullied by her old friend any longer. "We're thinking about getting married."

Kate's jaw dropped. "Getting married and having kids is the *next* level?" she sputtered. "Don't you think you're skipping a few steps? Like, maybe, dating a while? Finding out if you're compatible?"

Sophia threw back her shoulders and met Kate's fiery gaze. "We *have* been dating, Kate. For the past two years, in our own way. We know each other inside and out. I told you I'm the only woman Christopher's ever considered committing to. And after this weekend, he feels like he's ready."

"Why this weekend?" Kate countered.

"Because I'm more confident. I'm willing to take chances. I'm not so eager to please as I used to be." Sophia lifted her chin, feigning ignorance to what

Kate's question implied.

"Right. His sudden interest in you has nothing to do with you losing weight." Kate ground her bottom lip between her teeth, shaking her head.

Sam's memorial service was no place for a showdown. Clenching her fists, Sophia forced herself to keep her voice low. "I'm sure losing weight helped, okay? Is that what you want to hear? Then yes. Christopher *did* like the way I look. Why can't a man admit he's attracted to thin women?"

Kate's shoulders dropped as she threw her hands in the air. "What happens if you gain back the weight? Will he still want you then? Or do you have to starve yourself forever just so you won't lose him?"

Her tone was no longer angry. To Sophia's ears, it sounded pitying. Without answering, she bit her lips against her teeth and walked back to the kitchen. She rolled up her sleeves and ferociously scoured the empty chafing pans. *If Kate knows what's good for her, she'll leave me alone.* As the sink filled, she stirred the bubbles with a savage swirl of her hand, relieved Kate didn't follow her. Safe from the conversations on the other side of the door, she continued scrubbing with only her own thoughts to trouble her.

****

Sophia stood in the pantry an hour later, lining up salt and pepper shakers on the shelves. The last of the luncheon guests had drifted from the fellowship hall. She'd stayed behind to straighten the kitchen, hoping to leave unnoticed when the building emptied.

Kate opened the door and stepped inside, her face pale but set with a determined frown.

Trailing behind her was Jackson, his hands jammed

into his pockets.

Sophia's shoulders stiffened. What now? She clutched a salt shaker with unnecessary firmness.

"Pastor Thomas wanted to thank you for helping out today, Sophia." Kate pulled him forward by his shirtsleeve.

"Yes. Thank you for everything you did today, Sophia." Jackson cleared his throat. "Franny appreciated all of your help. She was telling me—"

"And he wanted to talk with you about something else," Kate interrupted. "Something important."

Sophia shifted her gaze from Kate to Jackson. The look he was giving Kate was an unmistakable warning.

Sucking in a breath, Kate looked squarely at Sophia. "He wants to talk to you about all the weight you've lost."

Jerking back, Sophia knocked over a group of salt shakers on the rack behind her. She stared at the minister, her jaw agape.

Jackson shook his head, running his hand over the back of his neck and avoiding her gaze.

Kate swallowed hard and cleared her throat. "I told him you've stopped having your periods because you're starving yourself."

Sophia gasped. The air in the small room was too thick to breathe. She reached for the metal bar of the shelf, needing to hold on to something. Her horrified gaze was glued to Jackson's face as it drained of color.

He tugged at his collar. "Your friend is worried about you." His voice faltered. "We...we're both worried."

As the room hummed with silence, Sophia's pulse thundered in her ears. Like a cornered animal, she glared at Jackson, then at Kate. Was this some kind of intervention for a poor, fat girl who couldn't even diet right? Her cheeks were on fire. She pressed her fingers against her lips and shook her head. "How pathetic you must think I am. Both of you." She strained to speak against the tightness of her throat. "Incapable of making my own decisions. Needing you to tell me what to do. My best friend. My minister." She flung the title at him like a curse.

Jackson held up his hand, but before he could speak, he was cut off by Kate.

"We just want to help you, Sophia. What you're doing is dangerous to your health. And you're doing it for a guy who doesn't even love you."

The words hung in the air.

Jackson's face was all the confirmation she needed for her shame. He struggled to find something to say, his gaze bleeding pity. Sophia put up her hand to silence him. With the precision of a robot, she removed her apron and hung it over a peg on the wall. "Stay out of my life. Both of you." Staring through them, she plucked her purse from the metal shelves and slammed past them out the door.

Chapter Ten

Air-conditioned coolness blasted Sophia's skin as she stepped into the nursing home lobby. The chill air relieved her raw nerves.

After the luncheon, she'd returned home, still choking on anger. Her best friend and her minister had forced her to stand before them, their expressions pitying. She'd never felt so naked and pathetic. Kate going behind her back and counting her monthly tampon supply was dirty dealing. But revealing something so intimate to the *minister*....Kate didn't know Sophia had already humiliated herself with Jackson. Still, sharing Sophia's personal information when Kate herself had no business knowing it—*that* was the final straw.

Channeling her fury, Sophia threw herself into housecleaning. On her way to the linen closet, she passed a framed photo of herself and Kate at the age of twelve. Two best friends squinting into the camera on a sunny day, draping their arms over each other's shoulders. *How dare you.* She grabbed the photo and slammed it into the bottom drawer of her desk.

She needed someone to talk to. But who? She couldn't tell Christopher what had happened. He didn't like Kate any more than she liked him. Besides, Sophia would never discuss her weight loss with Christopher.

She gazed for a moment at her parents' wedding

picture. She'd never missed them more, or so yearned for their guidance. She decided then to go see Hazel—not that she could help Sophia with her problems. But at least the old woman was company and would help Sophia get her mind off her problems.

Hazel's eyes clouded with confusion when Sophia entered the room with a bag from the bakery. "What are you doing here now?" She frowned as Sophia sat on the edge of her bed.

"I brought you a donut." She leaned forward to give Hazel a kiss on the cheek, squeezing Hazel's hands in her own.

But Hazel's lips quavered. "He's already getting me donuts." With a wavering hand, she gestured behind Sophia.

"Who?" Sophia jumped to her feet, a sudden suspicion flooding her with unease.

Jackson stood in the doorway, a plate with two donuts in one hand and a cup of coffee in the other.

His eyes were darker than ever, his face shaped into a mute appeal. She gazed back at him, her heart in her throat.

"The minister," Hazel said helpfully. "You know him. He came to your house."

"That's right." Sophia cut off Hazel before she divulged more details. "Well, I should leave you to your visit then." She stood at the foot of the bed, ready to flee.

Jackson put up a hand. "I'd like to talk with you, Sophia."

She shook her head, staring at a spot on the wall.

"To explain," he added.

Sophia crossed her hands over her abdomen,

gripping her wrist to keep from shaking. She wouldn't look at him.

In the uncomfortable stillness, he coughed. "Hazel, would you mind if I steal Sophia away for a little while?" He walked past the empty bed closest to the door to set the donuts and coffee on Hazel's tray.

Hazel shrugged. "You bring Sophia back, now." She lifted the donut to her mouth and took a messy, satisfied bite.

Sophia's face burned. "Thank you for getting Hazel's permission," she said, her words dropping like icicles in the quiet room, "but the last time I checked, I was a grown adult and make my own decisions about who I talk to." She sat on the end of the bed, her back rebuking him. Bitterness burning her throat, she tried to smile at the old woman.

Hazel slid her feet clear of Sophia and stared at Jackson in the doorway, then moved her gaze back to Sophia. Hazel's eyes lit up, and she fluttered her hands in excitement. "You kissed him on your couch. Him!" Cocking a thumb toward the doorway, she stage-whispered to Sophia, "The minister."

Her stomach churning, Sophia shot from the bed like a bird at the sound of gunfire. With a stern shake of her head, she gazed at Hazel with wide, imploring eyes. "No." She tried to inject her voice with the authority to stop Hazel's train of thought. But Hazel's eager smile told Sophia the memory had dug in. She dropped her chin, defeated. Could this day get any worse? Fighting the urge to lock herself in the bathroom, she picked up her purse. "I'll be right back. Watch TV, Hazel." Sophia whisked past Jackson in the doorway.

She gave him no choice but to follow as she

clipped down the hall toward the chapel. He hurried to grab the door as she yanked it open.

The small room was lit by a dim lamp almost obscured by silk flowers on the altar. Sophia sank onto one of the plain oak benches, grateful for the shadows hiding her face. Her skull pounded with resentment. "I will not sit here and listen to a sermon from *you*." Her voice was hard as bone. She'd been trapped.

Jackson balanced on the edge of the pew with his arms stretched in front of him, clasping his hands over the backrest of the next bench.

Both of them stared straight ahead in the silence. The heating registers hummed in her ears.

"I want to tell you about a man who lost his way." Jackson's voice cut through the protection of the darkness. "A man who's made a lot of mistakes. Mistakes that have hurt too many people." He turned to her. "Who wants to make amends, if he can."

Sophia glared at the altar, too angry for eye contact. She fought to find her words. "You protect yourself. The way you speak, in third person. You always get to step back and don the minister's role. Then you can pass judgment from on high."

Jackson shook his head. "Sophia, I know you're angry. But look at me." He sighed when she refused to turn. "Please."

She hesitated, moving her chin only enough to cast a glance in his direction. Her resolve wobbled.

A muscle convulsed under his jaw. "Let's talk, then. Man to woman." His voice rasped on the words.

Sophia nodded, pressing her lips into a line. She couldn't refuse the misery etched in his face.

Again, he faced the altar, staring at the glow of the

lamp. "When I was growing up, I never thought of being a minister. My Dad died when I was fourteen, and his death meant the family had to do whatever we could to survive. All of us—my Mom, my two older brothers, and me—did odd jobs, anything we could find in the farm town where we lived. All four of us had to work to pay the bills. And even that wouldn't have been enough if our pastor hadn't organized church volunteers to help us every step of the way."

He shifted on the bench toward Sophia but didn't look at her. "I saw how hard life could be at a pretty early age, but I also saw how much good the minister could do for my family when we needed it most. I wanted a career where I could help people, too. I could have been a social worker, but I didn't want to work for a bureaucracy. I wanted to be on the streets, helping people directly. So I decided to go into the ministry."

Despite herself, Sophia's distrust faded as she listened to him relate his past. "I always assumed people entered the ministry to answer a spiritual calling."

He barked a short laugh. "I had to work at the spiritual part. No one would ever have accused me of being a saint as a teenager. I was a typical, hormonal adolescent. But when I started in the ministry, I made up my mind to put it all aside."

His mouth twisted. "To be a spiritual leader, I had to be more than just an ordinary guy. My first parish was urban and poor. All they had was their faith. That's how I had to reach them. I threw myself into work, ignoring the demands of my physical body. I thought I was happy." He fell silent.

"Until you met your wife," Sophia prompted him.

161

The corners of Jackson's mouth lifted into a sad smile. "You might think so. But the truth is, I bumbled into marriage with Laura. We had a friendly working relationship until I found myself caught in a rumor mill. People assumed more was going on behind closed doors than just meetings." He splayed his hands before him. "Look, I was young, and I loved my job. I didn't want to jeopardize my position." He blew out a breath. "I wanted to protect her reputation." He gave an acid chuckle.

Sophia frowned. "You married her just so you could make an honest woman of her?"

He shook his head. "I was lonely, too. I thought love would develop in time. So yes, I asked her to marry me." Jackson shook his head. "Talk about a final solution to a temporary problem. I had no idea how to be a good husband. When my Dad was alive, he was always working. He was my model."

Sophia heard footsteps and voices in the hall. She tensed, afraid any interruption would jar Jackson back into reticence. But the sounds receded.

"I can't blame Laura for being frustrated. She'd say I was married to my job, not her." Jackson's voice was low and harsh. "And I couldn't earn a bigger salary, no matter how many hours I worked." He gripped his hands over the hard wooden pew in front of him. "She didn't understand why I wouldn't move to a wealthier parish, where we could live a 'normal' life. But I'd found my calling. I wanted to serve the underprivileged. So, I refused her." He bowed his head and lapsed into silence.

In the dark chapel, Sophia sat beside him, bemused. She'd assumed he'd wanted to discuss her weight loss. Or lecture her about her "dysfunctional" relationship with Christopher. Or, worst of all, address the line she'd crossed when they'd sat on her couch two weeks ago. Jackson's chronicle of his failed marriage was the last thing she'd expected. "I don't know why you're telling me this. Your past doesn't have anything to do with me." Her words sounded harsh, considering the humble posture he'd taken. But her heart was still hardened by the memory of their humiliating encounter in the church pantry.

Jackson raised his gaze toward the altar. "My past made me the man I am today, for better and for worse. The only way I can make amends for my behavior with you is to be honest about the things I've done." He straightened and turned to face her. "We need to talk about what happened at your house."

Her heart plummeted into her stomach. She shifted to avoid his gaze.

"I abused your trust. I'm asking for your forgiveness," he whispered.

Sophia whirled to face him. "Don't tell me— you're protecting *my* honor now. Does the marriage proposal come next?" She blanketed herself with a bitter laugh. Tears swam in her eyes. *Don't you cry, Sophia.*

Jackson winced as if she'd slapped him. "I deserve your anger. But don't let my stupidity change who you are."

"As if you know who I am." Sophia's throat closed over the words.

"Yes. I do."

At the tenderness of his tone, Sophia's eyes swam with tears. "Another hopeless girl throwing herself at her minister."

Jackson fell back hard against the bench, his face slack. "Is that what you think? Sophia…" he breathed, and his hand covered hers. "I walked into your house and found you suffering. Hazel had hurt you with accusations about your father. All I wanted was to comfort you—"

Sophia's face crumpled. She pulled back her hand. "And you gave me a hug, just like you did to Franny, to comfort her, but I—I misread it, and I kissed you."

"*I* kissed *you*, Sophia," he corrected her, his eyes dark and intense. "I never planned to. A minister should never cross the line. The problem was the minute I put my arms around you, I forgot who I was." He crossed his arms over his chest. "Man to woman, like we said." He hesitated. "I told you I shut down my physical side when I entered the ministry. And it stayed shut down for a long time. Almost twenty years. Right up until the day I saw a beautiful dark-haired woman breaking into the kitchen at church."

Was she dreaming, or was he saying he was attracted to her? "You hardly spoke a word to me." Her heart thudded against her ribcage.

"I didn't trust myself. I'd buried my instincts for so many years, and without warning, they popped to the surface again. Crazy thoughts ran through my head when I saw you. How do I make her notice me? How do I impress her? What if I carry all the heavy boxes?"

Astonishment washed through her. She remembered checking him out as he walked up the stairs, never imagining he'd been doing the same.

"I pulled myself together after you were gone. Resisting temptation is part of the package when you enter the ministry. But for all those years, I hadn't been tested. Experiencing desire was new territory." He stared at his feet. "I thought if I just got to know you, I'd see you like any other parishioner." He shook his head. "But the attraction didn't die. When I saw you walking down the runway in twenty different styles of lingerie, I wondered if Satan had sent you to test me."

No. Sophia gasped, her mouth dropping open.

Jackson closed his eyes and drew a hand down his face. "I was in the back. I tried to leave before you could see me."

"Oh, God," she whispered. "My minister saw me modeling lingerie."

"Yes, your minister." Jackson gritted out the title between clenched teeth. "Your minister, who asked you to help cook a picnic dinner for two old people in love, who couldn't stop thinking how beautiful you looked as you served them at the table." Jackson swallowed hard, his voice tearing. "Your minister, who watched a wife comfort her husband at the end of his life and wished the same thing for himself."

Sophia's hand rested over her heart. She couldn't remember putting it there.

He cleared his throat and dropped his gaze. "I was smacked back into reality when you told me about Christopher. You had your own life. Anyway, I'd already promised myself never to get involved with another woman. To keep my focus one hundred percent on my work. But I found another reason to spend time with you. I really did want your help," he added. "But even more, I wanted an excuse to see you again."

A flush of pleasure warmed Sophia's cheeks and radiated down to her chest. Jackson's head was bowed in the dim light of the chapel, reminding her of a man in a confessional. Nowhere else could she imagine him admitting his attraction to one of his parishioners.

He stared into his hands. "After I realized all the trouble I'd caused you with picking up Hazel, I wanted to make it up to you. A minister's job is to help people find strength when they most need it. But as soon as I touched you..." He flicked his fingers wide to mimic an explosion. "The minister didn't kiss you, Sophia. The man I'd buried all those years ago did. I had no idea how strong he was."

He raised his gaze to hers, his pupils enlarged and hypnotic. Her pulse throbbed in her throat as she fought to retain her senses. "When I saw you follow Kate into the pantry at the church today, I felt your pity. Not"— she gestured with her hand—"everything you've just told me."

Rubbing a palm over his brow, Jackson winced. "I couldn't explain to Kate why I shouldn't be the one talking to you about your love life. I tried to tell her you didn't need our advice, but she had her own ideas. I didn't even realize why she'd dragged me into the pantry until I saw you there."

Sophia raised a weak hand, beseeching him to stop. Her mind was reeling. She'd walked into this room dreading a mortifying mini-sermon on the proper relationship between a minister and a congregant. Or, after everything he'd heard from Kate, she wouldn't have blamed him for referring her to a psychiatrist. Instead, he'd opened up about his own past—his flaws, his failures. And now he'd confessed desire...for her.

Closing her eyes, she saw again his stiff shoulders as he shut the door and left her house that day. "But you walked out of my house without saying a word. How could you?" Sophia pressed her lips together to hide their trembling. Jackson rubbed a hand over his jaw as if he could scrub off the stain of guilt.

He gave a heavy sigh. "Because I felt like I'd fallen into the deep end of the pool. I had to save myself. I'd promised I'd never allow those feelings to rise again."

A million questions whirled through Sophia's mind as she struggled to understand. "Do you really believe you never deserve another chance at love just because your marriage failed?"

He folded his arms over his chest, his gaze hardening. "There was a baby."

Struck by his use of the past tense, she drew a quick breath.

"We were both happy about the pregnancy. For the first time, we bonded. I may not have been much of a husband, but I'd always wanted to be a father." At the corner of his mouth, a muscle twitched.

He wore the same haunted look she'd glimpsed over Franny's dinner.

"Laura lost the baby two months before he was due."

The words came slowly, like a drowning person dragged from a hole in a frozen lake. As she saw the pain rippling over his face, she had to stop herself from grabbing his hands and holding them tight.

"I was to blame. I'd stayed late at work instead of getting home. She carried the groceries up the stairs to our apartment." He lowered his forehead onto his clasped hands. "She fell."

Sophia's eyes stung with unshed tears. How he must have suffered when Sam told the story of saving

167

his son from drowning. Hesitating, she put a hand on his sunken shoulder. "I'm so sorry," she faltered. "I can't imagine the pain of losing a child." She blew out a soft, slow breath. Jackson had been so natural and gentle with the baby he held in the fellowship hall. The moment must have been an excruciating reminder of the son he'd lost, but he'd given no inkling. "But you shouldn't be so hard on yourself. You're a kind man and put others first."

Jackson straightened, shaking his head.

"What happened to Laura was a terrible accident," Sophia insisted. "You're not to blame any more than she was."

"The first job of a father is to keep his child safe. And I failed," he whispered.

Sophia shook her head. "No. Some things in life are beyond our control. All you can choose is how to deal with them."

Jackson gave a short, mirthless laugh. "Well, I didn't get to choose. Laura refused to see me after the accident. She wouldn't even let me come inside the hospital room or talk on the phone. As soon as she got out, she served me with divorce papers. So I gave her what she wanted—the freedom to walk away."

Her heart swelling at the anguish written on his face, Sophia gripped his shoulder. "She was unfair to you. No," she insisted as he began to protest. "I understand her suffering must have been tremendous. But you were husband and wife. You had a duty to comfort each other. Instead, she shut you out. And you've continued punishing yourself ever since. You can't live like this. You have to let go." She relaxed her grip on his shoulder, tracing her hand down his arm.

"Forgive yourself for mistakes made in the past. Focus on all the good you do now."

Jackson ran his hands through his hair, from his brow to the back of his head. "Thank you for offering absolution." He gave a shaky laugh. When he looked at her again, his eyes were wet. "But I came here today to ask your forgiveness for crossing the line between my vocation and my impulses. To promise you I'll never make that mistake again."

Sophia gave a tiny, bewildered shake of her head. He'd admitted his attraction. From the way she'd returned his kiss, he *must* know she felt the same. "Can't a man be a minister and have the joys of an ordinary life, too?"

A wave of sadness passed over his face. "I learned the hard way that *I* can't. And I'd never risk hurting you the way I hurt my ex-wife." Jackson sighed, his face lost in the shadows of the deepening evening as he leaned back against the seat.

Sophia held herself very still. From the start of the day, her emotions had pitched in too many directions. The disgrace of facing him after their forbidden kiss had been tempered by witnessing his tenderness toward Franny and her family, only to be followed by the humiliation of Kate's revelations in the pantry. She'd been furious with him for forcing her into this conversation, but when she heard him open up about his past, her anger was wiped away by the magnitude of his grief.

And in between, the way he spoke of her. *Beautiful. Desirable.* For a few wild moments, all the fears she'd clutched to her heart when they'd first entered the chapel had been replaced by the one emotion powerful enough to conquer them all—hope. Hope that the man whose face haunted her waking hours actually shared her feelings.

But his final words extinguished the flame. His feelings for her were a mistake, one he promised never to repeat. She trained her gaze on the lamp until her eyes watered, but she didn't blink. For a few blissful moments, she'd dared to believe in a fairy-tale ending. But real life wasn't like that. At least, not her life.

Blinking her eyes, she swayed to her feet. "I'd better get back to Hazel before the nurses start her PM care."

He nodded, looking forward.

At the door to the hallway, she gave one last look. Jackson's hands gripped the bench in front of him while his lips moved silently in prayer. His shoulders were as still as a statue's.

She closed the door, leaving him to the peaceful emptiness of the chapel.

Chapter Eleven

Jackson sat at his desk, puzzling over an old note he couldn't place. He finally tossed it in the recycling basket. In the week since he'd last seen Sophia, he'd kept busy organizing the piles of unfinished business on his desk.

Taking advantage of his unexpected change of focus, Donna had run in and out of his office all week offering him forms to sign and deliveries to expedite. Today, her plain face frowned as she waved a paper copy of an email. "Hazel Bracca wants to start coming to service again on Sundays."

On his desk sat a stack of mail he'd be lucky to sort through by lunch. "Would you mind putting a request for volunteer drivers into the newsletter? I'll ask somebody to pick her up this Sunday."

Donna snorted. "I'm sure if you ask Sophia Anton, she'll be *happy* to pick up Hazel."

What a witch. The words flew into his mind before he could stop them, and he shook his head. He was a minister. He had no business calling names, even in the privacy of his own brain. "I think I've asked enough of Sophia. We've got plenty of people who'd be willing to help."

Donna pushed her glasses over the bridge of her nose. "You're a sitting duck for women like her— women on the prowl," she sniffed.

Drumming his fingertips on the desk, he leaned against the back of his chair. "Is there a line of girls outside my door I don't know about, Donna? If so, by all means, show them in."

Donna scowled. "I'm just saying girls like Sophia only want one thing."

Hold your temper. He pressed his open hands on the surface of the desk and stared at his assistant.

Donna took a step backward. "She hasn't been to church in years, but as soon as she finds out we have a bachelor minister, she shows up everywhere you are."

Jackson lifted his palm to stop her. "I *asked* for her help because of her skills. On the very morning of the church festival, she was asked to make hundreds of sausages, and she got it done. She made a four-star gourmet meal when I asked her to cook for the Newes. I asked for her help finding a safe place for a confused old woman who wouldn't let me near her. Sophia came through again." Like a teacher taking a student to task, he listed off each of Sophia's accomplishments on his fingers. "Asking for someone's assistance and then assigning them ulterior motives when they agree to help seems pretty uncharitable."

"But she was in the kitchen during Sam's funeral lunch, and she's not even on the funeral committee," Donna persisted. "She visits Hazel in the nursing home. She's just finding ways to get your attention. Mark my words—she's hatching plans." Her lips puckered into a sour smile, jowls quivering.

Donna's face was a mask of malice. He threw up his hands. What did he have to say to make her understand? "Sophia helped in the kitchen after Sam's funeral because she *cares*. She visits Hazel at the nursing home—not when I'm there, but in the evenings—because she cares. Sophia 'shows up' where I am because she's doing the same work as a volunteer that I get paid to do as a minister." Jackson stopped short. What had he just said?

When he saw Donna's mouth open to retort, he waved her out of the room. "Just put the notice in the newsletter, please. And close the door on your way out."

He caught the affronted look Donna threw at him before he swiveled his chair to the window. He gazed at the door to the fellowship hall, the very door where he'd first met Sophia one short month ago. Again, he saw her as she fumbled with the doorknob, her dark curls spilling one by one from the top of her head as she struggled to open the lock with her hairpin. Her startled gray eyes, her heart-shaped face flushed with frustration. Her sudden smile breaking like the sun from behind the clouds, melting the walls he'd erected around his heart. Never had he allowed himself to consider a relationship. After experiencing the fiasco of marrying a woman who resented the demands of his job, he'd accepted the impossibility of dividing his attentions.

Not until the words left his lips had he fully comprehended what he said. *Sophia does the same work as a volunteer that I get paid for as a minister.*

He remembered the night at the coffee shop when Sophia talked about her career. She enjoyed the creativity of marketing, she'd said. But working for a corporation was less satisfying as she got older. She wanted to make a difference in people's lives. She wanted to do the kind of work he did.

Heart racing, he leaned back in his chair. Since Laura and he both worked in public service, he'd thought they had common values. But Laura had been fresh out of college. She burned out at her demanding job, wanting what he couldn't offer—expensive cars, exotic vacations, and a nice home in an exclusive neighborhood.

Sophia was older—old enough to know her own mind. She had a successful career, but she still found time to give back to the community. At the lobster picnic, Franny had named dozens of volunteer activities Sophia led over the years. He'd seen her dedication firsthand these past few weeks.

Could Sophia Anton be the one woman who could share his interests, his responsibilities…his life?

****

Jackson found Hazel sitting alone in the courtyard of the nursing home. She was so still he thought she was dozing, but her head turned as he approached, her eyes bright.

"Good afternoon, Reverend. Isn't it a beautiful day?"

Smiling, he squeezed her shoulder and sat in a plastic chair beside her wheelchair. White clouds reeled across the metallic blue sky. He'd heard storms would roll in later. "How was lunch today?"

Hazel drew a quick breath. "Tuna fish casserole and pineapple upside-down cake!"

"Sounds great," Jackson agreed. "Wish I'd been here."

Hazel's brow furrowed. "Maybe you can still order a plate."

"Oh no," Jackson said comfortably. "I've already

eaten. I'm surprised there aren't more residents out here enjoying the sun."

"The nurses offered to bring more people out here. But everyone wanted to go back to their rooms and nap. It's a pity when people choose to be unhappy." She gazed across the courtyard and pointed to the opposite wall. "Do you see it over there? The hamster. No, that's not it."

She continued to point.

Jackson squinted. "The chipmunk?"

Smiling, she nodded. "He's sitting on his haunches, looking all around."

Jackson was impressed Hazel could see the tiny creature so many yards away. Since she'd received a new set of prescription glasses, she participated more in the world around her. Three square meals a day helped, too.

"I've always loved chipmunks." She leaned forward in her chair, her gaze glued to the wall. "But they won't sit still. There he goes!" It dashed to the shrubs lining the brick walls of the courtyard and disappeared.

Leaning back his head, Jackson closed his eyes. A warm breeze lifted his hair from his forehead. He patted Hazel's wrinkled hand where it lay on the arm of the wheelchair. "I hear you'd like to attend Sunday services again." He kept his eyes closed, enjoying the heat of the sun on his eyelids.

"Yes, I would." She sighed. "But I'm afraid I don't know what's happened to my car."

He opened his eyes and smiled at her. "No worries. Lots of people in our congregation would be happy to drive you to church." He paused. "I thought I'd ask

Sophia if she could bring you this Sunday." For three days, he'd explored the idea of opening his heart to Sophia, but he still hadn't found the courage. After all, despite hearing everything he'd revealed in the chapel, she hadn't once told him what, if anything, she felt for him. Still, he felt her name on his tongue like an electric current. Saying her name felt as illicit, somehow, as touching her. *Not forbidden,* he reminded himself. *Unknown.*

Hazel turned to look at him. "Why, Sophia can't drive me. She's not in town."

"Oh." Jackson's chest deflated. He'd hoped to invite her to dinner tonight or tomorrow. Now he'd have to hold his feelings inside even longer. "I didn't realize she was away. I'll find someone else to drive you this weekend."

The chipmunk reappeared on the wall, scampering across the vertical surface and dashing back down into the bushes. "Just when I try to count his stripes, he runs off again," Hazel fretted.

Jackson patted her hand. "He'll be back." They continued watching the bushes as clouds overhead cast fast-moving shadows on the ground. "Do you know where she went? Sophia?" His mouth lingered over her name again.

"To New York." Excited, she sat straight. "There he is again! Do you have any food you can throw to him?"

A sick feeling churned his stomach, but he nodded to Hazel, patting his trousers for the saltine wrapper he'd pocketed at lunch. Tearing open the packet, he walked to the birdfeeder where the chipmunk had resurfaced. It shot back into the bushes at his approach.

Breaking the crackers, he trailed crumbs toward Hazel's wheelchair. "Maybe he'll run right up to you," he told her as he took his seat again.

"I hope so!" She sat forward in her chair, gripping the rests tightly.

Jackson cleared his throat, feeling like a teenager fishing for information about a crush. "You said Sophia is in New York?"

Her attention fixed on the empty sidewalk, Hazel nodded.

"Is she visiting someone?" Jackson asked.

Hazel nodded. "I should say so." Her shoulders tensed. "He's back. I don't think he sees the crumbs. Come this way!" She dropped her hand. "Maybe you should show him where they are."

Frustration swelled Jackson's lungs. He tried to crack his lips into a smile. "He'll sniff out the crumbs in a minute, Hazel. He's a rodent. He can smell food from a mile away."

The chipmunk ran like lightning to the line of crumbs. "He sees them!" Hazel yelled in triumph, cooing as it lifted tiny paws to its cheeks and chewed the food. "Isn't he adorable? Do you have more crackers?" She slapped sideways at Jackson's arm, her gaze riveted to the sidewalk.

"No." He pulled his arm away, his sense of unease growing. "Hazel. Please listen to me." He had an unholy urge to chase away the chipmunk with a broom.

Hazel turned, and her smile faded.

"Is Sophia visiting Christopher, Hazel?"

She nodded.

Blood hammered his eardrums. He was a fool. He'd told her he'd stay out of her life. Why should he be surprised if she'd gone back to Christopher? Jackson had been so busy imagining his happy future with Sophia that he didn't even realize she might make other plans.

He took a deep breath. Sophia had doubts about Christopher; she'd said so that night at the coffee shop. If Jackson courted her the way she deserved, he'd prove he wanted the whole Sophia, the real Sophia. He still had time to win her heart. "Do you know when she's coming back?" he asked Hazel.

She frowned. "Sophia's not coming back. She's on her way to Paris tonight."

Uncomprehending, he stared at Hazel. What was real, and what was fantasy? Sophia must have felt the same bewilderment when Hazel confessed her notorious affair.

"Why would she go to Paris, Hazel?" He strained to keep his voice low and steady.

"A dancer in the Paris Ballet Company broke his leg on an escalator. Christopher is taking over the role. He had to move to France right away."

"And Sophia is helping him settle in?" *Please, God, tell me she's there only for a visit.*

Hazel regarded Jackson like a slow-witted child. "Of course," she replied. "She can't work in France, so she'll be a housewife."

"A housewife." A lump of anguish lodged in his throat, and he repeated Hazel's words with difficulty.

"Yes. She came by here two nights ago to say goodbye. The only way she could go to Paris with Christopher was to marry him and get a temporary Visa. They got married at City Hall. Such a shame Sophia couldn't have a real wedding. She would have looked so beautiful in a gown and veil."

Jackson's gaze was fixed, unblinking, on the old woman. Thin blue veins lined the papery skin under her eyes, and wide pores climbed the side of her nose. A long white chin hair fluttered in a sudden gust of wind. He shook his head roughly. Was this another of Hazel's delusions? "I'm surprised I didn't hear Sophia got married." The words scraped his throat like sandpaper.

"She told me to keep it secret. Oh, I shouldn't have told you!" Hazel pressed her fingers to her lips to stop up the words.

A roaring silence pounded his ears. The dome of sky visible over the courtyard pressed down, an emptiness threatening to flatten him. He soothed Hazel using a mechanical tone. "I'm sure she'll forgive you." His gaze searched for an anchor. He didn't want to think. He loaded all his attention on the chipmunk at the edge of the sidewalk. "He's back."

Diverted, Hazel cooed as the tiny creature stole toward them. Inching closer, it fixed its beady, black eyes on the humans. A sudden gust of wind scattered the trail of crumbs off the cement and into the grass, sending the chipmunk running back to its hideout in the bushes. A shadow from the clouds overhead draped the courtyard in shade, and Hazel shivered.

He hadn't realized how the temperature had dropped. Forcing himself into motion, Jackson rose. He rolled Hazel's chair inside the building as the first few raindrops began to spatter. As he made his way to Hazel's room, he planted a smile on his face for the people he passed. He'd call Sophia as soon as he got home. She couldn't have married without everyone knowing. Hazel was spinning a dream into a story.

When Hazel was wheeled into her room, she pointed to a paper turned upside-down on the bedside table.

The room was too narrow to push the chair all the way to the table. He helped Hazel stand.

Painfully, leaning her hand on the bed's railing, she limped to the table and picked up the paper, clutching it to her chest.

"What is it?" Jackson's heart galloped. As soon as he asked, he knew he didn't want to look.

She waved the sheet with a cheery smile and handed it to Jackson.

Sophia and a man on the steps of City Hall smiled from the photo print-out. She was curled to his chest, laying her left hand against his lapel to show off a small diamond engagement ring nestled against a thin gold band on her finger. Sophia's curls were like ink against Christopher's ivory skin. His long blond hair was swept back from eyes dark blue, almost black. He wore a victorious grin, relishing what he hadn't earned.

Jackson gazed into Sophia's wide, gray eyes. Her face was laughing and happy, just as warm and full of life as the last time she'd smiled at him. His heart contracted, a painful twist subsiding into a bruised ache.

He placed the photo on the comforter of Hazel's bed, smoothing his hand over Sophia's face before he straightened. As he hastened from the room, he had just enough presence of mind to ask an aide to help Hazel into bed. Without saying goodbye, he strode through the halls of the nursing home to the lobby, emerging from the building just as the skies opened in a torrent. He yanked open the door of his car and slammed it shut after he slid inside. He fumbled for his keys and roared the engine to life, peeling out of the parking lot. Thunder concussed his eardrums as he raced into the lightning-streaked darkness.

Chapter Twelve

The day of Kate's wedding rehearsal dawned bright and scorching. "Carl's dad called it 'hotter than a billy goat with a blow torch.' I swear, my house feels like a barn before a hoe-down over here," Kate complained.

Sophia smiled, cradling the phone between her ear and her shoulder as she rinsed her toothbrush. "Bet you're wishing you'd sprung for hotel rooms for the wedding," she teased.

Kate groaned. "I should have run off to City Hall like you did. Now I'm stuck with a houseful of relations, and I don't even have a room for my own maid of honor."

"You and the boys need to get to know Carl's family. Besides, I'll be fine over here at Franny's. The woman is amazing. She lost her husband two years ago, but she hasn't slowed down one bit."

"Well, I'm glad *someone's* enjoying herself. I'd better get off the phone; I haven't even finished packing for the honeymoon. And I don't know how I'll ever get my house cleaned with all these people hanging around. Now they're shooting empty cans off the coffee table with rubber bands." Kate's outraged whisper wasn't likely to be heard over the loud hoots of laughter reverberating in the background.

"Don't worry about anything," Sophia soothed.

"When I get back to the house with the twins while you're on your honeymoon, I'll have plenty of time to clean up. You have enough to worry about the day before you get married."

Kate exhaled a long breath of air. "Thanks, Soph. Part of me wishes I could just stay home and recuperate with you and the boys. Carl could go on the honeymoon by himself."

Sophia laughed. "Come on. You just have to survive one rehearsal dinner and one little wedding ceremony. Then you're off to Hawaii for ten days of sun tanning and snorkeling. In less than forty-eight hours, you'll be sitting on the beach with a Mai Tai. Hang in there, pal!"

"I'll try," Kate sighed. "And even though I'm losing my mind in all this chaos, I know the boys are having the time of their lives while all their cousins are here. But they will *love* having Aunt Sophy all to themselves while we're gone," she added. "Now I really do have to run. See you at O'Grady's at one o'clock for the fitting?"

"Can't wait." Sophia's face dimpled with amusement as she dried her hands and turned off the phone.

In the two years since she'd last seen Sophia, Kate's life had turned on its head. Weeks after Sophia moved to Paris, Carl, the twins' father, suddenly resurfaced, asking Kate for a second chance with his sons. Clean and sober for twelve months, he promised Kate he was ready to shoulder his parenting responsibilities.

Kate had been slow to trust him. In fact, Kate's desperate plea for advice about Carl was the only reason Sophia agreed to talk to her friend again after Sophia's unannounced marriage to Christopher.

Furious at Kate for sharing with Jackson intimate details about her personal life, Sophia had moved to Paris without a word. For months, she blocked her oldest friend on social media and ignored phone and text messages.

Carl had done right by the boys *and* their mother. Following Sophia's advice, Kate demanded he attend Narcotics Anonymous meetings twice a week as a condition for visitation. She also insisted Carl find a steady job. He exceeded her expectations by enrolling in night school and finishing his degree in social work. He took a job as a counselor at a local drug and alcohol lab testing service where he had once been a patient. Before long, Carl was spending most evenings with his sons. He and Kate took turns making dinner and giving baths. Their cooperation as parents had unfolded into a deeper relationship between the two of them.

"I like having Carl around," Kate said simply to Sophia one evening on the phone. "The boys feel like they have a whole family for the first time. He may not be perfect, but he's right for us." Kate planned a simple summer wedding, asking Sophia to be her maid of honor.

Rubbing moisturizer over her cheeks, Sophia was still smiling. Kate had gotten more family than she'd bargained for when Carl's clan came to town for the wedding, complaining that she felt like the old woman living in a shoe. Her house overflowed with visitors: his parents, two brothers, their wives, and eight nieces and nephews. Carl's brother, Donny, had parked his battered RV in the side yard to house the crowd of bodies.

Franny Newes offered her spare room to Sophia and Christopher during their visit. But Christopher balked at the idea of missing dance rehearsal time. Since they'd moved back to New York four months earlier, he was away from the apartment more than ever. Long hours of practice were crucial to ensure his spot in the New York City Ballet, he told her. She didn't mind his absence during her first visit home in two years. Christopher wouldn't fit in at the wedding.

Wiping her lips with a hand towel, Sophia glanced at her reflection in the mirror over the sink. She'd changed since she was last in East Benson. Her face had rounded as she slowly crept back to her usual weight—and Christopher grew more remote with each pound.

Paris had been a lonely experience. Her efforts to create a home for her husband couldn't fill the space her work and friends had previously occupied. Pretending enthusiasm for his daily tips on diet and exercise, she waited until he left the apartment to buy herself home-baked treats at the corner bakery.

Sophia had always admired her mother's commitment to the home. She'd managed the household, supported her husband, and made sure her daughter knew she was cherished. But Sophia lived a different reality. She had no children, and her hopes to be a mother had faded.

She ran her fingers through her hair, frowning at her reflection. The roundness of her face didn't bother her so much—in fact, she finally saw traces of her pretty mother in her own face when she stopped being so thin. But the sadness in her eyes made looking in the mirror a little harder every day.

A quiet knock on the door roused her from her musings.

Franny stood in the hallway, looking fresh and trim in a yellow tank top and white shorts. "I just got back from tennis and put together a fruit platter for breakfast. Are you hungry?"

"Sounds fabulous." Sophia followed Franny into the small kitchen of her condominium. "I slept later than I planned."

"I'm not surprised, considering how late you got in last night." Franny handed Sophia a plate piled with berries and chunks of melon. She carried two mugs of coffee into the living room.

"When did you decide to move, Franny?" Sophia asked as she set the platter on an end table.

"About six months after Sam died." Sunshine flooded through the windows. Potted plants soaked up the light from shelves, tables, and the pergola flooring. A bookshelf crammed with titles left room for only a few family photos. In the corner below a window was a yoga mat, incense, and a small framed picture of Sam.

"But you had such a beautiful house. So many memories." Sophia remembered Sam's collection of music boxes and how family photos adorned the walls of the living room.

"Life moves forward, not backward." Franny's tone was brisk as she settled herself in an overstuffed brown leather chair, resting her feet on the ottoman with a contented sigh. "I didn't want to sit in our house and drown in my memories. Sam wouldn't have wanted me to, either. So I held an estate sale and moved in here. This little place has everything I need: an extra bedroom for guests, an office, my reading-and-yoga room"—she indicated the living room with a sweep of her arm—"one and a half baths, and a cute little kitchen. Housecleaning is so much easier now."

Sophia sank onto the cushion of a wicker rocker, placing a coffee mug beside the platter. "I love the peacefulness of this room." She sighed with pleasure as she raised a spoonful of blueberries and cream to her lips. "I haven't had berries like these in two years. Thanks so much for inviting me to stay, Franny."

"Two years! It *has* been too long." Franny shook her head. "Just let me sit here and look at you a minute. I'm glad you're not starving yourself anymore. I guess married life suits you."

Sophia forced a smile, her heart pressed by a familiar weight. She'd promised herself to keep a stiff upper lip around her old friends. No need to worry them with her problems.

Franny's bright blue eyes were fixed on Sophia. "I was looking forward to meeting your husband when Kate got married."

"He really couldn't get away. The wedding couldn't have come at a worse time for him." Sophia stopped short. "I didn't say that right. I only meant he has to work harder than ever to keep his place in this company. The New York Ballet is one of the most competitive in the world." She paused, making a face. "He and Kate don't really get along, anyway."

Franny nodded. "You can't force the people you love to like each other for your sake." She shrugged. "Still, is it too much to expect your husband to come with you on your first visit home in two years?"

Lifting her feet and curling into the chair, Sophia

wrapped her arms around a red velour pillow. "Every marriage has challenges. Living my life around Christopher's dance schedule is something I've had to get used to." She tried to keep her tone light. "I'm just relieved he's found a good job back in New York. I can't tell you how happy I am to be back in the States, with people who speak my language."

Franny pulled a stem from her mouth, her gaze curious. "Are you all settled in? Kate said your old house is still full of furniture."

"In Christopher's little apartment, my furniture didn't fit, in either meaning of the word. I'm not sure what I'll do with my stuff." Her fingers were clenched tight as she stared down at her mug. For two years, she'd delayed the sale of her townhouse, protecting a private plan of moving back to East Benson to raise a family. But with every passing day, her dream moved farther away.

She forced her fingers to relax. "Enough about me. What have you been doing with yourself the past two years? Besides yoga?"

"Well, I'm a working woman now," Franny replied. "I work at the church, as a matter of fact."

"You do?" Sophia was surprised. "What do you do over there?"

"I'm Jackson's office administrator."

His name jolted her like an electric current. How long since she'd thought of him? After moving to Paris, she used every drop of willpower she possessed to shut down lingering thoughts about the minister and dedicate herself to Christopher. In her lonely apartment, thinking about the few weeks she'd known Jackson Thomas would have been too painful. "What happened to Donna? Did she retire?" Sophia asked.

"I think she and Jackson made a mutual decision to part ways. And since he knew I wanted to find a job after Sam died, he brought me in to take her place."

"Good for you!" She marveled at the older woman's ability to roll with the changes in her life. "Do you like working there?"

Franny widened her eyes and smiled. "I love it! Jackson's been patient as I learned the ropes, and he told me about computer classes at the library to update my skills. Mostly, he needs help with administrative duties, but he always asks my input on classes and outreach efforts offered by the church, too. In my own small way, I feel like I'm making a difference."

Swallowing another spoonful of berries, Sophia sighed. "I'm envious." She contemplated the empty spoon in her hand. "I haven't felt like I made a difference in a long time."

Franny frowned. "So you're not working? Or are you just in the wrong job?"

"I've started looking for a job in merchandising in New York, but as you can imagine, I'm facing pretty stiff competition. I'm not even sure I want to work in retail any longer." Working at a fine department store in her hometown hadn't prepared her to compete for a job in the largest city in North America. Anyway, the whole glamor lifestyle had lost its appeal.

"What did you do while you were in France?" Franny asked.

Sophia shook her head. "I didn't have a worker's permit. *Or* any friends. And then there was the language barrier. Just going outside made me nervous, wondering what embarrassing situation I'd find myself in when I tried to speak French." She winced, remembering how her tongue would tie, forcing her to communicate with hand gestures. "Christopher's rehearsal days were long, even when he wasn't touring. I figured while I was in France I could at least do some cooking. I went to the market every day so I could come home and experiment with all kinds of different dishes. You can find almost any food in Paris. I got to know the butchers, the fish mongers, and the grocers within walking distance of our apartment."

She didn't tell Franny she ate alone most nights because Christopher rehearsed so late. To avoid sliding into a serious depression, she forced herself to take long walks every day, no matter the weather. "One day I wandered into the Latin Quarter by the *Fontaine Saint Michel*, a big tourist spot in Paris. Lots of teenagers hung out by the fountain and made money from the crowd. They'd turn on hip-hop music and get the tourists to dance the circle; then they'd pass a bucket for donations. I saw them go to the back of one of the restaurants afterward and ask for leftover food from the kitchens. They didn't get much."

She'd hurried back to her apartment and made sandwiches from leftover beef roast. When she returned to the fountain and offered sections to the teens, she was happy to see them accept without hesitation. For her part, using her halting French skills with young people made her much less self-conscious.

"I'd take them sandwiches twice a week. As the weather got colder, I made soups and stews. In France, cold weather doesn't keep anyone indoors. And those kids were tough. They were at the fountain come rain, shine, or snowfall."

"Even during school? Were they runaways?" Franny leaned forward in her chair, her eyes bright with curiosity.

"They seemed to be. My problem was, once again, the language barrier. They spoke enough English to communicate with me on a basic level, but to them, my French must've sounded like a little kid's." New faces replaced familiar ones from week to week. What brought them there? What were their stories? Because she didn't speak their language, she couldn't establish a real connection. "I just didn't have the words to really reach them."

She didn't tell Franny how the teens became an argument between Christopher and her.

"There's no reason for anybody to be homeless in France," he'd scold. "Half of my paycheck goes to this country's welfare system."

Instead, she twisted her lips into a smile. "Those kids were my only friends in Paris. I just wish I could have helped them find a way off the streets."

Vexed, Franny tapped the chair's armrests. "In this day and age, I can't believe the homeless are still among us. Sam used to say, 'If we can send a man to the moon, how can we still let kids go to bed hungry?'"

Sophia nodded as she ate a piece of sweet honeydew, wondering how many new teens were cooling at the *Fontaine Saint Michel* in the blistering August heat.

Franny gazed at Sophia with a thoughtful expression. "At least once a month I talk with Deirdre Haskew at the shelter for teens by Divine Mercy Hospital, helping arrange shipments of donated clothing and school supplies. They're always looking for volunteers to work with the kids. They need the kind of person who listens with her heart. You'd be the perfect person for the job—"

"Except I live in a different state." Sophia put up her hand to stop Franny. "Anyway, I didn't mean to hijack the conversation again. It's just so good to talk to an old friend who understands my language!" She laughed. "But you like your job?"

"Oh yes. I've learned so much about the lives of people who fall through the cracks in our county. We're lucky to have a minister who's so devoted to serving his community."

Sophia tried to stifle a small sigh as she gazed out the window.

For the second time, Franny noticed Sophia's face cloud at the mention of Jackson's name. *Interesting.* Franny had commented on the spark between Sophia and the minister during the lobster picnic, but Sam had warned his wife not to meddle. *You're not here to stop me now, love.* She stretched her arms and gave a luxurious yawn, looking up at the ceiling. "Yes, I love my job and helping to do the work of the church. Plus, I get to weigh in on the women Jackson's interested in." Hearing Sophia gasp, Franny bit into a strawberry before turning her gaze back to the young woman.

Covering her mouth, Sophia pretended to cough.

Franny watched her with polite concern.

"He's dating?" Sophia strained to keep her voice neutral.

Wiping the pink stain of strawberry from her lips with a napkin, Franny nodded.

"But I thought he was committed to celibacy. Kate said so," Sophia added hastily.

Franny harrumphed. "Maybe he discovered forever is a long time to be alone. I only know he belongs to an online dating service. I can show you his profile on lovematch.com if you'd like to see."

"The minister is dating online?" Sophia sputtered, dripping coffee as she banged her mug onto the end table. "Does the congregation know?"

Franny's eyebrows knit together. "I don't know. But what of it? Nothing in our faith tradition restricts him from marrying. Why shouldn't he try to find someone to love? Even a minister deserves happiness, I would think."

Sophia rose from her chair. Her hands shook as she carried her plate, rolling a berry dangerously close to the edge. "Breaking a vow of celibacy is a pretty big deal."

"People change, Sophia. Circumstances change."

Sophia avoided Franny's gaze as she walked to the kitchen. "I'm not very hungry after all. I guess I'm still a little tired from driving," she called from the kitchen.

"No trouble at all, dear. Maybe you should lie down for a while before you meet Kate," Franny suggested. A moment later, when she heard the guest bedroom door click shut, Franny leaned back in her chair and raised the coffee cup to her mouth, her lips curved into a speculative smile.

****

The familiar odor of floor polish under a mélange of fragrances assaulted Sophia as she entered the rotating doors of O'Grady's. She hadn't set foot in the department store since she'd given notice two years ago. Other than receiving occasional notifications on social media, she hadn't stayed in touch with co-workers, either.

She looked about for a familiar face, eager to think about something else, anything else, than her conversation with Franny. In the chapel of Hazel's nursing home, Jackson had delivered a long, tortured explanation of why, after his wife had lost her baby, he could never be with another woman. So tragic. So noble. But in the end, Jackson Thomas turned out to be a man like any other: a man trolling for women online.

Sophia gave her head a violent shake. What did it matter? She was a married woman. What the minister of her old church did in his own time was no concern of hers.

Then why did her heart feel like an old wound splitting open again?

"Sophia, up here!"

Raising her head to find Kate beckoning near the top of the escalator, she grinned, her heart flooding with happiness. She hurried to the escalator. Too impatient to wait for it to carry her to the next floor, she trotted up the moving stairs, then stopped in front of her friend and gazed with honest admiration. "You've highlighted your hair, you've lost weight, you're wearing stylish clothes, and you even put on makeup. Someone's been reading bridal magazines." Sophia put a hand over her heart in mock surprise.

Snorting, Kate shook her fist at Sophia before hugging her tight. "We don't have time for this." She released Sophia's shoulders and turned toward the back of the store. "Tiffany's only got an hour to fit you for your bridesmaid's dress." Kate ushered Sophia through a door marked Staff Entrance Only.

Inside, Tiffany's head of short, curly hair was bent

over a tablet, her lips pressed together in concentration as she scanned items on a list against the inventory on the racks. Her face broke into a smile. "Sophia Anton! How long has it been?" She dropped her tablet on a counter and hurried to the door. Taking Sophia's hands, she held them at arm's length and swept a critical glance from head to toe. "I'm thinking you're a size sixteen?"

"Probably," Sophia said, cheeks coloring with embarrassment. "I was a little thinner the last time you saw me…"

"Don't be silly. You look beautiful." Tiffany paced between the racks of dresses, glancing at labels. In a moment she'd found what she was looking for and held it out to Kate. "This should be perfect."

"Okay." Sophia raised her eyebrows. "Do I strip down right here, or am I squeezing into the supply closet for my fitting?"

Tiffany laughed. "Sorry, I didn't mean to rush you. I already knew what Kate had in mind, and I only needed to eyeball your size. You'll have to try it on in the bathroom. And since I know it's not as elegant as the fitting room in formal wear, I made sure to supply the most important part." From behind the counter, she pulled a tray with three glasses and a bottle of champagne.

"Now we've got a party," Kate agreed. "I really appreciate you taking the time to squeeze us in, Tiffany. *And* for letting me choose from the new line-up. All these dresses just came down from New York," Kate told Sophia over her shoulder as she carried her dress into the bathroom.

"Are you kidding?" Tiffany called. "I'm happy to

take a break from recording inventory. Yep, you're the first ones to see what anyone who's anyone in this town will be wearing in the next few months. Do you want me in there while you dress?"

Smiling, Sophia shook her head. "We can manage." She wasn't looking forward to undressing in front of Kate, let alone a second witness. She slid off her shoes while Kate hung the dress on the door and unzipped it. "Stay turned around and just hand me the dress when I ask," Sophia ordered.

Kate shrugged. "Whatever. We used to get dressed in front of each other all the time, though. Ain't nothin' I haven't seen before."

As she pulled her jersey over her head, Sophia grimaced. "I know. But the older I get, the less my body likes gravity."

Her back still turned, Kate snorted. "None of us are getting any younger. But don't worry: Tiffany knows how to pick a dress that hides your flaws and flaunts your best features."

In bra and panties now, Sophia reached for the dress.

Kate released it into Sophia's waiting hand. "Let me know when you need help with the zipper." She leaned sideways against the door, averting her face.

Sophia lifted the skirt over her head. She slid the lacy three-quarter-length sleeves down her arms, straightening the waistline and smoothing the skirt over her hips. She turned her back to Kate. "Ready for the zip."

Pulling up the zipper, Kate fastened a pearl clasp at the top, just at the base of Sophia's neck. Kate's face brightened as Sophia circled around. "Oh, Sophia," she breathed. "You have to see yourself." With gentle hands on Sophia's upper arms, Kate led her friend to the mirror over the sink.

Feeling shy, Sophia looked in the mirror. The dress was all-over sequin lace, antique pink, with an illusion bateau neckline. A bow ribbon belted at her waist. She smoothed her hands over the skirt. It fit snugly over her hips, the hemline resting just above her knees.

Kate was right—the dress flattered her finer points and camouflaged the trouble spots. Sophia turned, viewing her back from over her shoulder. "For a girl whose fashion sense used to end at black T-shirts and combat boots, you sure know how to pick a dress."

Kate's pleased face hovered inside the frame of the mirror. "I know, right?" she agreed. "Tiffany helped, though. After dressing you in all those fashion shows, she had a pretty good sense of what to choose. And she was right. I love this dress. What do you think?"

Before Sophia could answer, she heard Tiffany calling from the other side of the door. "What did you say?" she called back.

"Come out here and let me see!" Tiffany hollered.

Sophia opened the door.

Tiffany heaved a self-satisfied sigh. "Do I know my stuff, or what?" She tugged at the hem of the dress and slid her hands along the sides of Sophia's waist. "Fits like a glove. I don't think anything needs to be altered, do you?" she asked Kate while her critical gaze roved over every detail of Sophia's dress.

"I think it's perfect," Kate responded. "What do you think, Soph?" She bit her lip. "I don't want you wearing anything you're not comfortable in. I won't be one of those horrible brides you see on reality TV shows."

Sophia smiled at her friend. "You couldn't have made this easier on me. I *love* the dress. If you're satisfied, I'm satisfied."

"Yay!" Kate squeaked, grabbing and hugging Sophia.

Giving her friend a long squeeze, Sophia laughed. She'd never known Kate to be so affectionate. "I'd love to see you in your wedding gown."

Kate shrugged. "It's not really a gown. It's tea-length and lacy. I wanted yours to be lacy, too, to kind-of match mine. You always look so pretty in pale pink. Mine's a really soft heather green. Tiffany helped me pick the dress."

Tiffany nodded. "The silvery green was perfect for her skin tone. She wasn't interested in traditional white."

"Well, there's nothing traditional about my marriage to Carl." Kate clapped her hands together. "So if we're all agreed on Sophia's dress, the time has come for a champagne toast!"

Popping the cork from the bottle, Tiffany poured a bubbly stream into each of their flutes. "To Kate and Carl." She raised her glass.

"To old friends." Kate clinked her glass against Sophia's and smiled.

Echoing Kate's words and seeing her hazel eyes glow with affection, Sophia swallowed a gulp of champagne. For the first time in what seemed like forever, she felt as close to Kate as she had as a girl. Time had a way of healing old wounds. She sipped her drink, watching Kate answer Tiffany's questions about the upcoming wedding. Kate had never seemed so happy.

Did I look like that when I married Christopher? The warm glow inside her chest, powered by champagne and the company of good friends, sputtered at the memory of her wedding day.

He'd proposed so hastily—well, "proposal" wasn't exactly the word for it. "Suggestion" was more accurate. He'd had only a week to get his affairs in order and move to Paris, where he knew no one. What better time for them to start their life together? Maybe now was the time to take the plunge and get married. Sophia could settle them into their new home while he transitioned into the new ballet company.

She'd still been reeling from Jackson's confessions in the chapel. The one thing she knew was nothing would ever come from her feelings for the minister. Maybe in a new place, with only each other to lean on, she and Christopher could have a fresh start. She could put her hopeless desire for Jackson Thomas behind her forever.

"Are you all right, Soph? You look pale."

Sophia pushed her focus back to the two women.

Kate reached for her hand.

"I'm fine." Sophia shook her head, squeezing and dropping Kate's hand. "The champagne's going to my head. I should get out of this beautiful dress before I spill. Help me unzip?" She turned her back to the women, pinching some color into her cheeks. Back in the bathroom, Sophia rested her brow against the door. Why did she let herself think about the past? Nothing would change it now. Cooling her forehead against the pressed wood, she heard Tiffany say to Kate in a low voice, "I guess things aren't going so well for Sophia and her husband."

Sophia rocked back from the door. On second thought, she wanted to hear this. Pressing her ear against the wood, she held her breath to hear Kate's response.

"…know what you're talking about."

Kate's tone was stiff. Sophia blinked in gratitude to hear how uncomfortable her friend sounded. She strained to hear Tiffany's response. "I saw him at the Lincoln Center a couple of weeks ago. With another woman."

Sophia sagged against the door. When she and Christopher moved back to New York, she'd wondered if he'd see April again. Now she wanted to push the door open and question Tiffany herself.

"What'd she look like?" Kate's voice was quiet but steely.

"Long blonde hair. Late twenties, maybe. She was tiny."

"Like a dancer?" Kate whispered.

No response from Tiffany. Maybe she'd nodded her head.

"Mean faced, like a ferret?" Kate continued.

"Yeah, she definitely had the mean-girl look. You know her?"

"I've seen pictures," Kate whispered grimly.

April. The dancer Christopher had sworn was out of his system. Before his marriage, he'd turned to her again and again, no matter how many times he discovered she'd lied and cheated. And now, back in New York, the dangerous possibilities of April had been too sweet for him to deny.

Sophia sighed, a long exhalation of poisonous

gases pouring from her lungs. Tiffany's news should hurt. But instead of pain, she felt a loosening in the muscles around her heart. She lifted her chin and closed her eyes, breathing deeply.

"How are you doing in there?" Kate called from the other side of the door.

"Almost done," she lied, pulling the dress over her head and hoping she wouldn't rip the lace. If the women were still talking about her, they'd moved away from the door. Kate would no doubt blast her with Christopher's infidelity as soon as they left the store. Sophia sighed. Just when she and Kate were getting along again. Slipping back into her clothes and shoes, Sophia plastered on a bright smile as she pushed open the door.

Tiffany's and Kate's smiles looked as fake as Sophia's own probably did. The thought made her giggle. What was going on with her? Her worst fears about Christopher had just been confirmed, and instead of being destroyed by the knowledge, she felt only…"Liberated," she said aloud.

Tiffany nodded, pretending to understand, but Kate's face was a question.

Sophia turned toward the warehouse exit, the hanger of her dress clutched in her fist. "Let's go find some shoes!"

Chapter Thirteen

He'd dreaded this moment from the instant Kate Couvert had stopped by his office to arrange the details of her wedding. "Just a small ceremony, with Carl's family and a few close friends. Sophia will be my maid of honor *and* my whole family, I guess." She'd laughed, not noticing he didn't join in.

Every muscle in his body tightened with anticipation as he watched Sophia walk down the aisle of the church. Her face radiated affection for Kate's twins as they pulled her along by both hands. He stood on the altar with Kate, Carl, and his best man, a brother whose name Jackson had forgotten the instant Sophia approached.

"Drag her up here, guys," Kate ordered her sons. "Jackson, you remember Sophia."

He didn't trust himself to look at her face. Instead, he focused on the laughing eyes of the two boys as they pushed her up the landing. "That's no way to treat a lady," he scolded them, a smile at the corner of his lips. He reached for Sophia's hand to help her up the wide step to the altar. "Hello, Sophia."

"I'm fine." She ignored his outstretched arm and joined Kate on his right.

He'd forgotten, he realized when he dared to look at her face. He'd clamped down hard on his feelings after Sophia had gotten married, ruthlessly shoving aside any lingering memories whenever they would surface. In unguarded moments, when he caught the scent of lilacs in the air or saw the face of a woman smiling down at a child in her arms, images of Sophia would flood back into his mind.

But now, as he watched her murmur to Kate, he knew he'd forgotten the sweetness of her gray eyes and the dark eyebrows arched in amusement at the boys' antics. How could he have let himself forget the easy curve of her full lips, or the dimple carved like a half-moon to the right of her mouth when she laughed as she did now, her high cheekbones rosy with pleasure? His heart beating fast, he looked away. Thankfully, Sophia hadn't met his gaze.

Kate clapped her hands and gestured to Carl's parents in the front row. "Could you keep the boys down with you, Big Mama?"

He saw Kate glance sideways at Sophia and roll her eyes.

With a polite cough into the back of her hand, Sophia hid a giggle.

From the pews, Carl's mother, straining her buttons against the fabric of her patterned blouse, placed the circle of her thumb and forefinger against her teeth. A whistle pierced the air.

The boys froze in the stunned silence. With a sheepish look at their parents, the twins turned to the church and filed past the knees of a dozen family members to make their way to their grandmother.

Kate turned back to Jackson. "We'd better get this show on the road."

Jackson ran through the simple directions for the small wedding party. Kate had decided to forgo some aspects of the traditional ceremony—"I don't have a father to walk me up the aisle, and I don't need someone to give me away at the age of thirty-two"—so after the ring bearer and flower girl proceeded down the aisle, Sophia and Donny were to enter the back of the church from opposite sides. They'd meet at the center aisle and walk together. Kate and Carl would enter the church the same way, proceeding down the aisle arm-in-arm, and meet their sons at the altar to light a candle from their four tapers.

The rehearsal began amidst the usual confusion of getting a little boy and girl to walk down the aisle on cue. Jackson, usually amused by the kids, was impatient for them to do their part and sit with their parents. He wasn't aware of his sense of urgency, though, until Sophia re-entered through the door on the left at the back of the church.

Her hands clasped, she floated along the back row of pews in the characteristic slow slide of bridesmaids. Donny halted, mimicking her step. They were both laughing as they met in the center aisle. Sophia accepted his outstretched arm with a smile and a mini-curtsy.

Alone now on the altar, Jackson felt excruciatingly awkward watching the couple progress down the aisle. How could he stand here and smile when all he wanted was to knock Carl's brother away from Sophia and take his place?

He couldn't blame the best man for the stupid grin he wore as Sophia whispered to him. She was tall, regal, and composed as her long legs glided toward the altar; but the dimple in her cheek told Jackson her whispers were anything but solemn. She advanced down the aisle with supreme self-assurance. Her eyes sparkled as her gaze sought out Kate's boys, winking at them as she passed. She glided past him without a glance, arranging herself like a still, beautiful sculpture to his left.

Jackson swallowed hard. He tried to focus on Kate and Carl as they joined hands and walked down the aisle. Kate's simple wedding choreography appealed to Jackson more than the usual pageantry of a bride sailing down the aisle like a Thanksgiving float. Kate and Carl were just two people joining hands to stand before their loved ones and pledge their commitment to a shared life.

He walked them through the invocation, the exchange of vows and the rings, and the declaration of intent to be married. He picked up speed as he went, warned by the hissed scoldings of parents to children in the pews that patience was running thin.

As he watched the wedding party make their way off the altar and back up the aisle, he wished he'd fought harder against Kate's command to attend the rehearsal dinner. He'd at least laid the groundwork for leaving early by blaming evening visiting hours at the hospital. No parishioners were currently *in* the hospital—but Kate Couvert didn't need to know.

He wanted no more time than was absolutely necessary to witness Sophia Anton living her happy life without him.

****

Carl's large family filled the entire back room of the barbecue restaurant his parents had rented as their wedding gift to Carl and Kate.

Jackson had seated himself far away from the

couple, hoping to avoid awkward contact with Sophia, who sat at the bride's right.

This event was a little different from most wedding rehearsal dinners he'd attended. For one thing, the groom's family outnumbered the bride's by about twenty-five to one. The traditional toast from the parents of the bride and groom was discharged as an irritated command—"Well, go on and tuck in!"—by the groom's father when his wife prodded him to speak.

The conversation of Carl's young sons, nieces, and nephews was an improvement on the small talk Jackson engaged in during typical formal occasions. Even when the kids' exchanges were resolved with burps.

Wiping barbecue sauce from his fingers with a wet nap, he hazarded a glance at Sophia. She was talking to one of Kate's future brothers-in-law on her left. Why hadn't Sophia brought her husband? He knew Kate had disapproved of Christopher, but surely, after two years, Kate had learned to live with Sophia's choice.

He raised a glass of iced tea to his lips, still gazing at Sophia's profile as she listened with intent concentration to the man next to her. He hated to admit it, but marriage must be suiting her. The glow from her smile hadn't faltered all evening. Turns out she'd made the right choice when she'd decided on a future with Christopher in Paris.

"Excuse me, Pastor."

Carl's deep drawl startled him back to reality.

"I wondered if I might have a word with you privately."

Jackson pushed back from the table and dropped his napkin onto his plate. With a brief wave to Kate, pointing at his wristwatch with an apologetic smile, he followed Carl outside.

"It's hotter than the hinges of hell out here." Carl wiped his hand across his forehead. "Sorry to move you from the air conditioning, but I had to be sure we were out of Kate's earshot."

Jackson assumed his customary minister expression, his mouth relaxed and his eyes widened a tiny bit more than usual. He'd never heard Carl speak more than a few sentences. That the man trusted Jackson enough to tell him anything he considered private was a surprise.

From the back pocket of his trousers, Carl produced a folded piece of notebook paper and extended it to Jackson. "Kate chose the vows we practiced during rehearsal. She picked short ones so I wouldn't mess up." His mouth betrayed the ghost of a smile. "But I've done written my own vows. I'd be obliged if you could look them over and let me know if they're all right."

Jackson scanned the text, then raised his head and looked at Carl before handing back the paper.

Carl's shoulders dropped. "Won't work, huh?"

Jackson rubbed his jaw. "Are you kidding? You'll have your wife in tears. The whole church, probably." He'd underestimated this man. "Brides beg their fiancés to write their own vows. The guys go straight to the Internet and copy something. You just might be the first groom I've met who's willingly written his own vows."

Kicking the sidewalk with his toe, Carl shrugged. "I just want Kate to know how much it means that she's giving me a second chance." He cleared his throat. "My brothers say I'm whipped. They tell me I oughta put Kate in her place. They're gonna get a good laugh out of these vows." He folded the paper in neat squares and placed it back in his pocket.

Jackson put his hand on Carl's shoulder for a moment. "I've got brothers, too. They wouldn't have a good word to say to me if I cured cancer. Your brothers might give you a hard time, but they're all proud of you for coming back to Kate and stepping up to take care of your family." He dropped his hand to his side, scanning the parking lot for his car. He should go. "Men treat women like they're mind readers. But when you're in love with a woman, you need to let her hear it."

"Hey, Sophia."

A blast of air conditioning hit Jackson at the same moment he heard Carl speak. He whipped his head around.

Sophia stood poised in the doorway. "Am I interrupting something?"

"Nah," Carl said. "Just had to run something by the pastor. I told Kate I'd just be a minute. Better get back in there before she sets the dogs on me." With a nod to Jackson, Carl strode back inside as Sophia stepped out of the way of the closing door.

After a moment of silence, she spoke. "I just came outside to get my cell phone. I must have left it in the car."

Jackson nodded. "I was just leaving." They aimed polite smiles at each other, avoiding eye contact. "I'll walk you to your car," he offered.

"You don't need to," she responded, backing up a step.

He moved to her side and hovered his hand behind the small of her back to guide her into the parking lot. She didn't resist, to his relief; but the silence between them was charged with tension. He searched for a conversation opener. "Kate's glad to have you closer to home again."

"I can't wait to get her up to the city and show her a good time." Sophia's voice was bright and superficial. So different than he remembered.

"I thought I'd get to meet your husband tonight." The words rushed out before he could stop them. What kind of idiot was he? The last thing he wanted to hear was an update on her husband.

Sophia shook her head. "He's too deep in rehearsals right now. He's dancing for the New York City Ballet—one of the best dance companies in the country," she added.

"Yeah, Kate told me." Jackson fell silent, lifting his gaze to the gray clouds blanketing East Benson in sweltering humidity.

"So, how about you?" She turned to him with a painted-on smile, stopping in front of a small white car. "Any special girls in your life?"

He frowned as he watched her search the inside of her purse for keys. Why would she ask *him* who he was dating? He shook his head slowly. "No."

Fishing her keys from the bottom of her handbag, she clicked the pod to unlock the car. "So many women, so little time, huh?"

Was she taunting him? He opened her door so she could duck inside. He stood outside the door, his brow furrowed. Why was she asking him about other women?

With a flush of shame, he suddenly understood. She pitied him. The last time he'd seen her, he'd confessed his feelings. He'd never felt so vulnerable than when he told her how the man inside of the minister had come alive for the first time when he met her. How he couldn't control his desire to take her in his arms that day on her couch. How she made him wish for a life so different from the one he was living. But after hearing everything he said, she'd gone right back into the arms of her boyfriend.

True, he'd told her he was incapable of sharing his ministry with a wife. But the few short days before he realized how wrong he was proved to be too long— she'd already chosen Christopher.

Now she was back. And Jackson hadn't hidden his feelings from her any better than he could hide them from himself. What other reason could she have for asking if he was dating than she wanted to ease her guilt over her happy marriage to someone else?

Sophia stepped out of the car again, slipping her cell phone into her purse.

Jackson took her hand to steady her, feeling the old electric charge of his pointless attraction pulsing through him again. "Actually, I've got my eye on a couple of women." He brushed invisible lint off his shirt to avoid looking at her.

"Really?" Sophia drawled. "A couple." She folded her arms across her chest and stared at him, her gray eyes as hard as metal.

"Yeah." What if she asked who they were? Franny's dating website flashed through his mind. "They don't live here in town. Makes it easier." He crossed his arms and leaned back against the car next to hers.

"I'll bet." Sophia's smile didn't warm up her eyes.

She wasn't buying his story. He rubbed his finger

under his lip. In for a penny, in for a pound. "It's just for kicks." He shrugged again and grinned, feeling the inside of his gums sliding back from his teeth.

"Wow." A long moment passed before she spoke again. "So much for morals, huh? So much for being a spiritual adviser, resisting the temptations of the flesh. You're just"—her eyes narrowed and her mouth twisted—"living in the moment."

"Why not, Sophia?" he snapped, and then forced a smile. "As long as I put my job first, my private life is my own business."

Sophia stared, wide-eyed and drop-jawed.

Had he gone too far? Would she believe this about-face after everything he'd confessed in the chapel that night? Still…he'd rather she wrote him off as a total dog than pity him for loving her.

He gave her forearm an insincere squeeze, pretending not to notice when she flinched away. "Nice catching up with you, Sophia. See you tomorrow." He walked in the twilight to his car, his fists pushed deep into his pockets.

****

Parking in the guest spot in front of Franny's condo, Sophia flicked off the lights and jerked the keys from the ignition. She sat in the dark, staring straight ahead and struggling to control her emotions.

She'd been too uncomfortable during the wedding rehearsal to even look at Jackson. Instead, she'd mugged for the boys, flirted with Carl's younger brother as they'd walked down the aisle, and giggled like a moron on the altar. Anything to avoid the embarrassment of looking like just another love-struck reject from Jackson's past.

211

When she'd stumbled into Carl and Jackson outside the restaurant, she'd tried to flee, but Carl got away first. She wouldn't have said a word to Jackson about his online dating if he hadn't made the jab about expecting her husband to be with her. Did he have to rub her nose in the poor choice she'd made of a husband?

Then, to admit he was hooking up with women in casual relationships…! The tragic story about his lost wife and baby, his tortured attraction to Sophia, and his avowal to swear off love forever had been all an elaborate ploy to let her down easy. How had she not sensed, two years before, his insincerity?

She'd allowed herself to believe he cared for her too much to enter into a relationship. The truth was much simpler. The kiss they'd shared meant nothing. He lied to spare her feelings. For two years, she'd tried to put to rest the memory of Jackson's passion, refusing to relive the exquisite pain of what might have been.

She'd been played for a fool. By both Jackson *and* Christopher.

****

"Home already?" Franny's glasses slid down her nose when she looked up from her easy chair. She closed her laptop computer.

Sophia sank onto the rocker, grateful to close her eyes. "Thank God for air conditioning." She lined up her wrists and elbows on the armrests of the chair, trying to air out.

"How was the rehearsal?" Franny set the computer on the ottoman beside her feet, ready for a long chat.

A spasm of pain crossed over Sophia's face. She made a noncommittal noise, her eyes still closed.

Franny cleared her throat. She'd wondered if tonight would be difficult for Sophia. "I don't know about you, but I sure could use some wine." Hopping from the chair, she hurried to the kitchen and reappeared with a wine opener and two glasses. Selecting a bottle from the tabletop wine rack, brought it to her chair and opened it with the wine key. "Was Carl's family a hoot?" She poured wine into both glasses and then, on second thought, added a little extra into Sophia's. "What does Kate call them? Not the hillbillies..." She snapped her fingers as she tried to recall the name.

"The hickabillies." Sophia opened her eyes to accept the glass Franny offered. "They're colorful, all right, but they're very nice. You can tell how happy they are Carl's back in the boys' lives." Sophia took a deep sip of wine.

"Kate and Carl seem like they're really in love," Franny observed.

"Carl's devoted to Kate. She orders him around, and he doesn't say a word." Sophia's smile was wry.

"Sam always said it went better for him when he just did what I told him the first time." Franny chuckled.

Sophia took another drink of wine, swishing the liquid back and forth in front of her eyes. "Must be nice." She drank again, her focus turned inward.

Poor Sophia needed to unload whatever was bothering her, but she was so skittish whenever Franny tried to talk to her about her marriage. "You must be missing your husband," she finally ventured.

A snort of air flared Sophia's nostrils. "I wouldn't have to miss him if he'd just come along to this

213

wedding like I asked him." She lifted her wine glass, staring at it with moody eyes. "But Christopher's work takes priority over *everything*."

Franny rose to refill Sophia's glass, placing a comforting hand on the younger woman's shoulder. "I'm sure you'll work it out if you love each other." She sank down in her chair. "Every marriage has its ups and downs. What matters is being there for each other when you need each other most."

"Where is he now, when I need him? If I had a normal marriage, I'd have him here with me. But my marriage has *never* been normal."

The bitterness in Sophia's voice made Franny flinch. This was not the sweet Sophia who'd left for Paris two years ago. She stayed silent as Sophia drank from her glass again.

"I made a mistake, Franny," Sophia blurted. "I never should have married Christopher. I thought he'd learn to love me over time. But he hasn't. I'm more like a mother to him, taking care of things at home so he can live his exciting life and not worry about who's cooking dinner and cleaning the house. But the worst thing is, I'm starting to wonder if I ever really loved him, either."

Franny sighed. She'd been afraid of this. "Has he been unfaithful, Sophia?"

Sophia shook her head, her gaze darkening. "Maybe. I've heard rumors. He's gone all the time. I wouldn't know who he's with."

Franny took a deep breath and plunged in. "Have you noticed a change in the bedroom?"

Sophia rolled her eyes. "No. Because it's *always* been bad." She took a long swallow of wine, her cheeks flushing, and gazed at Franny. "My weight loss two years ago made Christopher attracted to me for the first time. I thought we had a chance to be happy. I knew we weren't ready to get married, but I could only go to France with him as his wife. I was afraid if I waited for him to come back, I might lose my only chance to have a husband and start a family. He was the one who suggested getting married. It wasn't much of a proposal, but I thought it was the best I would get." She grimaced. "But every time we were…intimate"—she said, flushing even more pink—"Christopher didn't…Christopher couldn't…"

"Seal the deal?" Franny asked drily.

Sophia laughed, a short, harsh exhalation. "Nope." She picked up her wine glass to take another drink.

"Maybe slow down on the wine a little," Franny suggested.

Sophia set down the wine glass and shrugged. "Gaining the weight back didn't help. We haven't even slept in the same room for months. I can't say I blame him, with the way I look."

"Nonsense, Sophia. You're one of the most beautiful women I've ever known at *any* weight. What's more important, you're beautiful on the inside. Christopher is a fool if he can't see it. Don't waste your life away wishing for things to change."

"I wanted children." Sophia gazed out the window at the dark night. "I thought any sacrifice was worth having a baby."

Sophia's face was so vulnerable. Franny needed to be gentle. "Is Christopher willing to make room in his life for children?"

Sophia sighed. "He used to talk about how

beautiful our kids would be."

Franny frowned. "Sounds like just another expression of his self-centeredness."

Sophia's shoulders sagged. The corners of her mouth trembled.

Franny cursed her own frankness. "I'm sorry, Sophia. I make a point never to bash a woman's husband. But, honey"—she leaned forward—"a marriage is about more than keeping house for your husband. An unconsummated union is not a marriage in the eyes of the law. If you wanted to leave, you'd qualify for an annulment, I think."

Clutching the pillow tighter, Sophia squirmed in the rocker. "I don't know, Franny. I never thought of myself as someone who would ever give up on my marriage." She looked down at her hands. "I haven't shared this with anyone else. I've barely even admitted it to myself."

Franny put out a placating hand. "You don't have to decide anything tonight. Time has a way of working things out. I'm sorry for getting you upset. Sam would wring my neck." She twisted her wiry hands around an invisible chicken.

"Oh, no," Sophia corrected her. "You don't know how good I feel getting this off my chest." She smiled at the older woman. "But let's talk about something else now. Did you have a good night?"

"I talked to Danielle for a little while. I was just playing around on the Internet when you came in. You're home a little earlier than I expected." Seeing Sophia avert her eyes again, Franny decided to probe. "Did you talk to Jackson much tonight? You two always seemed to get along so well."

Reaching for her wine glass, Sophia grimaced. "Not at all."

Franny lifted one skeptical eyebrow.

"I just mean, we didn't really know each other." Sophia paused. "I did ask him if he was seeing anyone."

She seemed to be weighing a decision. "Really?" Franny leaned forward with interest. "And?"

"There's someone who lives out of the area." Sophia's throat bobbed as she gulped a long swallow of wine.

"Really?" Franny's voice dipped up and down. Now *this* was intriguing.

"Well, there are a *couple* of women he's got his eye on," Sophia amended.

Franny sat back hard against her chair. "He told you this?"

Sophia nodded. "He's just looking to hook up." Lifting her wine glass, she drained it for the second time.

Franny was baffled. *Hooking up?* Jackson Thomas? Suddenly, she smothered a smile. Lifting her computer onto her lap, she hit a few buttons. She gave an ostentatious yawn as she set the laptop on her ottoman, lowering its screen halfway. "Time for me to hit the sack. Turn out all the lights when you go to bed, would you?" She walked close and kissed Sophia's cheek.

"I will. Good night, Franny." Still seated, Sophia gave the older woman an awkward hug.

"Good night, Sophia. Why don't you move over here to my chair? It's so much more comfortable than the old rocker." A smile played on Franny's lips as she left the room.

Sophia had had enough wine. But after she'd eased herself into Franny's comfortable chair, she poured the last of the wine into her glass anyway. Her mind was still restless even at this late hour. She didn't want to think about Jackson *or* Christopher.

How strange. She just now realized Kate had never brought up what she'd been told about Christopher. Sophia had been sure Kate would confront her with the report of Christopher's infidelity as soon as they'd left the warehouse. Yet during the forty-five minutes they'd shopped for shoes, Kate hadn't said a thing. How unlike Kate! Speculating on Kate's motives, Sophia tapped her foot against the side of the laptop. It slid across the leather ottoman. She lurched for it, pulling it to her lap. When she lifted the screen, she was still preoccupied with Kate's unexpected self-restraint.

One icon floating on the space-themed background caught her eye: a heart with an arrow pierced through. Lovematch.com. Franny hadn't been kidding when she'd said keeping an eye on Jackson's love life was one of her administrative duties.

Sophia clasped her hands together. Should she look? How private was an online dating site? After all, Franny had invited her to look at the minister's profile just the day before.

But why torture herself? She still couldn't believe he'd taken up online dating the minute she left town. Giving a guilty glance down the hall to make sure Franny's door was closed, Sophia clicked on the heart. A web page popped up bordered with tiny photos of loving couples posing for the camera. Text bubbles with testimonials by couples who'd found their "love matches" on the site floated around the sign-in box.

Sophia saw Jackson's user ID and black dots indicating a saved password. She hovered the cursor over the sign-in button, feeling like a child plotting to steal candy at a drugstore. She clicked. The screen dissolved into Jackson's home page. Sophia's eyes widened.

A photo of Jackson in a pair of ripped blue jeans, black scuffed boots, and a faded T-shirt as he leaned against a motorcycle filled a third of the page. His wavy brown hair was longer than she'd seen it, brushed back from his forehead and curling up on his neck. His arms, tanned and gleaming with golden hair, emphasized the muscles of his chest under a thin cotton T-shirt. He wore a lazy smile, and his eyes flirted at the camera.

Sophia's pulse pounded at the base of her throat. If she'd wanted evidence he'd been telling the truth earlier, she'd found it. His profile was written in dramatic italics: "Likes taking long walks in the moonlight with a special girl, cooking her dinner, running her bath, giving long backrubs when she's had a hard day. Looking for someone to climb on the back of my bike and ride off with me into the sunset."

Sophia slammed the lid of the laptop. She raised her hands to her burning cheeks. Up until the moment she saw the website, she'd hoped she was somehow wrong about Jackson. Grabbing her wine glass, she ran to the kitchen and poured the rest of its contents down the drain.

She needed a good night's rest to prepare for a long day tomorrow. After the wedding and reception, she would take the twins back to their house and stay for ten days while their parents honeymooned. Six-year-old boys would have zero sympathy for her fatigue tomorrow.

But her sleep was fitful, mocking her with the self-assured smile from the computer screen, even in her dreams.

Chapter Fourteen

Sophia walked down the aisle to the soft strumming of a mandolin, wondering at her friend's unexpected soft side. A few well-placed pots of overflowing lavender perfumed the sanctuary. Kate had placed a curved white trestle from her own garden at the end of the aisle. The ring bearer and flower girl stood on either side, smiling shyly in their wedding finery as Sophia approached arm-in-arm with Carl's brother.

Standing at the rear of the archway, just before the steps to the altar, were Josh and Randy, hair slicked back. Carl had taken the boys' sides when they'd fought against wearing suit coats and ties, allowing them to wear white short-sleeved shirts and khaki pants. They each held an unlit tapered candle.

Sophia shot a cool glance at the minister as she moved up the left steps of the altar. She'd handled herself badly yesterday. Nothing would shake her commitment to make this the happiest day of Kate's life.

Kate and Carl met in the center of the aisle at the back of the church.

Sophia caught her breath as Kate began her slow glide down the aisle. In a vintage heather green trumpet dress with a short-sleeved lace overlay, Kate was a vision of femininity. She'd scorned the idea of a veil or a train, carrying a small bouquet of miniature white roses in one hand. Her other hand was tucked into the crook of Carl's elbow.

Sophia's heart twisted when Carl closed a protective hand over Kate's. Carl's shoulders were thrown back, and his smile was broad. Watching them walk together down the center of the church toward their sons, Sophia marveled at how relaxed they both looked. Like they'd been waiting a lifetime for this day. As they passed through the garden trestle, they each tousled the hair of the child who stood near them. After reaching their sons, bride and groom picked up tapers from the small round table in front of the altar.

Jackson tilted his candle 'til theirs were alight. Each parent lit a candle for their son. Then all four leaned toward the pillar candle on the table and lit it in unison: four individual flames combined into one. With a kiss for each boy after they blew out their candles, Kate and Carl mounted the steps to the altar while the twins sat with their grandparents in the front pew.

Throat tight, Sophia smiled as Kate took her position. As a child, Kate had been so tough and aggressive, afraid to show vulnerability in a world she faced alone. Sophia would always be grateful she was the one person who Kate let in all those years ago.

She was ashamed now to remember how angry she'd been at Kate for "butting in" on her relationship with Christopher. True, Kate had a way of stepping over the line when she worried about a friend. But she'd been right about Christopher all along. Christopher had never really loved Sophia. He only wanted her to take care of his needs.

Sophia felt a tug on her wrist.

Kate had turned to her with widened eyes, trying to thrust her wedding bouquet into Sophia's hands.

Sophia grabbed the stems. Preoccupied with her thoughts, she'd missed the invocation. Kate and Carl were already stepping forward to exchange vows.

As they joined hands, Kate looked at the minister standing between them. Carl dropped Kate's hands and reached into his breast pocket.

Kate, Sophia could tell, was alarmed. This was not part of the ceremony.

Carl raised the paper to read, and his hand was shaking. "Kate Couvert, I fell in love with you the first time I met you."

Kate gasped.

Carl cast her a pleading glance. "Just let me read it, Katie. I'm nervous enough as it is."

A light laugh ran through the pews.

Carl cleared his throat to begin again. "Like I said. You were tougher than a one-eared alley cat, and I had to ask you out about a hundred and ten times before you said yes. I knew you were the one woman I wanted to spend the rest of my life with. But I messed up, Kate." At this point, Carl dropped the paper and held both of Kate's hands fast in his.

"I blew it. I walked away from the only person who was ever strong enough to say no to all my crap— pardon the expression, Pastor. Instead of protecting you and taking care of you when you got pregnant with our sons, I ran off and left you to take care of my responsibilities." Carl's voice broke on the last word. He swallowed hard before continuing.

Kate's eyes were wide.

For once, Sophia realized, her friend had no idea

how to respond.

"And for all those years, you raised our boys by yourself. No one could've done any better by those boys than you did." He paused again. "I came crawling back to you after almost five years, but you didn't have to let me back in their lives. God knows I hadn't earned the right to be their father." Carl swallowed hard before he spoke again. "But you took a chance on me. Again. You let me start over, even though I know most people were telling you to kick me to the curb. Your belief in me saved my life." Carl gripped Kate's hands tightly.

Sophia watched, fascinated, as Kate's composure crumpled. In all these years, she had never seen Kate cry. Sophia's throat thickened, and tears welled in her eyes.

Carl pulled one hand away from Kate's to retrieve his paper from the floor. He lowered his gaze to read it, and then looked back at Kate before he continued.

"I, Carl, promise you, Kate, to be your husband from this day forward. To never quit on you. To be faithful and honest in every way. I promise to respect you as the mother of our boys and the wife who's way out of my league."

Murmured laughter came from the pews, a balm for the eruptions of sniffles Carl's words had triggered.

"I promise to support the work you do, and to stand behind you when you try new things. If you ever fall down, then I'll be there to catch you. I'll take care of you when you're sick, and I'll take the night shift with the boys when they get sick." Carl let the paper drift to the floor once again as he took Kate's hands.

His were no longer shaking, Sophia noticed; but Kate's were.

"However much time the good Lord gives us in this life, every second of every day I have left, I'll try to prove you and our family are more important than anything in the world. From this day forward, and for the rest of our lives," he whispered, his gaze resting on Kate's tear-filled eyes.

Kate sniffed. "I could use a tissue!" she called, her glance wild.

Sophia, dabbing at her eyes with the one tissue she'd tucked in her sleeve, hastily thrust it into Kate's hand.

With a shaky laugh, Kate held up the tattered tissue.

Carl's mother hastened up the altar to hand Kate a handkerchief.

When he confirmed Carl's mother had taken her seat and Kate had blown her nose, Jackson continued the service. "Thank you, Carl. Kate?" He nodded to the bride.

Kate's eyes widened. "I got nothing!" she protested.

A murmur of laughter rose from the pews.

Jackson held up his hand. "My mistake," he said hastily. "Kate Couvert, do you take this man to be your lawfully wedded husband, to have and to hold, in sickness and in health, from this day forward and for the rest of your life?"

"I do." Kate wiped a tear from the corner of her eye before joining hands with Carl again.

They exchanged rings, Carl's voice steady and Kate's quavering as they repeated the words of the minister.

Sophia wiped at her tears with the back of her hand

and cheered with the rest of the guests when the couple kissed. She stole a glance at Jackson as he introduced the new couple. Wearing a black suit with a simple gold monogrammed stole, he held himself with easy elegance as Kate and Carl lifted their entwined hands into the air. His eyes, too, looked damp. Her heart stirred as she remembered again the intensity of those brown eyes gazing into hers, his hand rough against her cheek as he drew her mouth toward his own.

As if he could read her thoughts, Jackson turned his head and looked directly at Sophia. His eyes hardened, and his lips compressed into a thin line.

He nodded: her cue to leave. Sophia straightened her shoulders and joined Donny at the center of the altar. They followed Kate and Carl back up the aisle.

Only when she took her place in the receiving line beside Kate did she realize Jackson was gone.

****

"Sure am glad Kate agreed not to have a full-blown reception," Carl remarked to Sophia as they stood to the side of the fellowship hall kitchen. Both had drifted there to take a break from socializing. He tugged at his collar. "Can't wait to get out of the monkey suit."

Sophia glanced at her watch. "Only one more hour. By the way, those vows you wrote…" She put her hand to her heart. "*So* beautiful."

"Much obliged." He dipped his chin, sweeping his lank brown hair off his forehead.

Carl wasn't a handsome man, but he had beautiful brown eyes that reminded Sophia of a deer. "And here I was all prepared to give you the speech about what I'd do to you if you ever hurt my best friend again." Though her smile softened her words, she was serious.

"I know you realize what a special woman she is. Thank you for promising to bc thc person she can count on for the rest of her life."

He shook his head. "Not the only person," he reminded her. "She's always had you in her corner. It's me who should be thanking you for helping her take care of my sons. When I came back two years ago and asked Kate for a second chance with the boys, I know you were the *only* person who told Kate to let me try."

"Everyone makes mistakes. Yours was really big," she acknowledged. "But Kate knew Randy and Josh deserved a daddy, if you could get yourself clean. There's nothing Kate wouldn't do to give them the kind of family life she never had."

They were interrupted as one of Carl's nephews slammed open the kitchen door.

His mother grabbed her son by the collar before he could escape, jerking him back hard. "Act like you got some raising!" she hissed, swatting him once on the bottom as a warning before she released him.

Carl winced. "They're gonna get some family, all right. Maybe more than Kate bargained for."

Stepping through the opened kitchen door, Sophia could see her friend in the center of the fellowship hall handing out slices of wedding cake. Josh, Randy, and three cousins near the same age were crouched near her feet, pushing miniature cars back and forth to each other. "Are you kidding?" Sophia asked. "Kate's in her glory. Her boys have cousins now, and aunts and uncles and grandparents. Don't believe her griping one little bit. She's going to *love* being part of your family."

Before Carl could answer, a familiar voice rang out from the entrance to the hall. "Sophia Anton! Yoo-hoo!"

Sophia's gaze traced the hand waving above the crowd to the diminutive woman beneath it. "Hazel?" She hurried over to the old woman. Despite the heat, Hazel was dressed in a blue velour sweat suit and wore a visor over her eyes. Her face wrinkled in delight as Sophia bent down for a hug.

"Look at you, running around without a walker!" Sophia exclaimed. "I'm so glad to see you! I was a little worried when you stopped writing after Christmas. I hope you've gotten my cards?"

Hazel pointed to her chest. "It was my fault. I moved after Christmas, and I still haven't unpacked everything. Your address is in a box somewhere." She gave a vague wave.

"Where did you move to?" Sophia asked. "I thought you were happy at the nursing home."

"Well, I had a better offer." Hazel signaled to a woman who stood near the entrance.

Tall and broad, clad in black slacks and a plain brown jersey, the woman approached Sophia and Hazel with a smile.

Hazel took her hand. "This is my sister, Marie. I've moved to her house in Florida."

The cropped gray hair was different than Sophia remembered, but she recognized her smile. "It's been a long time, Marie." Sophia extended her hand.

"You're all grown up," Marie remarked, her voice an octave lower than her sister's. "You've got your dad's height but your mother's face. They made a good-looking kid."

"She's a *beautiful* girl," Hazel insisted.

With a resigned grin, Sophia shook her head.

Marie's smile widened. "She is," she acknowledged. "Hazel's told me all about you."

But then Hazel caught sight of Kate. Before her sister could continue, Hazel darted across the room.

Sophia laughed as she watched Hazel push her way among the guests. "She sure is getting around a lot better than when I last saw her."

Marie nodded, crossing her arms over her chest and leaning against the wall as she watched her sister. "I hear you're the one I have to thank for it. Pastor Thomas told me you were the one who got her off the streets."

Sophia colored. Between being forced to listen to Hazel discuss her affair with Sophia's father, followed by the humiliation of kissing her minister on the couch, she preferred not to remember that day. With an effort, she changed the subject. "How wonderful for Hazel to live with you again." Sophia paused. "If you don't mind my asking, how had you two lost touch for so long?"

Marie grimaced. "Love, I guess you could say." She paused. "Hazel didn't approve of the person I fell in love with. When she found out, she said she'd never speak to me again." She hesitated.

A sudden suspicion flooded Sophia's mind. "Don't tell me you were involved with my father, too," Sophia blurted out.

Marie's eyebrows lifted like a drawbridge. She gasped with laughter, bending her heavy torso to lean her hands on her knees for support.

Sophia stood still, wearing an uncertain smile as Marie regained her composure.

Pulling a tissue from the back pocket of her slacks, she wiped the tears from her eyes and looked at Sophia, a smile on her broad face. "Do I look like the type of woman your father would be involved with?" She wheezed with laughter a little longer.

Sophia gave a weak smile in return. Was Marie implying Sophia's father had a type?

"You're barking up the wrong tree, sweetie," Marie assured her. "I fell in love with a woman, a fact Hazel could not accept. When I moved out of state, I couldn't get Hazel to talk to me on the phone or answer my letters. I thought she'd come around eventually, so I let some time go by. The next time I reached out, I couldn't locate her. No one knew where she was. I checked all the hospitals and nursing homes. The obituaries, too." Marie's eyes dimmed for a moment. "When I couldn't find her in any of those places, I had to believe she was still alive and might try to reach me someday."

"And she did?" Sophia asked.

"Not her." Marie tsked, tempering her criticism with a fond smile. "Too stubborn. Pastor Thomas found me. He visited Hazel at the nursing home, and at some point, she told him about me and Nancy, my partner." She grinned ruefully. "She wanted to confess *my* sins, I suppose."

Sophia shook her head. Hazel had turned her back on Marie for all those years, preferring to be homeless, rather than reach out to her sister. What a shame.

Marie was still smiling, unruffled. "The minister reminded Hazel about the Golden Rule and doing unto others. I'd said the same thing for years. I guess she just needed the reminder from someone with more moral authority than her sister." She chuckled. "So I have the minister to thank for getting back my sister."

At the mention of Jackson, Sophia's stomach dropped again. She glanced around the hall. She would have thought he'd put in an appearance at the short reception. "He's devoted to his work," she agreed grudgingly. When she'd first met him, she'd admired his zeal for reaching out to the community's most isolated and needy. He'd demonstrated such care and tenderness toward Hazel, toward Franny and Sam. *Toward me.*

Was it *all* an act?

"But he couldn't have helped Hazel without you." Marie's homely face wore a grateful smile. "Pastor Thomas told me he couldn't get close to her until you broke down her walls. You were the only person Hazel trusted."

Sophia waved off Marie's gratitude. "I loved getting to know Hazel. I always enjoyed visiting her at the nursing home."

Her smile ironic, Marie raised her eyebrows. "Not so easy getting her *into* the nursing home, though, or so I heard."

Sophia shrugged, her smile guilty. "Okay, I admit I found Hazel a little hard to handle in the beginning." She paused, not sure if she should continue. But she was enjoying her conversation with Hazel's sister. Her shoulders tensed as she decided to take the plunge. "She told me about her affair with my father."

Marie honked with laughter, causing heads to turn at several tables. She wiped tears from her eyes for a second time, then shook her head as she locked her gaze on Sophia. "Honey, your father never had an affair with my sister."

For two years, the question of her father's

faithfulness had niggled at the back of her mind.

"Hazel's never had a relationship with anybody, sad to say," Marie sighed. "We all could see she had a little crush on your dad. Your mom knew it, too."

Sophia cocked her eyebrow.

"Oh yeah, Estelle knew. When we all worked in the kitchen together, your mom would put your dad to work with my sister because Hazel got such a kick out of it. Estelle Anton was never threatened by Hazel, believe me. She could afford to be nice to Hazel and the other church hens. She knew no one would ever come between her and your dad."

As she listened to Marie, Sophia felt a weight she hadn't realized she'd carried lift from her shoulders. She leaned forward and gave the older woman a tight hug. "I am *so* glad you came back to East Benson."

Marie's answering hug was bashful. "We're only here this week. We wanted to stop by the church and say hello to Pastor Thomas before we left. When Hazel heard you were at Kate's wedding reception in the fellowship hall, she made a beeline right over here. I had to run to catch her."

So, he was still at the church. Why hadn't he dropped by? She gave herself a tiny shake, chiding herself for wondering. She should be relieved, not disappointed, at his absence.

Kate and Hazel gestured to Marie and Sophia from across the hall. She hurried over to the wedding cake, grateful to leave behind unwelcome thoughts of Jackson threatening to rise to the surface. She needed to stay in control.

Because after the events of the day were done, she needed to think of only one person. And that was her husband.

****

"Aunt Sophie! Look at me!"

From high atop the tower of couch cushions, clinging like an oversized frog to a lily pad, Randy held on with whitened knuckles, fighting to maintain his balance as the cushions slid slowly out from under him.

Sophia slapped her hand over her eyes to avoid witnessing him tumble to the floor. "Of all the perilous, life-risking ways you boys entertain yourselves, this game has got to be my least favorite." She raised two fingers to peek and make sure no skulls were fractured. She'd already moved the coffee table, end tables, and the de-cushioned couch far out of the way of the play area, and she'd haggled with the boys over the maximum height of the tower—"four cushions, max."

"What about sliding down the steps in a laundry basket? I thought *that* was the game you hated most." Josh's clear blue eyes were wide and curious.

"I hate them all," Sophia growled, grabbing him and hugging him.

Hearing Josh's giggles, Randy propelled himself into her lap like a cannon ball.

"Oof!" Sophia gasped. "How has your poor mother survived you boys?" She winced, rubbing her hip. With a glance at the clock, she gave a decisive clap of her hands. "Cushions back on the couch. Time to brush your teeth and go to bed."

"No!" they wailed in unison. Randy flung himself face-first on a cushion and lay still, squeezing his eyes shut. Josh followed suit, falling backwards onto a cushion and lying still.

"Come on, guys." Sophia adopted her most

authoritative tone. "Don't make me tell your parents you wouldn't mind me."

Josh's eyes shot open. He sat up. "Why did everyone cry today when Mommy and Daddy got married?"

Sophia tossed a cushion on the couch and hoped the boys would follow suit. "Sometimes grown-ups cry when they're happy."

"That's stupid." Randy's voice was muffled by the cushion.

Sophia pulled up Josh by his hands, kicking the cushion out from under him before he could fall down again.

"Mommy was *really* crying. She must have been the happiest of all," Randy observed, springing up and launching his cushion toward the couch.

Sophia smiled. "I think she was. After all, your Dad said some pretty nice things."

"About getting up with us if we get sick in the middle of the night. That was probably her favorite part. She hates it when we wake her up at night." Josh placed a lopsided cushion on the end of the couch.

Sliding the end tables to their usual spots, Sophia chuckled. "I think she also liked the part about being the most important person in the world to your dad, forever and ever." She turned and looked at the boys, who had collapsed on the couch to wait while she straightened the room. She lifted a mocking hand. "Oh no, boys, don't even *think* of lifting a finger to help me."

Randy pinched his lips tight. "How come we've never met your husband, Aunt Sophie?"

Sophia slid the coffee table onto the center of the

oval rug, grateful to have a reason to avoid his eyes. "Well, he doesn't get much time off from his job."

"Did you cry when you got married, Aunt Sophie?" asked Randy. He twisted the hem of his pajama shirt around his thumb while he gazed up at Sophia.

He didn't look the least bit tired. She stood and swiped her hand across her brow, pushing her hair back from her face. She sighed. "I don't think I did."

"Why not? Didn't your husband call you the most important person in the world, forever and ever and ever?"

Sophia froze, struck by Randy's unintentional insight. Anxiety raced through her bloodstream. She couldn't delay her conversation with Christopher any longer. "Who wants a piggyback ride to bed?" she called, jogging over to the stairs.

Cheering, the boys clambered onto her back, Randy plastered against her with Josh squashing him from behind.

After passing another half-hour supervising reluctant teeth brushing, reading two picture books, and telling one made-up story, Sophia closed the boys' door and walked the darkened hall to Kate's bedroom. She flicked on the overhead light. Kate's queen-sized bed was folded back with fresh sheets. Sophia sank onto the mattress, gathering her courage.

On the bedside table sat Kate's and Carl's engagement picture. Their arms were around each other, with Carl's face in profile and Kate facing the camera. Sophia's breath hitched to see the tenderness in Carl's eyes while he looked down at Kate. Her serene smile conveyed a contentment Sophia had never known in her friend.

Sophia reached for her phone on the foot of the bed. Tapping her Contacts page, she exhaled, staring at Christopher's picture. Long blond hair draped his face, and his sculpted shoulders were bare. She'd taken the photo in the early days of their marriage, when she'd still thought the beauty of his face mirrored what was inside.

Tears fell from her cheeks to the bed, darkening the pale yellow daisies embroidered in the comforter. She drew her fingertip back and forth over the dampened flowers, rubbing teardrops into the fabric. "Goodbye, Christopher," she whispered and pressed the button to call him.

Chapter Fifteen

Exiting her marriage proved to be almost as simple as her hurried entry into matrimony had been two years before. As they shared no assets and no children, completing the paperwork for a summary divorce was easy. Maybe she should have felt insulted by Christopher's readiness to dissolve their marriage. But for once, she was grateful to be a low priority in his life.

She chose a day to collect her belongings when he would be tied up with rehearsals until late in the night. Her furniture and appliances were still inside her old townhouse, awaiting the day when she and Christopher would buy a family home in Brooklyn. Christopher hadn't made much room for her belongings in his New York City apartment, but his lack of consideration worked in her favor now.

He'd promised to stay out of the apartment for just one day, so she worked fast. Pausing only to gulp a hot dog from a street vendor, she made short work of hauling boxes of clothing and cooking supplies into the back of her rented moving van.

Early in the evening, she pulled away from the curb in front of Christopher's apartment.

Her memory drifted to another night, two years ago. She'd climbed in the car to drive home the day after the premiere: the fateful night they first kissed. She'd just pulled out of her parking space when she saw

Christopher run across the street. He stood on the boulevard median of Seventh Avenue, waving goodbye until she was out of sight.

Like opening a present wrapped in gorgeous papers and finding nothing inside, Sophia thought now as she crossed the bridge. With Christopher, the beauty was all just packaging.

She glanced in the rear view mirror at the quiet street, resting her gaze one last moment on the battered front steps of his apartment building. Turning the corner, Sophia settled in for the journey home.

****

Franny opened her door with a wide smile. She pointed to a basket at her feet. "We're going for a ride in the country. I've packed a picnic." Her tone brooked no argument.

Sophia had moved back into her old home three months ago, but restarting her life in East Benson hadn't left much time for friends. Franny phoned earlier in the week demanding a "girls' night." With a wistful look at her paint swatches—a fresh start called for a new look in her home, and Sophia was gradually repainting every room—she'd agreed to come to Franny's for dinner on Friday.

"Leave it to you to turn a quiet meal at home into an outdoor adventure," Sophia grumbled as she slid Franny's wicker basket into the backseat, but her smile belied her words. Winter was around the corner, and Sophia was happy to be forced outside to enjoy the fall weather. She marveled at the colors of autumn in East Benton, as if seeing them for the first time. After two years of city living, her soul thirsted for the colors of nature's palette. For the past week at work, she'd admired the beauty of Virginia Creeper and poison ivy twining like red filament up the oak tree outside her window. The buckeye trees in her neighborhood had faded from green to gold. The maples were just beginning to turn, flaming red in too many hues to count.

Sophia opened the passenger door for Franny. Clad in a colorful Fair Isle sweater, her blue jeans tucked into ankle-high hiking boots, the older woman looked as jaunty and vibrant as a woman half her age.

Whenever Sophia needed a reminder to put the past behind her, she only needed to look at Franny. Sophia took her place behind the wheel and fastened her seatbelt. "Which way, *kemosabe*?"

Franny pointed toward the overpass. "Let's go south. We'll find the perfect spot in the country."

Sophia headed out of the condominium complex to the On ramp, cracking the back windows to circulate some fresh air. She wore her favorite sweater, a long-sleeved cabled pullover in goldenrod yellow. Its slouchy neckline made the most of her fading summer tan, but the cool breeze coaxed goosebumps from her exposed skin.

"So, how do you like the new job?" Franny asked.

Sophia smiled. "I *love* it."

After she'd moved from the New York apartment, she secluded herself in her townhouse to watch a string of sad movies and eat too much ice cream.

Franny allowed Sophia only one week of self-pity before dragging her back into the land of the living. Reminding Sophia to "share her God-given gifts with the rest of the world," Franny directed Sophia to Port in a Storm, a youth shelter for runaway teens.

Volunteering allowed Sophia to forget her own unhappiness and help troubled youth assimilate back into society.

Her cooking classes taught the teens how to prepare simple meals in bulk to freeze and eat later. No matter how wary or hostile, the teens enjoyed learning to cook. Once she earned their trust in the kitchen, she taught other life skills: balancing checkbooks, writing resumes, and preparing for job interviews.

To support underfunded Port in a Storm programs, she solicited local businesses and organizations for donations. The many contacts she'd made as events coordinator at O'Grady's helped get her foot in the door.

She loved her volunteer work, but she couldn't live without a paycheck much longer. She'd have to decrease her hours at the shelter and find a full-time job, she told Deirdre Haskew, the program director.

But Deirdre countered with an unexpected offer. "The extra funding you've brought in has allowed us to create a new position: Outreach Coordinator, who will supervise the volunteers and interns, manage the Street Outreach project, and raise our profile in the community. You're the perfect candidate."

Although the hours were longer and the pay was less than she'd earned at O'Grady's, Sophia accepted the job without hesitation. In her first two months, she worked twelve-hour shifts and went weeks at a stretch without a day off. And she was happier than she'd ever been. She squeezed Franny's hand. "This job has been my lifeline, and I owe it all to you."

Franny clicked her tongue. "I only told you about the place. You won the job on your own merits. If you want to thank anyone, you should thank Jackson for getting our congregation involved with the teen shelter."

Sophia pulled her hand back to the steering wheel to merge onto a two-lane rural route. How she wished the mention of Jackson's name would stop making her heart somersault. Her frenetic work schedule kept her too busy to dwell on the minister's deception, but whenever she spent time with Franny, the conversation always seemed to return to him.

Attending Sunday services at St. Jerome's would have been a comfort, if only *he* weren't there. The thought of listening to Jackson Thomas deliver some pious sermon, all the while knowing he trolled for women online after he'd rejected Sophia two years before—she shook her head, swallowing hard. *Men. I sure can pick 'em.* She shook her head. She'd better concentrate on navigating the curving country road.

At a swell in the road, bordered on the right by a thick grove of oak trees, Franny directed her to turn left. The crumbling blacktop was narrow, and rows of corn stretched out on either side as far as Sophia could see.

"Just how far out into the middle of nowhere do you want to go?" she asked, eyeing the gas can icon flashing on her dash.

"We're almost there. At the end of this road, before you start going down the hill, turn left into the little lane."

They passed a large white farmhouse, and the road began to descend. Sophia slowed the car and steered onto a graveled lane running along the top of a yard. She pulled up to a barn at the far end of the drive. Dilapidated and picturesque, it reminded Sophia of a photograph she'd once seen, probably on a postcard.

"Not here," Franny directed. "Go down the driveway."

Sophia swung the car to the right and coasted down the driveway diagonal to the lane. She stopped behind an old station wagon. "Is someone expecting us?"

Without answering, Franny jumped from the car to drag the picnic basket from the backseat. "A friend lives here. She's not home, but she told me we could come over. She's got a beautiful view of the countryside from her back porch—the perfect spot for a picnic. Just leave your keys in the ignition. We're not in the city anymore. Hurry!" she chided the younger woman.

Sophia stood beside the car, casting a doubtful look at the old log cabin. Shrugging, she tossed her keys on the front seat and hastened after Franny, following her onto the front porch and through the screen door.

Franny popped from behind an archway leading to a kitchen. "Come out back," she ordered, lugging the basket over the linoleum and disappearing through a door at the other side of the room.

What was the rush? Sophia would have liked to walk around the low-ceilinged living room instead of rushing by. From the looks of the walls, their weathered white plaster split by unfinished wooden planks, she speculated the house to be at least two hundred years old. But she didn't want to snoop, and Franny was already out the door. Sophia followed the older woman's path through the kitchen, emerging onto a balcony.

Franny was right; the view was spectacular. The back yard was a steep hill bordered by thick woods.

Pine trees reached down to a valley cut by railroad tracks. From there, the land swept upward into ploughed fields. Like dominos, more hills piled up behind the field. The sun, a hazy yellow-orange orb hovering over the horizon, cast a warm glow over the wooden balcony.

She leaned over the porch rail, soaking in the warmth of the autumn sun. To her left, a tractor miniaturized by distance labored across the steep fields, its engine a faint hum. Just beneath her, a pair of cardinals chirped on a bird feeder suspended from a laundry post. She closed her eyes, feeling the sun wash her face with its rays. What a blessing to be back in her hometown during the most beautiful season of the year, savoring the scent of leaves' slow withering as it traveled along the cooling afternoon air. She sighed, opening her eyes at last, and turned to Franny behind her.

Sophia gasped. Franny had placed a red-checked cloth on the picnic table. At the center sat a bottle of white wine and two crystal glasses. A delicate bud vase cradled a red rose. Franny had unpacked a basket of fried chicken, fruit salad in a cut-glass bowl, a homemade loaf of wheat bread, and a platter of sweet potato fries. "Franny!" Sophia breathed. "Who else have you invited? This is too fancy for just us!"

Franny smiled as she placed the plates, napkins, and cutlery. She stood back to inspect her work, giving an exaggerated snap of her fingers. "I've forgotten the coleslaw! I'll just run to the store now. Why don't you sit and have some wine" Franny whisked back into the house.

"Are you kidding?" Sophia called inside. "Stores

don't stay open late out in the boondocks. Anyway, everything is perfect!"

Her answer was the heavy bang of a screen door from the front porch. A moment later, she heard her car back out of the driveway and spin gravel as Franny reversed toward the barn. Sophia held her breath, sure she'd hear the back of her car slam into a building. But when the car's engine receded away, she shrugged. "Crazy old broad," she said aloud, opening the bottle with the wine key and pouring herself a glass. Being alone to watch this beautiful vista was fine by her.

Strolling back to the railing, she sipped from her glass. The quiet of the evening was marred only by the buzz of a motorcycle's engine on the road behind the house. Sophia smiled. She remembered her mother, after a day of dirt bikes jumping ramps in the field near their house, saying, "I'd like to take a giant fly swatter to all of them!" The engine hum ceased, and the early evening stillness settled around her shoulders like a silk sheet.

Her gaze followed the cardinals in their ritual of devotion. The male flew from the feeder to the line of trees, and his mate followed. They hopped from bush to bush, separate yet together, circling back to the feeder to eat side-by-side.

Sophia raised her glass to them in a silent toast. Humans could learn a thing or two from the fidelity of birds.

The door behind her creaked, and she jumped, splashing wine on the cuff of her sweater. She brushed at the fabric, surprised she hadn't heard Franny pulling into the driveway. "Did you come to your senses and realize you'd never find an open store?" she asked, wiping her fingers against her blue jeans as she turned to the house.

Her breath caught in her throat as she froze, staring at the door like a cornered animal.

Wearing engineer boots, faded jeans, and a black crewneck sweater, his hair flattened on top and curling around his face, Jackson looked like a biker, not a minister. He held the doorknob in a vise grip, the tendons of his hand pushing white against his knuckles. He gazed at Sophia, an upside-down V pressed between his eyebrows from the force of his stare.

Like a bad dream, the awkwardness of the moment stretched on as Sophia stared back with a mixture of guilt and defiance.

"What are you doing here, Sophia?" His deep voice ripped a hole in the serenity of the balcony. Startled, the cardinals below them flew from the feeder.

"What are *you* doing here?" Sophia countered, setting her glass on the railing. Her hand trembled, and more wine spilled over the side.

His frown deepened. "I live here." The door swung shut behind him as he crossed to the table and handed Sophia a napkin. "Used to, anyway. This is my mother's house."

"Oh," Sophia whispered. Wiping her hand, she silently begged it to stop shaking. "Franny brought me." She hated the revealing flush of blood climbing up her neck to her cheeks. How many times would this man see her embarrass herself? She crumpled the napkin in her fist, avoiding Jackson's gaze. "Franny said we'd been invited to come over, even though her friend wasn't home. She never mentioned who the friend was." Sophia paused, narrowing her eyes. What was

Franny up to? "She forgot the coleslaw, so she ran to the store."

He raised his eyebrows. "Do you know how far the closest store is?"

"I tried to tell her she was crazy." Sophia gestured toward the table. "But she really wanted everything to be perfect." How could Franny have forgotten to tell her this was Jackson's mother's house? Sophia's eyes widened. Hit at last with the dawning recognition of the older woman's intentions, Sophia clamped her jaw shut and crossed her arms. *Franny, I could kill you.*

Jackson surveyed the table, picking up the bud vase and staring at the rose. He set it down, trailing his finger over the bread basket. He looked up at Sophia, the hint of a smile at the corners of his mouth. "The food's getting cold. Why don't we sit and eat?"

Her arms huddled over her cable sweater, Sophia placed a nervous hand on her throat. "Look, I'm really sorry we came out on a night when you planned a visit with your Mom. I know Franny wouldn't have wanted to intrude." She choked out the last word. Intruding was exactly what Franny had planned. "Just let me clean up, and we'll get out of your way." Sophia picked up a plate and put the other on top, clattering them together in her haste.

Jackson's rough hand closed over hers. She froze, helpless against the rising swell of attraction she felt every time he touched her.

"I have to disagree with you." He was so close, his breath stirred the hair over her ear. "Franny wouldn't want the food going to waste. There's plenty here for three of us. Let's go ahead and eat. We'll leave her some." He released Sophia's hand and slid onto the bench opposite her. Picking up the bottle of wine, he poured more into her glass before filling his own.

Sophia wavered. She wanted nothing more than to flee, but Franny had her vehicle. She lowered herself onto the bench, her hands in her lap. *What else can I do? Hitchhike my way out of here?* She watched as Jackson served Franny's food, spooning portions onto Sophia's plate and then his own. He seemed far more comfortable with the strangeness of the situation than she felt. He asked about Kate and Carl.

"They're doing well." Sophia struggled to speak in a normal tone of voice, even though her heart was beating so fast, she was afraid he could see it pounding against her chest. "The boys are happy having both parents at home every day." She forced a sweet potato fry into her mouth.

Neatly pulling apart his chicken breast with a fork and knife, Jackson's gaze was fixed on her. "Franny tells me you're working at Port in the Storm now."

Sophia nodded, her shoulders stiff as she lifted her glass for a sip of wine. "I've never had a job I loved more."

He set down his cutlery, placing his hands flat on either side of the plate. His smile was open and disarming. "Franny told me this was the job of your dreams, but I'm glad to hear it from your own lips." His gaze drifted to her mouth, and then rose.

She covered her lips with her napkin. Inwardly, she seethed. *No wonder I misread his signals. The guy is a player.* But *she* refused to be a pawn any longer. With a stony smile, she speared a strawberry on her salad fork, chewing with a defiant tilt to her chin.

Leaning forward, Jackson cleared his throat. "I was

sorry to hear about your marriage, Sophia. Sorry it didn't work out."

With more force than necessary, Sophia tore a piece of bread in two. She spread a thin layer of butter on one bite before she looked at Jackson. "I'm happier now than I ever was with Christopher," she forced out. She couldn't even taste the bread as she fought to swallow.

Jackson nodded again.

She supposed her answer pleased him. After all, he'd disapproved of Christopher from the beginning. *He's probably congratulating himself for forecasting the failure of my marriage.* She took a sip of wine, her throat raw with resentment.

Jackson swallowed a mouthful of wine and set it down. Tearing a piece of bread, he smiled. "I don't think I've ever seen you eat this much, Sophia."

Sophia's mouth tightened. Her reply was icy. "Now that we've agreed my marriage was a failure, the only thing I'm less interested in discussing with you is my weight gain." Throwing her napkin onto the table, she bolted from the bench to escape through the door.

But Jackson was too quick. He grabbed her arms and forced her to turn toward him.

She struggled, but her wrists were locked in his hands. "Let me go!" She glared up at his face.

His brown eyes pleaded as he dropped her hands. "Don't run away. I can't lose you again."

She flinched at the intensity of his hoarse voice. Her own voice shook. "Is this what you say to all the girls?"

Jackson's head jerked back, and his jaw dropped.

If she didn't know better, she'd think she hurt his

feelings. But she'd made the mistake before of believing he had a heart. She pressed her lips together and glared.

Jackson closed his mouth. The furrows on his brow smoothed, and the strain around his eyes relaxed. "Sophia," he whispered. "There aren't any other girls."

His face was so persuasive. Not to believe him was almost impossible. But she'd be damned if she'd let any man fool her again. She threw back her shoulders, her spine straight as a steel rod. "You told me yourself, remember? Not that I was surprised. Franny had already told me you joined an online dating service." Would he admit the truth or keep lying?

His clouded gaze cleared. He tilted his chin, his lips curved into a mocking smile. "Did she?" His words were a slow exhalation. He folded his arms over his chest and leaned against the railing.

Sophia flinched. Far from being embarrassed, he looked confident. Cocky, even. "Yes, she did. I saw your profile picture. You were standing in this same pose, leaning against your bike in front of a barn." *No wonder the barn out front looks familiar.* "'Looking for a woman to take long walks on the beach at moonlight, someone who'll ride off into the sunset on your motorcycle.'" Her words dripped with sarcasm— enough, she hoped, to mask the tears bubbling just behind her voice.

Leaning back farther, he crossed one boot over the other. "Can I tell you something?"

She shrugged. She'd never let on how much he'd hurt her. *Never*.

The mocking expression was gone. His brown eyes were honest and serious. "You know a lot more about the website than I do, because I've never been on it. Not once."

Sophia's shoulders sagged. Why was he bothering to deny it? How gullible did he think she was? She swallowed, afraid to trust her voice. "I don't know why you're lying," she whispered. "Your love life is your own concern."

"Sophia." His voice was sharp. "I didn't join any website. Franny signed me up. Franny and my mother." He caught her hand as she tried to sidle to the door. "No, you listen to *me* now. My mom and Franny struck up a friendship when she started working in my office. My mom knew there'd been a woman in my life, but she didn't know who. Franny suspected something had happened between you and me, but no way in hell would I talk about it. You'd left town, so they decided to find me another girl. Franny signed me up for an online dating service, and every so often she'd come to me with print-outs of women who'd responded to my profile."

Sophia's mouth was agape. Was he delivering another elaborate cover-up, or could he be telling the truth?

"They had good intentions." He shrugged. "I was willing to humor them if it meant they'd stop sniffing out my feelings for you. So I'd take the profiles Franny printed, and as soon as I saw her leave the room, I dumped them into the recycling bin. I haven't dated anyone or even thought of anyone but you since before you were married."

Eyes wide, Sophia put her hand over her mouth. Like a fire flaring in a cold draft, her heart flooded with hope. Did she dare to believe him? She narrowed her eyes. No. His story didn't add up. "What about the 'out of town' girls? The ones you were seeing 'for kicks'?"

Jackson's face reddened. He swept his hand over his forehead, avoiding her gaze. "There *were* no 'out of town girls.' I lied to you at the rehearsal dinner, because I thought you were happily married, and I didn't want you to know how much I missed you." He swallowed, passing his hand over his eyes. "I'd already lost you. I couldn't handle your pity." He turned his gaze to Sophia.

Sophia searched his face, seeing the plea to be believed and wishing she could see into his soul. Never in her life had she wanted so badly to believe—but all trust in a man had ever brought her was heartache.

"Why do you play with me this way?" Her words spilled out like a bleeding wound. "I've been down this road before. You tell me how much you think about me, you even *kiss* me, and the next minute you pull away. How can a minister be so cruel? How can a *man*?" Trembling, she pushed past him to lean on the railing, her eyes awash with tears.

His fingers wrapped over her shoulders, turning her face to him again. "I'm not playing games, Sophia." He bent his head, his breath against her ear.

She shivered at the wave of heat his face released against her cold skin.

"I told you I could never be with another woman again, but I was wrong. You're the only woman who could be part of my life *and* part of my work. Once I realized my mistake, I wanted you more than I've ever wanted anything in my life." Easing back, he squeezed his eyes shut, his hands tightening on her shoulders before he opened his eyes again. "But I missed my chance. You were gone."

Sophia's pulse battered her throat. "But you were sure you couldn't balance work and love."

He shook his head. "I was fighting my feelings. I couldn't expect you to share my life—not with all the demands of my work." He slid his hands over Sophia's, clasping her cold fingers within his rough palms. "But I finally saw the truth. You minister to people every day of your life. You're the one woman who could understand my calling. Two years ago, I lost you because I didn't speak up. I can't lose you again. Sophia," he breathed.

His gaze, naked with hope, pierced her heart.

"I'm in love with you. I knew it from the second you opened the music box at Sam and Franny's house."

Sophia's heart skipped, remembering the four of them holding hands around the table. Jackson had been haloed by the rays of a waning sun. She felt an almost unbearable fullness in her chest. Almost since she'd met him, she'd yearned for more than he could give. She shook her head in wonder. Was this moment really happening? The last rays of the setting sun glowed bronze in the curls around his face.

"After we talked in the chapel, I finally allowed myself to hope you might have feelings for me, too." A shadow passed over his eyes. "But I waited too long. And you went back to him."

Sophia clung to Jackson's hands, hardly daring to trust the hope his words ignited in her heart. "I thought Christopher was my last chance at having a family. I never should have married him. We never truly loved each other. Not like—" Her fingers tightened around his. "I never dared believe you loved me. I felt like a schoolgirl with a crush." She lifted her gaze to his, gathering every ounce of her courage. "But when I was with Christopher, I thought of you. I pretended you were holding me. I made believe I was"—she blushed deeply—"loving you, instead of him."

He lifted Sophia's hands and kissed her palms. "Sophia, are you telling me you love me?"

She shivered as he grazed his lips over her skin. Her throat was so thick with emotion she could barely breathe. "I've loved you ever since we first kissed," she whispered. "I couldn't shut it down no matter how hard I tried. I've never felt love like this before."

"Sophia," he groaned with a little laugh, burying his face in the soft curls along her neck. "If we'd just told each other the truth two years ago!" He pulled back, and his eyes shone. "I could have been holding you in my arms all this time." His gaze dropped to her lips, and he lowered his mouth to hers.

Sophia's lips parted under the urgency of his kiss. She'd returned to the sweetest of dreams: the unforgettable scent of his skin, the roughness of his cheek brushing hers, and the warmth of his strong arms wrapping her inside his embrace. She pressed closer, sure for the first time that he wanted her as much as she wanted him.

His mouth roved over hers, straying to her earlobe as his hands gathered the curling tresses at her nape. Her heartbeat was wild. *Too wild.* She drew back from his kiss, opening her eyes and resting her palms over his chest.

His heart hammered against her fingertips. Stroking his fingers through her thick hair, he slid his palms to the small of her back, locking her within the security of his embrace.

As she felt his heart slow against hers, she reveled in the sanctuary of his arms. The image of her parents on their wedding day flashed through her mind. She'd always yearned for a man like her father, strong enough to lean on. But when Hazel implicated him for being unfaithful, she made Sophia doubt true love for the first time.

Jackson tipped her chin with his thumb, stroking the soft skin of her cheek. "What are you thinking?"

She smoothed her palms over his shoulders, gazing up at him. "I spent the past two years chasing the wrong man, the wrong dream. I pretended to be someone I wasn't, locking myself into a prison *I* designed. I'd almost given up on happiness." She traced a fingertip over his jawline, feeling smitten with each bristle. "I needed to come home to remember my real purpose in life."

Jackson's arms tightened around her waist, drawing her even closer. "We both had to take a leap of faith." He kissed her again, lingering over her lips until she pulled away with a smile.

She rested her head against his shoulder, feeling his cheek caressing the top of her head. Now she was home again. She would work at the side of a man who loved helping others as much as she did. The man who loved her as much as she loved him.

He took a step back, lifting Sophia's hands and entwining his fingers in hers. "I never want to be apart again, Sophia." His voice was low and tender. "I want to stay by your side forever, if you'll have me." He paused. "Will you, Sophia?

Her heart was too full for words. She nodded.

"Yes, Jackson," she whispered.

He pulled her back into the circle of his arms, lowering his face against her dark hair. Leaning back into the security of his embrace, she lifted her face to his kiss.

Epilogue

Sophia glanced at the time and slid her cell phone back into her purse. She was a few minutes late, but she wouldn't take any other calls today. She hurried across the parking lot to the fellowship hall, huddling her elbows against her sides. Warm weather was taking its time arriving this spring. For most of April, the gray skies camping over East Benson had brought daily rains. She lowered her face from the fine mist chilling the breeze, relieved to reach the lobby doors.

The odors of garlic and onions assaulted her senses when she walked inside. She stopped, closing her eyes to take a few deep breaths. An arm came around her shoulders, and she rested her head against it before opening her eyes.

Jackson's forehead was creased, his eyes clouded with concern. "Is anything wrong? Should I take you home?"

Sophia slid her arms around his waist and squeezed, shifting her abdomen slightly to the side to snuggle in closer. She shook her head and smiled. "No, darling. It'll pass in a second. I thought I was done with morning sickness after the first trimester, but I'm still nauseated by certain smells."

Jackson drew her away from the noise and bright lights of the fellowship hall into the entrance of a darkened hallway. Wrapping her in a loose hug, he stroked her hair while she closed her eyes and slowed her breathing. When the nausea passed, she lifted her chin and opened her eyes.

"Better?" He couldn't resist stroking his thumb against her soft chin.

"One hundred percent." She stretched up and placed a soft kiss on his lips.

"What did they say when you told them?" His voice hushed as a family wandered out of the fellowship hall toward the exit.

Sophia beamed. "They were thrilled for me." After she'd told her boss she was pregnant, Sophia was the guest of honor at Deirdre's celebratory luncheon including the small staff.

"Did you talk about your plans to work after the baby comes?" His hands massaged the sides of her arms.

"I didn't have to." Sophia relaxed beneath his touch. "Deirdre told me she'll be totally flexible with my schedule during and after the pregnancy. We even talked about training one of the interns to be my assistant this year, so she'll be ready to step up and fill in when the baby comes. She'll be a real help when I go back to work part-time after the baby comes, too."

Jackson squeezed her hands. "Did she suspect you were pregnant, like Kate did?"

"I think Deirdre expected it to happen at some point." Sophia chuckled. "If she noticed I was getting a little thicker around the middle, she was too polite to tell me."

Sophia and Jackson had agreed to keep secret the news of their pregnancy until the first trimester ended. They'd been lucky, in a way, that the months following their December wedding had been so busy. Not having time to see Kate prevented her from witnessing how often Sophia became nauseated and rushed to the bathroom.

But last week, when Kate saw Sophia at her new house for the first time in months, Kate had guessed. "Either you're eating a few too many *cannolis*, or you're pregnant!" she'd proclaimed as soon as she walked in the door.

Sophia shook her head, trying to keep her face stern. "You just can't let me have my big moment, can you?"

Kate's hazel eyes filled with tears. "Finally!" she crowed, hugging Sophia hard. She warned Sophia she could keep a lid on the news no more than twenty-four hours. The dinner Sophia had scheduled to announce the news to Lou Anne and Franny the following week had to be moved to the following night.

Jackson pressed his lips against Sophia's temple. "I got back at Kate. I put her in charge of the Italian sausages tonight. Clean-up, too."

Sophia laughed. "Serves her right." Without thinking, she straightened his clerical collar. "I'll always be thankful to sausages for introducing me to the man I love, but I couldn't possibly stomach one tonight."

"Then let's just go watch Kate hand them out to the crowd." Jackson stepped out from the shadows, reaching his hand to Sophia.

She smoothed her sweater over her hips. "The twins are already here with Carl?"

"They're at the table with Mom and Franny. They saved a place for us."

Clasping Jackson's hand, Sophia walked toward the bright lights of the church hall. Her family waited.

A word about the author…

Nell graduated from Temple University with a degree in English literature. While home-schooling three children through high school, she also taught students with dyslexia in a local public school. She lives in Ohio with her husband and youngest son.